TWO WEDDINGS AND A MURDER

Books by Alyssa Maxwell

Gilded Newport Mysteries
MURDER AT THE BREAKERS
MURDER AT MARBLE HOUSE
MURDER AT BEECHWOOD
MURDER AT ROUGH POINT
MURDER AT CHATEAU SUR MER
MURDER AT OCHRE COURT
MURDER AT CROSSWAYS
MURDER AT KINGSCOTE
MURDER AT WAKEHURST
MURDER AT BEACON ROCK
MURDER AT THE ELMS
MURDER AT VINLAND

Lady and Lady's Maid Mysteries
MURDER MOST MALICIOUS
A PINCH OF POISON
A DEVIOUS DEATH
A MURDEROUS MARRIAGE
A SILENT STABBING
A SINISTER SERVICE
A DEADLY ENDOWMENT
A FASHIONABLE FATALITY
TWO WEDDINGS AND A MURDER

Published by Kensington Publishing Corp.

TWO WEDDINGS AND A MURDER

ALYSSA MAXWELL

KENSINGTON
PUBLISHING CORP.

kensingtonbooks.com

KENSINGTON BOOKS are published by

Kensington Publishing Corp.
900 Third Avenue
New York, NY 10022

Copyright © 2025 by Lisa Manuel

All Kensington titles, imprints, and distributed lines are available at special quantity discounts for bulk purchases for sales promotion, premiums, fund-raising, educational, or institutional use. Special book excerpts or customized printings can also be created to fit specific needs. For details, write or phone the office of the Kensington Special Sales Manager: Attn. Special Sales Department, Kensington Publishing Corp., 900 Third Ave., New York, NY 10022. Phone: 1-800-221-2647.

Library of Congress Card Catalogue Number: 2024946454

KENSINGTON and the K with book logo Reg. U.S. Pat. & TM. Off.

ISBN: 978-1-4967-3492-1
First Kensington Hardcover Edition: March 2025

ISBN: 978-1-4967-3495-2 (ebook)

10 9 8 7 6 5 4 3 2 1

Printed in the United States of America

To the readers who have followed this series from its beginning, and who have written to me over the years to express their enjoyment of it. I appreciate your kind words, your support, and your encouragement, and I hope this last installment leaves you smiling.

ACKNOWLEDGMENTS

A huge thank you to my agent, Evan Marshall, everyone at Kensington, especially my editor, John Scognamiglio, for the opportunity to write this series. It's been an adventure and a joy, and your support and your confidence in me has been greatly appreciated.

CHAPTER 1

June 1922

A tingle of anticipation raced along Phoebe Renshaw's spine as she regarded the shimmer of alabaster satin draped over the dress form in her bedroom. The fabric, unadorned but for its flawless sheen, was draped to one side and held in place with what appeared to be a diamond-encrusted brooch the size of a man's hand, but was, in fact, a hook-and-eye closure beaded with crystals and embroidered in silver. The arrangement lent the gown a clever asymmetry that declared it as modern as could be. Although the current trend was for shorter wedding dresses, Phoebe had opted for full length. She delighted in the gown and counted the hours until she felt its cool glide against her skin.

Her grandmother, on the other hand, sighed yet again, a sound that prompted Phoebe to turn away from her wedding gown and regard the woman who had raised her since she had turned six. "Grams, even you must admit it's a work of art. And that it suits me. And that it's going to play an essential part in the happiest day of my life."

Grams tilted her head, as if that slight change in perspective might suddenly reveal the dress in a new light. "If only it weren't quite so *plain*."

Phoebe reached out to pet the Staffordshire bull terrier lounging on the floor beside Grams. Given to them as a puppy two years ago by Owen, Mr. Fairfax had immediately gravitated to Grams's side and had rarely left it since. "What do you think, sir?" she asked the dog, stroking the luxurious patches of brown and white down his back. "You like it, don't you, boy?"

Mr. Fairfax thumped his tail, sniffed at Phoebe's hand, and gave an approving lick.

Phoebe's elder sister, Julia, rose from the foot of the bed and sauntered over to the full-length mirror beside Phoebe's dressing table. "I'm afraid I have to agree with Phoebe, Grams. The dress is charming on her. Anything else— anything with tiers or petticoats or flounces—would have made her appear short. Because Phoebe *is* a tad short." She flicked an unapologetic gaze at Phoebe. "No offense."

She smiled. "None taken."

Grams sighed again. "I don't see what would have been wrong with a smidgen of lace or a ruffle or two."

"Don't worry, Grams." Phoebe's younger sister, Amelia, did a little pirouette before plucking a shortbread biscuit from the tray Eva had brought in earlier. "You still have my wedding to look forward to, and you know I adore lace. My wedding dress shall have oodles of it."

"You're much too young to think about marriage," Grams admonished, but not without a fond look at her youngest granddaughter. At nearly twenty years old, Amelia was not at all too young to consider marriage, but Phoebe understood Grams's fear of too many changes at once. "And don't use words like 'oodles,' Grams added. "It makes you sound American."

Phoebe crossed to the easy chair by the window, crouched before Grams, and took her hand. "I know you wish me to be married in a dress I love, and I love this one. Besides, the lace will be in my veil, as you well know." As Julia had for her first wedding, Phoebe would don her great-great-grandmother's Honiton lace, a wedding tradition begun by Queen Victoria herself. Perhaps it didn't truly go with the design of Phoebe's gown, but Grams's disappointment would be manyfold if she didn't wear it. Besides, Eva, her lady's maid since before the Great War, would work an artistic miracle incorporating the veil with the crystal orange blossom headpiece Phoebe would wear.

She rose and glanced at the dress with longing. They were all still in their wrappers, their hair in curling pins, but in only two hours she would slip into its elegance, slide into the backseat of the Rolls-Royce beside Grampapa, and make her way to the village church.

Where Owen would be waiting.

The door swung open. Eva had left only minutes ago for a fresh pot of tea, but as she burst into the room now, her hands were empty. "It's Lady Cecily," she said breathlessly. "She's missing."

"What?" Phoebe, her sisters, and Grams spoke at once. Grams came to her feet—or sprang, Phoebe would say, with the energy of a woman half her age. "What do you mean *missing*?"

Before Eva could form a reply, a voice could be heard from somewhere down the corridor. "We must find her immediately! Immediately, I tell you! Raise the alarm!"

"That's Lucille," Grams said, and hurried from the room, Mr. Fairfax streaming out behind her. Julia darted after her like a startled jackrabbit. Only Phoebe and Amelia hesitated, staring at each other in dismay. A missing Great-Aunt Cecily could seriously hamper the day's proceedings. And if anything happened to the octogenarian, who also happened to be Julia's great-aunt by marriage—well, a weight of dread dropped in Phoebe's stomach.

Amelia rallied herself with a too-bright smile. "Don't worry. She'll be found. She's probably gone belowstairs to hunt down a treat or two. You know what a sweet tooth she has. Let's just hope she hasn't swiped a finger across the frosting on your cake."

Phoebe hoped—prayed—Amelia was right, yet a sinking feeling suggested this latest crisis would not be so easily resolved.

Eva had followed Julia into the corridor. Now she strolled back in bearing a smile that resembled Amelia's in its artificial optimism. "Don't you worry about a thing. It looks as though every available hand is joining the search. Lady Cecily will be found presently, I'm quite sure of it."

To that, Phoebe blew out an exasperated breath. Eva crossed the room to her and grasped her firmly by the shoulders. "Now, none of that. You're not to give the matter another thought. Let everyone else in the house worry about Lady Cecily. You're to concentrate on one thing, and one thing only: your happy day. Now then, Phoebe, take a seat in front of the mirror and I'll do your hair."

Sometime over the past year, the last vestiges of employer-servant protocol had dissolved between them, leaving them on familiar terms. Eva had dispensed with calling her *my lady*, and Phoebe was glad of it; glad to have a true friend in Eva, rather than merely someone who showed her deference because of wages paid. She needed that friend today, far more than she needed a lady's maid—albeit no one could arrange her hair the way Eva could.

Phoebe did her best to hide her qualms as Eva led her, like a docile child, to her dressing table and gently pressed her onto its tufted bench. Sure enough, as each curling pin came out to ping on the tabletop and Phoebe gave herself over to the magic of Eva's ministrations, her cares melted into a swirl of excitement.

Two hours later, Eva paused for a breath at the bottom of the servants' staircase. Lady Cecily and been found, and the family and their guests were now piling into the automobiles, with Phoebe and her grandfather waiting until everyone else had left. Eva would go to the church with the servants, but first she wanted the details about Lady Cecily. She followed the trill of excited voices into the servants' hall, where the staff were gathering before setting off together.

"Where was she found?" she asked while simultaneously pinning on her best hat, a gift from Phoebe, covered in pale rose silk and trimmed with a grosgrain ribbon and matching rosette. She tipped the asymmetrical brim cunningly low to one side as Vernon, the under butler, offered a reply.

"On the High Road, walking back from the village." He stood up from the table, giving the coat of his Sunday best suit a tug.

Eva's hands, still fussing with her hat, hung in midair. "She walked all the way to the village and back?"

Vernon shrugged. "Don't know if she made it all the way there. I only know she was walking back when I found her. Just ambling along the roadside, hands full of wildflowers. Like this were any normal Sunday morning."

"What did the dowager marchioness have to say when she saw her aunt?" Eva wanted to know. Lady Lucille Leighton, dowager marchioness of Allerton, was Lady Cecily's niece.

As Vernon shrugged, Mrs. Sanders, the housekeeper, turned briskly into the room. "I do hope you're not gossiping. You know the rules about gossiping about our betters."

That last word produced more than a few winces from

those in the room, Eva included. Since the war, fewer and fewer of them took for granted the traditional view of servants being inherently beneath their employers—a view Eva once shared—and instead acknowledged that one's circumstances owed much to the luck of one's birth, and that while service was certainly an honorable occupation, there were other choices to be had. Looking around the room, Eva saw the evidence of this new philosophy in the dwindling numbers of Foxwood Hall's servants. So many young people these days opted to find work in the cities.

Dora, once Foxwood Hall's scullery maid but now an assistant to the cook, gathered up her hat and handbag. "Mrs. Sanders," she said with far more self-assurance than she once would have shown, "we're only concerned about Lady Cecily and hope her niece didn't suffer too much of a fright."

"And then there's Lady Phoebe," added Connie, who also had enjoyed a recent promotion and was now head housemaid. "Such a tumultuous start to her wedding day. Is she quite settled now, Eva?"

"Quite." Eva set her own handbag on the table and stood before it. She gave a sideways glance at Mrs. Sanders. "And I did glimpse an enormously relieved Lady Allerton— the dowager that is. Although, Lady Allerton the younger, as was our Lady Julia, was vastly relieved as well."

"All right, all of you. The disaster has been averted." Mrs. Sanders clapped her hands together. "We'd best be off or we'll be late for the ceremony. Some of you will have to walk, as we can't all fit in the farm lorry and the motors are all needed for the guests."

The three footmen and Vernon indicated they planned to walk. That left the maidservants, Mrs. Sanders, Eva, and dear old Mr. Giles to ride in the lorry, which in fact wasn't a farm lorry any longer, since Lord Wroxly had it

TWO WEDDINGS AND A MURDER 7

fitted with wooden benches along the sides of its bed for the express use of the servants on Sundays.

Mrs. Sanders waved the male servants on, admonishing them to hurry on their way. As Eva piled along with the others into the back of the lorry, she found herself seated next to Mr. Giles. The Renshaws' longtime butler, the kindly man had become rather unsteady and forgetful in recent years. Lord Wroxly kept him on officially as butler, although it was Vernon who did most of the work. It warmed her heart when he reached for her hand and held it fast.

"Why, I'm finding myself quite nervous, Miss Huntford. One might think it was my wedding we're off to."

"I completely understand, sir." Eva's fingers tightened around his in reassurance. "I want everything to go perfectly for Lady Phoebe. This is a happy day for all of us."

Except that, once at the church, Eva's own happiness dimmed a fraction. She stood outside St. George's, Little Barlow's ancient Anglican church made of honey-colored Cotswold stone, and gazed up and down the High Street. Everyone else had gone in to take their seats, and now the organist began playing softly to encourage people to settle in. Lady Phoebe and Lord Wroxly would be arriving at any moment.

But where was Miles?

She and Miles Brannock had been stepping out together these three years or so, and he had promised to meet her here promptly at ten forty-five. Surely on this glorious morning in this sleepy village there could not have been a crime to keep him away. Then again, Little Barlow wasn't nearly as peaceful as it often looked; Lord knew, as did Phoebe and Eva, that evildoers struck at the most inopportune times and in the most unlikely of places. Still, nothing but serenity pervaded the curving High Street, the pavements swept clean, the window boxes outside the shops teeming with spring blossoms, the sky overhead a stretch of bright blue velvet punctuated with pearly clouds.

No, surely nothing bad could happen on such a day as this. Miles would be here shortly. But to ensure Eva wasn't standing outside when Lady Phoebe arrived, she hurried in and took her seat near the back of the nave with the other servants, saving a space for Miles. The pews were packed, with as many of the villagers as possible having squeezed in. The front pews had been reserved for the family, including aunts and uncles who hadn't been seen in years, along with Lady Julia's mother-in-law, Lucille Leighton, and her aunt Cecily. On the other side of the aisle sat Owen Seabright's parents and a handful of relatives.

At some invisible signal, the organist slid into the opening notes of the bridal processional. The congregants stood. A door to one side of the transept opened and out strode Owen Seabright and, right behind him and standing in for Lord Owen's deceased brother, was Phoebe's brother, Fox. Eva felt a surge of pride in the young man. Only a few years ago an arrogant terror in an Eton tailcoat, Fox Renshaw, at eighteen, with his golden-brown hair slicked back from his chiseled features, looked every inch the earl he would someday be.

A burst of spring air flooded the church as the doors at the back swung open. All turned their gazes to the vestibule, and when Phoebe, on Lord Wroxly's arm, stepped through, a collective, delighted gasp echoed through the church. Phoebe had been right about her gown. It was a statement in simple elegance, unequaled in quality, and set off her best features. Dearest Phoebe had always considered herself plain, but in that gown, with its sleek asymmetry and gentle folds gathered at her right hip, even Julia, long considered the beauty of the family, paled in comparison. Beside her, Lord Wroxly walked straighter, stood taller, and his shoulders spread wider than they had in years. Tears pushed at the backs of Eva's eyes.

Amelia and Julia followed, and another gasp was heard. They wore palest yellow silk, vividly mirrored by the little bouquet of primroses and celandine they carried. Amelia had donned a headpiece studded with amber stones that caught the candlelight, with golden ribbons trailing down her back. The outfits were similar, yet where Amelia's dress had been fitted and tucked and had the darlingest short sleeves, Julia, as matron of honor and in the family way, wore a looser-fitting garment with three-quarter sleeves, and instead of a circlet, she wore the smartest little chapeau with a shallow crown and a flat brim.

Yet, even in Eva's joy for her lady, a worry slipped through. Miles should have been here. Had Chief Inspector Perkins refused him the morning off? Eva's gaze slid past Phoebe and her sisters into the vestibule. Perhaps he had arrived late and didn't wish to interfere with the procession. Perhaps he would slip in as soon as Phoebe reached the altar . . .

The slimmest shadow fell over Phoebe's happiness as she passed Eva on her way down the aisle. Tears of joy glittered in her friend's eyes, but then, for an instant, Eva's gaze slid past her and a worried look crossed her features. And in that moment, Eva's concerns became Phoebe's.

But only until Owen, standing at the front of the church between Fox and Mr. Hershel, the vicar, filled her vision and blocked out all other thoughts. In his morning suit, broad at the shoulders and trim at the waist, and the dove-gray trousers that tapered to the shape of his legs, he stole her breath. The look in his eyes, as his gaze locked with hers, brought tears to her own. She was about to become this man's wife, and she had never been more certain of anything in her life. Before entering the church, Grampapa had leaned close and whispered in her ear, "You're sure?" She had replied with a steady smile and a kiss on his dear cheek.

The people around her blurred into a mosaic of bright colors, all of them wearing their finest, while the organ music took up the very rhythm of her heart. A few faces did stand out. From the front row, Grams stared back at her with brimming eyes—not at all typical of her stoic grandmother. Owen's parents, Lord and Lady Clarebridge, looked as pleased as they had the day Owen and Phoebe had made their announcement to them. They had held nothing back in welcoming her into the family, although Phoebe knew they hoped she might cure him of his penchant to "dabble in business and industry," as they liked to put it. With a small inheritance from his maternal grandmother, Owen had invested in the wool industry. His mills had helped clothe the British forces during the war and continued to supply clothing manufacturers throughout Great Britain. Phoebe, alas, would prove a disappointment to Lord and Lady Clarebridge, as she had no intention of dissuading Owen from continuing in the business he had built.

From the corner of her eye, she also caught a brief glimpse of Great-Aunt Cecily standing at Lucille Leighton's side, her expression angelic and her chin tipped at an innocent angle as if nothing out of the ordinary had occurred that morning. As if she hadn't put the entire household into a high state of alarm. Thank goodness she had been found, unharmed. When Phoebe thought of what might have happened . . .

No. She would not allow such thoughts today.

The aisle seemed endless, and then, suddenly, she reached Owen's side, Grampapa having kissed her cheeks and her bouquet having been handed off to Julia. The vicar spoke, but Phoebe barely heard the words. Owen slipped the ring on her finger—like her dress, it was smooth, sleek, and un-adorned but for the inscription and two linked hearts inside—and before Phoebe could take a breath his lips were on hers. Warmth and love and joy filled her—not the kind that made one breathless, but which settled deep inside and would keep her contented for a lifetime.

The music swelled, the congregation applauded, and Phoebe, her arm linked through Owen's, found herself re-tracing her steps down the aisle. Outside, a shower of rice and flower petals greeted them, along with the joyous faces of family, friends, and villagers.

And Eva, of course, was standing off to one side with the other servants, a handkerchief crumpled in one hand, her cheeks still wet. Always Eva, friend and sister and mother, there through the most difficult times of Phoebe's life. All Phoebe wanted now was to see Eva find her own happiness.

Upstairs in Phoebe's room, Eva and Lady Julia's maid, Hetta, attended to a steady stream of female guests who needed touch-ups on their cosmetics or hair, or a bit of lace or trim sewn back into place. They also applied cold compresses to two ladies who had developed headaches, and prepared a bicarbonate of soda for one suffering a bout of dyspepsia. Eva and Hetta mostly attended to the younger relatives and friends of the sisters, while Lady Wroxly's maid took care of the matrons.

A little after noon, Dora came up with a tray laden with selections from the wedding breakfast, which was really more of a lunch. A couple of times, during quiet intervals, Eva and Hetta had tiptoed to the upper gallery and peeked down on the festivities, which spilled from the dining and drawing rooms into the Great Hall. Eva could have watched Phoebe and her new husband dance for hours, they looked so blissful together. Or, when the six-piece band struck up a lively foxtrot, Eva marveled at how perfectly synchronized they were. Phoebe had removed her veil, the effect of which was to transform her wedding dress into a chic gown worthy of any social event. Such a shame she couldn't wear it again.

Soon enough, other guests came drifting up the stairs in need of their ministrations, and Eva and Hetta would resume their tasks. It was late into the afternoon when things quieted downstairs and Dora reappeared, this time with a tea tray.

"Thought you two could use it," she said, and poured them each a cup.

"I could use to put my feet up," Swiss-born Hetta replied, plunking down into a chair near the hearth. "Such a busy day, *ja*? But a *gut* day. A very *gut* day. I am happy for your lady, Eva."

Hetta pronounced Eva's name in the German way, with a long *A* sound. When she had first begun to serve Lady Julia, she and Eva could barely understand one another, but after being in England only a few years, her English had vastly improved. But no wonder. It had turned out that Hetta had understood much more than she initially let on, believing—perhaps rightly so at the time—that Lady Julia preferred a maid who was unable to eavesdrop.

Eva handed Hetta a cup and saucer after Dora poured, took one for herself, and settled in the chair beside Hetta's. "I'd say we've made a job well done of it today."

"The day's not over yet." Dora stood before them, her arms crossed. "Don't forget we get to celebrate, too. So drink your tea, go upstairs and freshen up, and come down for the real party."

Eva and Hetta traded weary glances. But as soon as they had drained their cups, they pushed to their feet and did as Dora bade them. It was on Eva's way down the back staircase that Miles creeped back into her thoughts. Anticipation that he'd be waiting below sped her steps.

Yet amid the voices and faces filling the corridor and servants' hall, his was not among them. Worry mingled with slight annoyance, until Eva remembered that Miles wouldn't have stayed away without a good reason; he certainly wouldn't have forgotten today's importance, and that made her worry all the more. She pretended to enjoy the festivities. Douglas, recently promoted to head footman, played the upright piano in the back corner of the servants' hall, and even Mr. Giles regaled them with the old songs that were popular before the war as though he had sung them only yesterday. Mrs. Sanders had changed out of her housekeeper's black serge and into the dress she had worn to the ceremony. In the kitchen, the worktable did duty as a buffet, overloaded with goodies from the reception. On the counters, temptingly, sat two huge bowls of punch, one with fruit floating on its surface, the other with a good dash of port. Eva opted for the former even though Mr. Giles urged her to live a little.

After about an hour, footsteps announced an imminent arrival. Douglas ceased his playing and voices quieted until Lady Phoebe and Lord Owen reached halfway down the stairs, whereupon cheers broke out.

"We wanted to thank you all for making our day such a success," Phoebe said once they'd descended the rest of the way. Another cheer went up. "Everything was perfect."

Lord Owen added his thanks as well. Then Mr. Giles urged them to the punch bowl, specifically, Eva noticed, the one with the port. "You'll not have had any of this upstairs," he told them conspiratorially. "Our Mrs. Ellison's secret recipe. I implore you both to try some."

"Don't mind if we do." Rather than waiting to be served, Lord Owen reached for the ladle. He poured some for

Phoebe and the two of them raised their cups. "To all of you, with our deepest gratitude."

For a few minutes the pair were separated, Lord Owen surrounded by the manservants, Phoebe by the maidservants. Eva noticed Phoebe's gaze wandering a couple of times, a slight frown forming. Finally she made her way to Eva and took her aside.

"Where is Constable Brannock?"

"I wish I knew. Something important must have come up." She tried to look unconcerned, but rarely could she fool Phoebe Renshaw.

"I didn't mean to make you worry."

"Worry about what?" Lord Owen had joined them, and Phoebe explained. With a look of concern, he said, "If he doesn't show up soon, I could make some calls, find out what's kept him." Phoebe nodded her agreement with this plan, and while Eva didn't wish to impose, especially on their wedding night, she couldn't help nodding her accord.

"If it wouldn't be too much trouble, my lord."

"Not at all—"

"Miss Huntford, you've a visitor." Vernon announced this from the kitchen doorway. At the sight of Miles behind him, Eva ran to him and threw her arms around his neck.

His own arms encircled her waist. "I'm sorry, I wanted to be here," he was saying, as Eva pressed her brow to his cheek.

"You're all right, then?" she asked more than once, until he eased away, took her hand, and led her out of the kitchen. They walked a little distance down the corridor.

"I'm fine, but something *has* happened." The deep timbre of his voice sent a wave of dread through her. Before she could ask, he said, "It's Chief Inspector Perkins. He's been murdered."

CHAPTER 2

Phoebe knew by the pallor of Eva's complexion that something dreadful had happened. She braced for distressing news, but at the same time, the past several years had taught her that a level head achieved much more than a panicked one. She calmly waited for Miles Brannock to explain.

After he and Eva had briefly left the kitchen, Eva came back and quietly asked Phoebe and Owen to accompany them to Mrs. Sanders's parlor. She and Owen had drained their cups of punch, thanked everyone again, and, hoping no one followed, joined Eva and Constable Brannock in the other room.

He explained what he had discovered that morning. "He was late for work," the constable said in a brogue that had lessened since he had first arrived in Little Barlow near the end of the war. "Isaac Perkins was many things, but he was never late for work. So I went to his cottage, expecting perhaps to have to wake him from a sleepy hangover. But that was another peculiar thing about him. The man could polish off a fifth of whiskey at night and be at the station first thing in the morning." His gaze dropped, and when he looked up, it was with a look of chagrin. "Sorry. Shouldn't speak ill of the dead. But the truly troubling thing is that he was shot, and it appears to have been with his own gun."

Eva, sitting beside him on Mrs. Sanders's wooden, spindle-backed settee, touched his shoulder. "Could it have been suicide?"

The constable shook his head. "Even without an autopsy, the angle of the wound rules that out. Besides, he wasn't a man to ruminate over his life or regret his decisions. No, this looks like murder, but with precious few clues as to who might have done it. No break-in, no signs of a struggle, not even much blood. What there is suggests he died quickly right there in his favorite chair." He slapped his knees and started to rise, then stopped when Phoebe spoke.

"You said you found him first thing this morning. What time do you suppose this happened?"

"The coroner estimated sometime after dawn and before eight thirty. In fact, the remnants of his breakfast were on a small table beside him, along with a mug of coffee and . . ." He shrugged. "A bottle of whiskey."

"Do you think he was drinking so early in the morning?" Eva asked. "Or could it have been there from the night before?"

"No, the mug bears witness that Mr. Perkins poured a splash into his coffee this morning, as he probably did every morning."

"A functioning alcoholic," Owen concluded. "Have you questioned the neighbors?"

"Of course. No one saw anything unusual. They were all busy with their morning chores."

Phoebe's gaze connected first with Owen's, then Eva's. They both nodded, clearly able to read the direction of her thoughts. She said, "I know someone who might have seen something."

Constable Brannock's eyebrows quirked. "Don't keep me in suspense, please."

"She's not the most reliable witness, but my sister's great-aunt by marriage, Lady Cecily, apparently went for an early morning walk today." Phoebe came to her feet, prompting the others to do the same. "Most of the guests are gone. I'll find you a quiet place where you can ask Aunt Cecily a few questions."

She brought the constable upstairs to the library, tucked into a corner at the far end of the Great Hall. A complete refurbishment had erased all evidence of the tragedy that had occurred there the previous year, but not the memory burned into Phoebe's brain. The constable's too, she was certain, but at this time of day, the room ensured the privacy he needed for his task. She left him there while she explained to her grandparents what had happened, found Lucille and Aunt Cecily, and brought them both to the library. When she thought the constable would ask her to leave, he did the opposite.

"It might help her ladyship to have two familiar faces here," he explained.

"While I understand what this is about, Constable," Lucille Leighton said in her most authoritative, dowager marchioness tone, "I cannot guess what my aunt has to do with any of it. I cannot allow you to upset her with such unpleasant business."

"Who is going to upset whom, Lucille, dear?" Aunt Cecily, who still wore the hat she had pinned on for church that morning, smoothed the wrinkles in the lap of her dress. "No one is going to upset anyone."

With a glance at the constable for permission, Phoebe added, "Aunt Cecily, do you remember going for a walk this morning?"

"My, it was a fine day, wasn't it?" Aunt Cecily broke

into a fond smile. "Such a beautiful bride. And the ceremony was positively sublime. Didn't you think so, Lucille?"

Lucille didn't answer, but instead patted her aunt's hand.

"Lady Cecily, I understand you were out early today, before the wedding. Is that right?" Constable Brannock sat ready with his pencil and notebook.

"Why, I did, didn't I?" She appeared bemused, as if learning of her morning jaunt for the first time. "What an extraordinary thing for me to do."

"Was it extraordinary, Aunt Cecily?" Phoebe leaned forward in her chair. "While you were out walking, did you see something terribly interesting?"

"Why, yes. The wild lavender is lovely this time of year. Don't you think so, Lucille?"

"Good heavens." Phoebe let out a long, albeit quiet, breath as she attempted to rein in her impatience. Conversing with Aunt Cecily was never easy. Usually, she let the woman talk and played along with whatever fantasies inhabited her mind at the time. Yet occasionally, such as the other day when the Renshaw and Leighton ladies had gone to tea at the village tearoom, Cecily enjoyed perfectly lucid moments. Phoebe's hopes that she might experience one now were dashed.

"Did you see any villagers while you walked?" The constable, apparently, remained optimistic. "Pass anyone on the road? Anyone walking in the bordering fields?"

"Hmm . . . about that." Aunt Cecily held up a finger, nodded vigorously, and scowled. "An invitation to tea would have been most welcome, but apparently some people are too busy to remember their manners."

The constable and Phoebe each sat back in their chairs. Obviously, Cecily had seen what the constable had seen that morning: neighboring farmers completing their morning chores. None of them would have taken note of her, and they certainly wouldn't have invited her to tea.

After a few more routine questions, the constable tucked his notebook and pencil away, thanked Aunt Cecily and Lucille, and went belowstairs to find Eva.

"I'm sorry Lady Cecily proved unhelpful," Eva commiserated after Miles described the interview. They stood in the service courtyard, relatively alone but for the new hall boy, Larry, sweeping the area. "I'm afraid she's been suffering from a bit of a mental miasma for several years now, poor dear."

"Just a bit." He glanced up at the purpling sky, or was that a roll of his eyes? Not that she could blame him for expressing his frustration.

"Some evidence will turn up. You'll find whoever shot the chief inspector."

He reached for her hand. "You're right. No murder is unsolvable. This killer was clever, but the ones who get away do so because the authorities miss something vital and eventually move on to other crimes. I don't intend to do that."

"I have every faith in you." Eva moved closer and enjoyed the brief luxury of brushing up against his woolen uniform coat, like a wall of security against her. But with a glance at young Larry, she just as quickly opened space between them. The boy might be pretending to be sweeping away every speck of dust and every dried leaf from the courtyard, but she knew very well that he watched them from the corner of his eye. Otherwise, he'd have realized he just swept the same area for the third time.

Miles noticed him, too. "Let's take a walk."

She let him lead her by the hand through the courtyard gate and past the kitchen gardens. The two hothouses lay in darkness, their panes reflecting the evening sky. Miles led her past them, to an open sweep of lawn bordered by a yew hedge that marked the boundary of the formal gardens. They stopped beside it, safe in the shadow cast across the grass.

"An awfully deserted spot, Constable," Eva teased. "If I didn't know better, I'd think you were planning to take advantage of me."

"Just stealing some moments alone. Really, truly alone, as we can never be at the house." He ran his fingertips up and down her arm and leaned in for a kiss. "But what I really wish is . . ."

"What," she prompted when he hesitated.

He shook his head. "We can't. Not yet."

She knew he was speaking of marriage, and how financially they weren't yet able to manage it. A constable didn't make enough to support a family, and even if Eva could juggle a home and her position with the Renshaws, once she became with child that would no longer be possible.

As in the courtyard, she perceived his frustration, but this time for a very different reason. He glared down at the ground between them, his face a shadowed study in grim lines. "Perhaps if I were to—"

She pressed her fingertips to his mouth. "Stop being a policeman? Never. You love your work."

"Not as much as I love you, Eva."

She went stock still. He had never said it before, not like that. Oh, it had been assumed. He had shown her in countless different ways, but Miles Brannock was not a man to put into words what he felt in his heart. That he did so now jarred her to her very core.

"Our time will come, Miles." She smoothed the russet hair back from his brow. "We must be patient."

He gathered her to him, his torso truly a rigid wall until gradually he relaxed and they molded themselves one to the other. He began to hum a tune Eva recognized but couldn't name, something old and Irish that had them both swaying in a leisurely two-step.

"I owe you a dance," he whispered. "The one we should have had in the servants' hall today, if I hadn't been so late."

"No one was dancing."

"We would have." He bent his head to her, and she felt herself absorbed by his kisses until, once again, he eased away. This time, however, he was grinning. "We'd better get back, Miss Huntford, or I'll not be responsible for my actions."

"Nor I for mine." She felt deliciously wicked admitting it, but there it was.

That evening, Phoebe and Owen bid his parents good-bye with promises to see them soon in Yorkshire. They were staying at the Calcott Inn in the village, but would be setting off early in the morning.

"We couldn't be happier, Phoebe dear." Owen's mother gathered her in a warm embrace. A handsome woman in her early fifties, she had from the start endeavored to welcome Phoebe into the family and set her at ease. "Brides have enough to be nervous about," she had said when Phoebe and Owen had first announced their engagement, "so you needn't ever wonder if we believe you're right for our son. You are. Perhaps more than he deserves," she had added with a wink. Phoebe liked that about her mother-in-law. Though as entrenched in the old traditions as her grandparents, Madeleine Seabright always seemed able to bring a touch of humor to even the most serious matters. Her husband, on the other hand . . .

"We're confident you can talk sense into him," George Seabright, Lord Clarebridge, said after kissing Phoebe on each cheek. "Textile mills, indeed. He's made his money.

He's proved his point. Now it's time to invest that money and live the life of a gentleman. His responsibilities are to the Clarebridge title, not the clothing industry. And to you, of course."

The man had long been disappointed in Owen, once his second son, but now his heir owing to the death of his elder brother during the war. It's true that Owen had never wanted a title or the responsibilities that went along with it. And Lord knew, he didn't need the entailed fortune, such as it remained in the light of the postwar economy. On the contrary, he had wished to make his own way in the world, prove his own abilities, and he had, in abundance. But Phoebe knew that didn't mean he wouldn't accept the responsibility when it came, or that he wouldn't do his best to preserve the Clarebridge name and traditions. If only his father could see that as well and have a bit of faith.

Later, after wishing the rest of the family and guests good night, she and Owen made their way across the estate in his brand-new Rover, an electric-blue sedan roofed in black.

"The place is finally getting some use," Phoebe mused as he maneuvered the drive that twisted through the surrounding trees and ended at her grandfather's former hunting lodge. The front garden had been laid mostly to lawn, with little ornamentation besides the encroaching forest that bordered the property. "I remember my grandfather's and father's hunting parties, how we all rode out in the mornings, but in the afternoons, the women would return to the main house while the men came here to . . ." She stole a glance up at him as he came around and opened her door for her. "What is it men do in hunting lodges?"

His solicitous expression became a wide grin. "I'm not sure you want to know. It involves copious amounts of brandy and talk your grandmother would never have countenanced." He handed Phoebe out of the car and kissed her. "I was at a few of those parties. My father, brother, and I."

"I remember. Well, then. Shall we have brandy and say scandalous things that would turn Grams scarlet with indignation?"

He leaned to press his forehead to hers, then kissed her again. "Talk is cheap, my darling, and I don't plan to do much of it tonight."

Those words sent a delightful shiver through her.

Inside, Eva and Douglas awaited them to see to any needs they might have. In time, Phoebe and Owen would have their own staff, although they didn't plan to have more than a cook, housemaid, and perhaps a footman. As for valets and lady's maids . . .

Phoebe couldn't imagine replacing Eva. She had no wish to, even though Eva would remain in Little Barlow when Phoebe and Owen took up residence in Yorkshire. With Amelia out in society now, she would need Eva not only as a maid but as a trusted friend. And since Phoebe and Owen would be splitting their time between Yorkshire and here, it wasn't as if she were bidding a permanent farewell to her friend.

The house, though small compared to Foxwood Hall, boasted a salon, dining room, breakfast room, and study, all paneled in rich woods, with beamed ceilings and wide, stone fireplaces. Several bedrooms lay upstairs, with one serving as a billiard room. The entire house had been renovated and the furnishings were new, chosen mostly by Phoebe with help from Grams and Julia. The lines were simple, clean, and modern, and made Phoebe smile. Whenever she and Owen were in Little Barlow, this would be their home.

Douglas laid out the light supper sent up from the main

house by Mrs. Ellison, before discreetly retreating to the kitchen and not appearing again, at least not while they were in the dining room. Neither Phoebe nor Owen ate much.

"After today I don't know when I'll be able to look at food again." Phoebe pushed her plate aside. Despite the long dining room table, they sat beside each other. Owen reached for her hand.

"Nervous? About tonight?" His voice hitched slightly, as if his throat had gone dry. Phoebe smiled a reassurance.

"Not particularly, no."

He frowned and looked puzzled at the same time. "Well, I am."

"Why?"

"You know why. We've never . . . and we're going to . . ." He cleared his throat. "I want tonight to be perfect for you, Phoebe."

"It will be."

"I want to . . . I want you to be . . ."

"Happy? How could I not be?" She pushed her chair back and got to her feet. "I'm going up now. Eva will be waiting to help me change. You come up in a little while, yes?" Without waiting for an answer, she leaned in, kissed him firmly, and calmly left the room.

In truth, she *was* a little nervous, but wasn't that simply part of the excitement of starting their new life together? Whatever happened tonight, and she had a fairly clear idea of what *would* happen, it would be entirely theirs and no one else's; theirs to mold and shape to be exactly what they wished it to be. Not that it would be perfect right away, but in time. Time together was something they would have plenty of from now on.

Eva, at the dressing table laying out Phoebe's comb, brush, perfumes, and other toiletries, jumped when Phoebe opened

the door, her uneasy gaze locking on Phoebe's. Was everyone apprehensive about tonight?

"I didn't mean to startle you," Phoebe said with a
chuckle.

"Are you quite all right? Today was . . . not completely
what it should have been."

"No, you're quite right about that." Phoebe perched at
the edge of the bed, hung with deep crimson curtains tied
back against the four substantially square, fluted posts.
Douglas had obviously been up, as a robust fire crackled
and leapt in the hearth. "Poor Mr. Perkins. No one deserves such a bad end. No matter his deeds in life," she
couldn't help adding in a murmur. Then a wave of remorse
made her shake her head. "I'm sorry, I shouldn't have said
that."

"Miles said something similar," Eva said as she came to
sit beside her. "Chief Inspector Perkins was what he was.
We can't change that any more than we can change what
happened to him today. And you're right. No matter his
faults as a police inspector, he surely didn't deserve to be
murdered."

Phoebe slid from the bed, and Eva stood to help her out
of her gown and into a wrapper. Eva had a hot bath ready
for her, steaming and scented with oil of rose hip. Phoebe
hadn't realized how tired she was, or how her legs ached
from dancing, until she sank into the delicious warmth up
to her shoulders. She closed her eyes and tipped her head
back against the rim of the tub.

The water both relaxed her and revitalized her. As soon
as she was back in her wrapper, she went to sit at the
dressing table. As Eva began extracting the pins from her
hair, they spoke to each other through the mirror. Phoebe
asked, "Who do you think might have done it?"

Eva exhaled a long breath. "He didn't seem a man with
much of a family life, nor many friends, for that matter. I'd

say it was most likely someone from his past. Some criminal who wanted revenge for being arrested. Probably someone the chief inspector helped send to prison."

"Yes, that makes the most sense, unless he'd gotten into some difficulty more recently."

"Corruption, you mean?"

"Here I go again, speaking ill of the man." Phoebe ran her hands through the hair Eva had released from its coif. "But how many times have we gotten involved in a murder case because Isaac Perkins didn't do his job properly? How many innocent people might have gone to jail because he followed the wrong clues and set his sights on the wrong suspect?"

"Quite a number of times." Eva picked up the silver-backed hairbrush and began taking long, even strokes down Phoebe's reddish-gold hair. "The difference this time is that Miles is in charge. He'll do what's right."

"Thank goodness for it. Owen and I leave for Cornwall in two days. I don't have time to investigate a murder." She spoke in mirth, but truthfully all the same. The last thing she wished to do as a new bride was spend the first days of her marriage tracking down a killer.

Eva plaited Phoebe's hair and tied the end with a ribbon. Phoebe stood and, turning, regarded the silk negligee spread carefully across the foot of the bed, so gossamer she could see the coverlet beneath both layers of the garment. She suppressed a smile at the thought of Owen seeing her in it . . . and then out of it.

Eva caught her staring at the nightgown and placed her palm against Phoebe's cheek. "Do you have any questions about what will happen tonight?"

Phoebe bit back a grin. The concern on Eva's face was far too sincere to make any jokes. Yet, she couldn't help asking, "And you know all about it . . . how?" In the next instant her hand flew to her mouth. Perhaps Eva did know—perhaps she'd had this experience—and here Phoebe was embarrassing her about an exceedingly private matter. "Eva, I'm sorry, I—"

But Eva was laughing. "You needn't be. You're absolutely right. I've no more experience in such matters than you, except for some things I've read, and from listening to my sister, Alice. She's quite the expert, or must be by now. She's got four little ones now, you know. This last was another boy. A shame Alice isn't here."

Phoebe joined her in laughter. Then Eva turned serious and cupped Phoebe's face in her hands. "Your parents would be so proud of you, Phoebe. So very proud. As I am, though really, I've no right to be."

"You have every right, my friend. You've helped raise me these many years, and I'm who I am as much because of you as my parents and grandparents. But this won't be goodbye, even though you're staying here for Amelia. Owen and I will visit so frequently you'll hardly know I've been gone."

"I hope so."

Phoebe tossed her arms around Eva's shoulders. "It's a promise."

The concern reentered Eva's eyes. "Do you want me to stay here tonight?"

Phoebe shook her head. "No, go back to the Hall with Douglas. Owen and I will be quite fine on our own. I'll see you there in the morning."

CHAPTER 3

Phoebe stretched her arms over her head, basking in the multitude of sensations humming through her. Muscles she didn't know existed ached, but in the most delicious way. She opened her eyes to the half-light peeking around the curtains. Dawn hadn't yet arrived, and she was glad—glad to be able to lie here wrapped in the warm sheets, with Owen's soft, steady breathing tickling her shoulder.

He lay sleeping beside her, his body relaxed, his face more serene than she had ever seen it. She blinked away a sudden tear, but at the same time stifled a bubble of laughter as their activities of last night came flooding back. He had been nervous—truly, endearingly nervous—in his desire to make everything perfect for her, to show her a pleasure she never could have imagined. She had been nervous, too, in her desire to do the same for him. With his help, she had been a quick learner, and all the evidence pointed to her having been gloriously successful.

She breathed the mellow scent of him deep into her lungs. She loved him so much more than she had realized even yesterday, when she had stood before Mr. Hershel, her family, and the congregation and became his wife. She whispered it to him now, and was startled to see his lips curl in a smile.

"Likewise, my darling," he murmured, his voice sleepy and rumbling. "More than I ever dreamed possible."

Phoebe struck him on the shoulder. "I thought you were asleep, you faker."

"Mmm . . . I am . . . sort of. I don't want to wake up." His arms went around her and he dragged her the necessary few inches across the sheet to tuck her against the angles and planes of his body. "I could stay like this forever . . ."

Yes. Phoebe wanted that, too.

For the first time since before the war, Eva didn't go to Phoebe's room first thing in the morning to bring her a cup of tea. Instead, she went to Amelia's room, and after closing the door behind her, she stopped in her tracks, nearly sloshing the tea into its saucer. She had always found the resemblance between the three Renshaw sisters remarkable, but now her breath hitched at how like Phoebe her younger sister appeared in repose. The main difference between them was the color of their hair, Phoebe's being a reddish blond and Amelia's being a darker gold, the color of antique jewelry.

Eva set the cup and saucer on the bedside table and opened the curtain, letting the sunlight pour in. Amelia groaned and opened her eyes, first one and then the other, and peered through her lashes at Eva.

"It's rather early, wouldn't you say?"

"You never were a morning person. But with Phoebe at the lodge, I came here first thing. Would you rather I wait an hour or so before waking you from now on?" After all, with Amelia now her mistress, there might be a number of changes in Eva's routine.

Amelia turned her face into the pillow but nonetheless

said, "No, it won't do for me to be a lie-abed. I was always up and dressed this time of morning at school. Here shouldn't be any different. I've things to do, haven't I? I must be up and ready to help Grams entertain our house-guests, and I promised Phoebe that whenever she and Owen are away in Yorkshire, I'll take over her work with the RCVF."

The Relief and Comfort of Veterans and Their Families. Phoebe had barely been out of school herself when she founded the organization in the first year after the war ended. Through her efforts, money was raised and supplies collected each year to ensure the area's war veterans—and their families—had enough to eat and warm blankets and clothing to see them through the winter months.

"You'll have me to help you with that, don't forget, and any other project you might wish to take on."

Amelia studied her face with a solemn expression. Then, quietly, she said, "Everything will be different now, won't it?" When Eva nodded, she pushed herself up against her pillows. "Certain things will be up to me now. As the last remaining Renshaw sister in Little Barlow, I must rise to the occasion, mustn't I?"

"To whatever extent you wish to." Eva sat on edge of the bed and brushed some stray hairs back from Amelia's face. "It's up to you to determine the role you wish to take on. You don't have to be Phoebe or Julia. You only have to be Amelia."

"Hmm . . ." She tilted her head as she considered this, and Eva suppressed the urge to smile at her again. She realized she was witnessing a formative moment for Amelia, a serious one, and Eva must not make her feel as though she were a child. A moment later, Amelia sat up straighter and swung the covers aside. "Eva, help me dress. It's time to start my day."

An hour later found Eva on the road to the village. Amelia would be busy helping her grandmother entertain the house-guests and wouldn't be needing her until it was time to dress for dinner. And Phoebe had indicated she and Owen would prefer to be on their own this morning.

She went to the police station. Miles was at his desk, shuffling through a sheaf of notes when she came through the door. He tossed them down and stood to embrace her.

"I'm glad you're here."

"Have you discovered anything since last night?"

"Nothing. Whoever did this wiped the gun clean, so no fingerprints. I've sent to Gloucester for help on this one. An extra man or two if they can spare them, and I've also inquired who has been released from prison recently."

"You think it's someone Mr. Perkins arrested in the past?" Eva answered her own question. "That it's some-one recently released would answer the question of why now. But could it have been a more recent run-in with someone in the village?"

Miles pointed to the papers on his desk. "I was just going over our recent files, refreshing my memory as to our most recent cases. There are a few, but nothing that seems serious enough to warrant murder."

Eva walked over to the desk and glanced down at the topmost file. "Let's see what you have." She bent lower to read. "This one concerns that tavern brawl you told me about. Luke Ivers and Stuart Branson. Shows violent ten-dencies in both men."

"They were let off with a warning. No charges were filed after they agreed to pay for the chair and bottles they broke."

"All right." Eva put that page aside. "And this one? Something about sheep?"

"Conner Dawlish was grazing his sheep in Edgar Wilson's north field again. Was warned to cease and desist. Hardly worthy of killing anyone."

Eva nodded, moving on to the next page. "What's this? Shoplifting at the dry goods store. And only the day before yesterday. I don't recognize the offender's name."

"Serena Blackwell is a member of the Romany caravan encamped on the edge of Lord Wroxly's forestland."

"My word, with the wedding I'd practically forgotten about them." Eva picked up the page to study it closer. "I was surprised when Lord Wroxly allowed them to stay. He believes they're harmless, but *Lady* Wroxly isn't sure she agrees." She looked up at Miles. "What do you think about them? And what happened with this Serena Blackwell?"

He pulled out his chair for Eva, then brought over the one from Mr. Perkins's desk for himself. "Generally, I believe Lord Wroxly is right. In Ireland they call themselves Travelers, and it simply means they travel about the country and refused to be tied down to one area."

"But how do they earn the money they need to live? Surely such a lifestyle makes it impossible to maintain employment."

"They have skills that they put to work wherever they camp. The men do repair work, carpentry, and the like. The women make and sell jewelry and other crafts, and, of course, some of them tell fortunes." He must have seen Eva's dubious expression, for he added, "The stories of thievery, kidnapping, drunkenness, and heathenry are just that. Tales invented by people who don't understand their ways. They've never been welcome in most places, but that doesn't dissuade them from keeping up their traditions."

"Did Mr. Perkins share your views?"

"He most certainly did not. He wanted them out of Little Barlow. As do others in the village. But since they're on Lord Wroxly's land, there's not much anyone can do to evict them."

"Well, it's not as if they'll be here permanently," Eva remarked. "So I don't see why people should fret about them.

"Nor do I. But getting back to Mrs. Blackwell, she claimed innocence. Said she didn't know how the stolen items—a pair of leather gloves, a tin of Fortnum and Mason tea, and a small can of tobacco—ended up in her shopping satchel. Says she came in for milk powder and rice, set her satchel down a moment, and the next thing she knew, she was being accused of theft."

"Again, though, not exactly worthy of committing murder. Was she arrested?"

"Perkins was all for it, but since they got their goods back, Mr. and Mrs. Fielding told her to get out and never come back."

"If she *was* innocent, I can see how that would be mortifying." A thought made her frown. "Could she have been telling the truth? If someone wants the gypsies out of the village badly enough, what better way than to make them appear to be thieves, just like in those old tales."

"You've a point there . . ."

The door opened, and tall man with jet-black hair and a short beard strode in. Eva suddenly realized that at some point she and Miles had joined hands. They quickly released one another and Miles came to his feet. "Can I help you?"

The man wore a faded bowler and a checked suit covered in dust from the road. He also possessed a directness of gaze that made Eva guess at his profession. His reply to Miles proved her correct. "Mick Burridge, Metropolitan Police." A strong London accent lent a knife edge to his speech. "Your people over in Gloucester called me in about the Perkins matter. You're to stand down and allow me to take over. I'll need to see all the information you've managed to gather so far, all the files, and any physical evidence there is. So then . . ." His gaze shifted back and forth between them. "What have we here?"

Phoebe left her bedroom—her former bedroom—thinking how strange that not only the room was no longer really hers, but the house itself. It was no longer that abstract sense of comfort called home. Home from now on would be the hunting lodge and Owen's Yorkshire estate. They had, weeks ago, pored over lists of potential interior decorators Phoebe would work with to make each abode *theirs*, and not hers or his. The hunting lodge was certainly theirs—especially after last night. The thought sent heat rising to her face and she fanned herself with her hand lest she give herself away when she rejoined the ladies downstairs.

She descended to the Great Hall and started through to the drawing room when nearby voices raised an odd sensation at her nape. Though she couldn't hear what was being said, the low murmurs sent a shiver of foreboding through her.

They were coming from the dining room, where no one should have been so long after breakfast and well before luncheon. She recognized the voices almost immediately as the two uncles who had stayed on at Foxwood Hall after most of the other guests had left. A word, or rather, a name, sent her closer to the doorway while remaining out of sight.

"Yes, the earl may be slipping a bit, I'll give you that. It comes with age." It was Uncle Bert, Mama's eldest brother. Phoebe narrowed her eyes. What on earth did he mean to imply? That Grampapa was no longer competent? The very notion sent the blood pulsing in Phoebe's temples.

"He's driving this place straight into the ground," the other voice complained. Uncle Greville, Papa's younger brother, whom the family had not seen since before the war. He dared criticize his own father? Greville Renshaw had lived in Italy all during the war, hiding from the dangers, instead of coming home and joining up as Papa had done. In plain words, he was a shirker, even if he did manage to obtain documentation from the Italian government stating that he had filled an administrative role in their military.

She wanted to storm in and give him a piece of her mind. But she remained where she was, listening and speculating on why Uncle Greville had come home now. She did not believe his primary concern had been to attend her wedding.

"I tell you," he went on to murmur, "soon there won't be anything left for anyone to inherit. These old coots need to get their heads out of the Victorian age and join the modern world. But heaven forbid they listen to anyone, ever. Not even their own financial advisers."

That, Phoebe knew, was a lie.

"It's nothing new, is it, old boy?" Uncle Bert employed a placating tone. "A man inherits a pile, and it's his to do with as he pleases."

"That's wrong and you know it. Each generation is supposed to safeguard the estate for the next."

"True, and might I remind you, Grev, that you're not the next generation. Fox is."

At that, Uncle Greville groaned. "This place will be

wasted on that insolent whelp. The rest of the family might as well kiss this place goodbye, lock, stock, and barrel. Of course . . ."

In the ensuing pause, Phoebe heard the trickle of a liquid being poured, then the light scrape of a glass against the tabletop. The interlude continued until she heard an "ahhhh."

"One thing I'll say for the old boy," Uncle Greville said, "he knows his cognac."

"He does at that."

Their glasses clinked.

"You do realize, though . . ." Again, Uncle Greville paused. Another sip? Then continued, "Should anything ever happen to Fox, none of the girls will inherit a thing, nor their husbands. No, should our dear Fox leave this earth without issue, we both know who gets the lot."

"Grev, you're drunk, and I suggest you go sleep it off before you land yourself in permanent trouble."

"Bah. Now, old Theo certainly lucked out when Henry gave up the ghost."

Phoebe suppressed a gasp. That Uncle Greville could speak so blithely of another man's death—

"Henry Leighton was murdered, Grev. I don't think Theo considered that a stroke of good fortune."

"No? I beg to differ. He not only inherited the title of Marquess of Allerton along with the estate, he inherited Julia as well."

Phoebe's hands fisted at her sides. On the table beside her sat a Meissen vase she would have loved to hurl at her uncle's head. But Uncle Bert was right. Uncle Greville was drunk—she could hear it in his voice—and there was no reasoning with a man not in his right mind. She moved to go, then froze.

"If I were you, Grev, I'd be on my best behavior here.

Should your past come back to haunt you, you won't be around to enjoy anything, whether an inheritance or whatever bounty you manage to wheedle out of the earl. You'd do best to climb out of your cups and keep your wits about you."

"Shhh! Good grief, shut your yap, Bert. You swore . . ."

"And I've been true to my word. Trust me, I don't want anyone finding out what happened either."

"That's right." Uncle Greville sounded not only mollified, but shrewd. "You were in it up to your ears. If I go down, you go down with me."

Uncle Bert retorted with something Phoebe wouldn't care to repeat. Then he said, "Say, old man, you didn't . . ."

"Good grief, no! I was here, like I said. I had nothing to do with . . . that."

A chair slid back. Her eyes gone wide, Phoebe threw herself into motion, running on tiptoes into the drawing room. She could see the ladies through the terrace doors. Could she make it across the room and outside before either of her uncles saw her and surmised she had been eavesdropping? She hurried while glancing over her shoulder, and nearly ran into the tall woman blocking her path, whose sensuous lips formed cunning smile.

"And where are you running off to, dear niece?" Giovanna de Tusa Renshaw was Uncle Greville's second wife—or perhaps third. Phoebe never cared to keep track. They had met in Italy during the later war years and had married in enough of a hurry that the family had wondered. Yet, there hadn't been a child, so it hadn't been that.

Phoebe regarded the woman who was technically her aunt by marriage, but whom she found nearly impossible to think of in such close familial terms. Giovanna Renshaw was voluptuous and tall, with a smooth, olive complexion, glossy black hair, and dark eyes that hinted at stormy passions within. She was also a good decade and a half younger than Uncle Greville, which made Phoebe ponder what the beautiful Giovanna had seen in an older man with little fortune and a penchant for drinking far too much.

Was she the reason Greville had decided to return to England after so many years away?

"Giovanna, I . . . er . . . didn't see you there."

"*Zia* Giovanna. *Auntie*, if you like. And no, you did not see me because you were not looking where you were going. It makes one think you're up to something. Were you still a child, I would demand to know what that something is." Giovanna laughed, showing nearly all of her large, white teeth.

Her teasing made Phoebe's skin crawl. She would never deign to address this woman as *zia*, auntie, or any other term of familiarity, much less affection. "If you'll excuse me, my grandmother and the others are waiting for me. Are you going back outside?" She hoped not.

"Not just yet. I'm looking for my husband. Ah, Bert." Giovanna's sultry gaze traveled past Phoebe's shoulder. Phoebe spun around to find Bert standing just beyond the doorway, watching them. "Do you know where that husband of mine has gotten to?"

Bert signaled with his thumb. "Dining room."

"Ah." Giovanna gave Phoebe one last assessing glance and strode off, her hips swaying with each step, the hem of her silk dress swishing about her shapely calves.

When she had passed, Bert beckoned. "Phoebe."

"Not now, Uncle Bert. I'm needed on the terrace." She didn't give him a chance to beckon twice, but continued to the doors and stepped out.

Later, during a croquet game Phoebe found interminable, she managed to tell Owen what she'd overheard, speaking in whispered snippets.

"Much of it angered me," she said, tucking a whisp of windblown hair behind her ear, "but knowing Uncle Greville as I do, not unexpected. Not until that bit at the end. I don't believe they were discussing a gambling debt or unpaid bills. It was something serious. Perhaps even illegal. And then, with Uncle Bert somehow being implicated . . ."

"Are you sure he wasn't simply playing along with Greville, trying to avoid any sort of confrontation?"

"No. You didn't hear their voices. They were deadly serious, both of them. Equally. Whatever it was, it sounds as though they could both be in a lot of trouble if they were found out." Phoebe stole a glance at them now across the makeshift croquet court. They were standing with Theo and Julia, talking and laughing as if nothing in the world could be amiss. Grams and Grampapa had teamed up with Lucille and Great-Aunt Cecily who, despite her habitual malaise, retained the croquet skills of a professional.

"Are you two paying attention?" Grams called over to Phoebe and Owen. Mr. Fairfax added a bark to ensure she had their attention. "Because it certainly doesn't look like it."

"Sorry, Grams," Phoebe called back, and raised the score sheet and pencil in her hands. She and Owen had begged off playing by volunteering to referee and keep score, for the precise purpose of stealing this time to talk.

Grams, all six feet of her swathed in half mourning even after these half dozen years since Papa's death, prepared to take her turn. As soon as she positioned herself and her mallet at the ball, Phoebe turned back to Owen. "It's got me wondering if whatever they were talking about has anything to do with recent events."

He eyed her sharply. "You mean Perkins's murder?"

Phoebe nodded. The tap of the mallet raised a round of applause, and Phoebe looked over to see that Grams had deftly sent the ball through the wicket. "Very nice, Grams!"

"Whatever you overheard this morning took place years ago. Before the war." Owen paused, thinking. "How could that have anything to do with now?"

"I don't know . . ." She watched as Greville strolled onto the court, swinging his mallet at his side. He took his shot; it went wide. "But why would Uncle Bert even have brought it up after all this time?"

"Probably because Greville's been gone all these years. He hasn't been home to Foxwood Hall since he left, has he? Not even for a visit."

"No, you're right about that. But of course, had he come home, he'd have had to join the war effort like everyone else. In Italy he could be an administrator without risking his precious life."

Owen put an arm around her waist. "You don't much like Greville, do you?"

"I thought I did when I was young. He was great fun. But after he left it became apparent that he and Papa had never got on. They were too different, with Papa being the responsible one and Greville . . . well . . . I know he caused my grandparents quite a lot of grief over the years. Being sent down from Eton, then Oxford, and Grampapa always having to intervene. And then suddenly leaving and never coming back . . . until now." She pursed her lips. "I don't wonder why he's come. You can be sure it isn't to celebrate our marriage."

"Is it our business, though? Really?"

Her chin came up. "It is if he's here to swindle money out of Grampapa."

"That should be between the two of them, my darling. Despite what Bert and Greville might believe, your grandfather is no fool. If Greville is attempting to bamboozle him, the earl will know and act accordingly. As he sees fit, I might add."

"I suppose you're right . . ."

He tipped her face up for a quick kiss. "But just in case, we'll keep an eye out. And when you and I leave for Cornwall, we'll ask Theo and Julia to keep watch. And Fox and Amelia, for that matter."

"Yes, I'm worrying for nothing. I'm sure everything will be just fine."

CHAPTER 4

"To him, I'm just a copper on a beat," Miles complained as he and Eva walked hand in hand along the High Street. "He tells me nothing, not even when I ask."

The setting sun turned Little Barlow's creamy Cotswold stone to burnished gold, as if the entire village were made of precious metal. Eva admired the window boxes on nearly every storefront window, framing the colorful displays inside. "Detective Burridge did tell you he was questioning those village men and the Romany woman, didn't he?"

"Yes, but only that. He won't share what he's learned. I might as well be a civilian." He had removed his police helmet and, with each word, slapped it against his thigh. "He must think I'm an idiot. A country bumpkin."

"I'm sure he doesn't think that."

"No? Then why not let me help with the case?"

"I'm sure he has his reasons." But Eva couldn't think of any, except that perhaps the Scotland Yard detective believed all local constables to be incompetent. Miles was far from that, but how to persuade Detective Burridge? He certainly wouldn't listen to Eva.

"I can only hope he solves this case soon and goes back where he came from."

"Yes, we all want that." Eva didn't ask the question foremost on her mind, and undoubtedly on Miles's as well. What would happen then? Once the chief inspector's murder was solved, would a new inspector be assigned to the village? Or would Miles move up in rank? Would the possibility then exist for the two of them to marry?

She let out a sigh, then quickly covered it with a cough. She wished to marry, but she simply wasn't sure the time was right. He didn't seem to notice, being caught up in his ruminations about being supplanted by Detective Burridge. Eva understood his frustrations. If another woman attempted to supplant her with her ladies, she would put up no end of a fight.

"I should bring you back to the Hall," he finally said, breaking the silence but for the evening birds and the children playing on the side lanes, outside their cottages.

"Yes, all right." They walked back toward the police station, but when Miles moved to help Eva into his police motorcar, Mick Burridge stepped out the door of the police station.

"Where do you think you're going?"

Miles and Eva traded puzzled expressions. Miles said, "I'm off duty now and I'm about to bring Miss Huntford back to Foxwood Hall."

"No, you'll not be doing that, I'm afraid."

"If you need the motor, we can walk." Eva looked at Miles. "I wouldn't mind. It's a glorious evening."

"It's not the motorcar I need," Detective Burridge retorted. He held up a pair of handcuffs. "It's our constable here."

"What on earth?" Eva stepped in the detective's path as

he approached, putting herself between the two men. "Have you lost all reason? You surely can't mean to—"

"Arrest your beau? That I do, Miss Huntford. Now, kindly step aside."

"Is this your attempt at a joke?" Miles nearly smiled, but the effort fell short. "What is this about?"

"This is about your being arrested on suspicion of the murder of Chief Inspector Perkins."

Eva fought the urge to slap sense into the man. "You'll do no such thing!"

Miles placed a hand on her shoulder. "I'm sure there's been a misunderstanding. We'll get it cleared up soon enough. Burridge, you can put those things away. I don't know what you're on about, but I'm no flight risk."

"Sorry, we're doing this by the book." The detective reached out to grab Miles's forearm. Roughly he spun him around and shoved him face-first against the motorcar. He wrenched one of Miles's hands behind his back, then the other, and snapped on the cuffs. Then he pulled Miles upright and turned him again. "Miles Brannock, I'm arresting you under suspicion of murdering Chief Inspector Isaac Perkins. Anything you say will be written down and used as evidence against you . . ."

"Stop this at once!" Eva shouted. "Have you gone mad? He hasn't done anything . . ." As she watched, Detective Burridge half dragged Miles by the arm into the police station. Not to be cowed, Eva strode in behind them. And just as well. They had drawn a small crowd of onlookers; villagers, their eyes gone wide, stood frozen on the pavement on either side and across the road.

"Miss Huntford, it would be best if you leave now," Detective Burridge said before the door had closed behind her. "Nothing you do or say is going to help Constable Brannock."

"You think not?" She crossed her arms and drew a sharp breath in through her nose. "Wait until Lord Wroxly hears about this. I assure you, he shan't stand by and allow you to bully an innocent man."

"Eva . . ." Miles's right arm jerked as he tried to reach out, only to be thwarted by the restraints. "Perhaps it is best if you go. For now."

She turned to him, and though it wasn't directed at him, her eyes sparked with ire. "I refuse to leave until this man explains himself and his abominable actions."

"I'd be pleased to, Miss Huntford." He pulled the chair out from Miles's desk and gestured for him to sit. "First of all, there are no other viable suspects, as you yourself admitted, Constable."

"Miles—Constable Brannock—is certainly not a viable suspect either." Eva struggled to keep the panic from turning her voice shrill. "He worked with Chief Inspector Perkins. Why on earth would he want to kill him?"

"Because the good constable here has *been* a constable since before the war ended," Detective Burridge said. "Surely you expected to have moved up by now. Must stick in your craw that you haven't." He leaned down closer, his face inches from Miles's own. "Perkins refused to put your name in, did he?"

Miles met Burridge's gaze without blinking. "It never came up and no, it didn't stick in my craw."

"I'll bet not." Burridge leered at Eva over his shoulder. "And what about her?"

"*Her* name is Miss Huntford," Miles said between gritted teeth.

"Wouldn't you prefer her name to be Mrs. Brannock?" Burridge ignored Eva's indignant gasp behind him. "But you can't likely make that happen on a constable's salary. However, an inspector's salary is quite another matter."

"And you think I'd risk our future by committing murder?" Miles scowled. "You're completely off the mark here."

"Am I?" Burridge finally straightened, gazing down on Miles as if from a great height. "It was you who found the chief inspector, already dead, or so you say. You know what I think? I think you found Perkins very much alive. Found his gun. Fired it. Then wiped it clean before going on your merry way, only to double back and pretend to discover the heinous crime." Those last two words dripped with sarcasm. "That's motive and opportunity."

"This is so ridiculous as to be contemptible," Eva charged. "It'll never hold water. You've nothing to prove any of it."

Burridge smiled, baring his teeth, yellow against the black of his beard. "Except the facts, Miss Huntford. A man with a sweetheart can't afford to marry, because another man stands in his way. Perhaps you knew or suspected, or perhaps you didn't. Doesn't much matter. I have my murderer."

Tears pushed at Eva's eyes, but she refused to blink them away or let them fall. "This will never stand. I'm going to speak to the earl immediately." Coming forward, she crouched in front of Miles, ignoring Burridge when he told her it was time to leave. "Lord Wroxly will fix this, I'm sure of it. So will Phoebe and Lord Owen. They know you. They know you could never be guilty of any illegal act."

"We'll see about that, won't we?" Burridge chortled.

Eva rose and gave Miles's shoulder a squeeze. She would have liked to kiss him, but she refused to give the detective something else to sneer about. "I'll be back, Mr. Burridge. And when I do, I won't be alone."

Phoebe was at dinner with the family and guests when Douglas, serving the fish course, whispered a message in her ear that made her whisk her napkin onto the table. She came to her feet, prompting the gentlemen at the table to do the same. "Please excuse me. There's a matter I must attend to."

"Phoebe, what on earth?" Her grandmother sounded both annoyed and alarmed.

"So sorry, Grams. Something important has come up." Without giving Grams another chance to question her, Phoebe hurried through the butler's pantry. Owen, already on his feet, was quick to follow.

"Phoebe, wait a moment. What's happened?"

They started down to the servants' domain below. "I don't know yet. Douglas only said Eva urgently needed me."

Owen didn't ask further questions. At the landing, they headed for Mrs. Sanders's parlor, where they found Eva ensconced in the housekeeper's favorite overstuffed chair. Mrs. Sanders herself handed Eva a cup of tea as Phoebe and Owen came into the room.

"Phoebe." Without taking a sip, Eva set the cup and saucer aside and sprang to her feet. She threw her arms around Phoebe. That Eva had addressed Phoebe simply by her given name in front of others, especially another of the house staff, spoke volumes as to how upset she was.

"Eva, what is it? Are your parents—"

"Not my parents. It's Miles. He's been arrested." Tears spilled over. "For the murder of Isaac Perkins. But he had nothing to do with it. He—"

"Of course he didn't." Phoebe smoothed a hand up and down Eva's back. "Take a deep breath, drink some tea, and tell us what happened."

"Shall I bring in more, my lady?" Mrs. Sanders started toward the door, but Phoebe put her hand up to stop her.

"No, thank you, Mrs. Sanders. But perhaps . . ."

"Of course, my lady. I'll leave you alone. If you need me, I'll be in the servants' hall."

Eva, fortified by several sips of the strong tea Mrs. Sanders had made her, poured out the story of how Miles Brannock had ended up behind bars tonight. Before she'd quite finished, the parlor door opened and Phoebe's grandparents came in, followed by Mr. Fairfax. He greeted each occupant of the room with sniffs and licks, then, apparently sensing Eva needed consoling, stationed himself at her knee.

"I hope we're not intruding," Grampapa said, "but for Phoebe and Owen to rush off as they did, we knew something must be terribly wrong. How can we help?"

"Bless you, Lord Wroxly." Eva came to her feet again, dabbing at her eyes with a handkerchief—one of the ones Phoebe and her sisters had embroidered for her several Christmases ago. Once more, she explained what had happened. "That odious man insists Constable Brannock is guilty, but I know he isn't."

"We all know the good constable could not be guilty," Grampapa said gently.

"Good heavens, no," Grams agreed with him. "Why, even if we had no knowledge of him ourselves, simply your faith in him would be enough for us, Eva."

Phoebe nodded emphatically to that, even as Eva's tears began to flow again. While she expressed her gratitude, Phoebe whispered to Owen, "We can't possibly leave for Cornwall now. Not yet. Our honeymoon will have to wait."

"But . . ."

"We're needed here."

The resistance ebbed from his features, replaced by resignation, and then determination. He nodded. "We'll get to the bottom of this."

"My husband and I shall go to the village first thing in the morning and have a word with this man, this muckety-muck from London," Grams was saying.

Phoebe was torn between reacting to Grams using a word like *muckety-muck* and protesting a delay till morning, but Grampapa settled matters.

"I think we should go tonight, right now. An innocent man shouldn't spend the night in a jail cell. Does anyone know where this detective is staying?"

"I believe the Calcott Arms," Eva said with a sniffle. "I'll come with you."

"Eva, I think it best if you wait here. Phoebe, stay with her. I happen to know the magistrate is a bit of a night owl, so we should find him awake. We'll collect Burridge and go directly to see him." Grampapa turned to Grams. "My dear, I'll understand if you prefer to wait here. Owen and I can handle this."

"I'm coming." She gathered herself taller, until she towered over Grampapa. "I will not countenance some high-and-mighty from London coming to our village and tossing his weight about. Who does he think he is? I intend to give him a piece of my mind."

"Grams." Phoebe placed a hand on her wrist. "Please let Grampapa handle this. Perhaps you should stay here."

Grams exhibited all the signs of an inner debate. Her brows gathered, her lips compressed, and her gaze fixed on some point beyond Phoebe's shoulder. Finally, with a glance down at Mr. Fairfax, she issued a sigh. "Perhaps you're right. You men will speak more frankly without a lady present. Threaten this detective if you must. You might be a country nobleman, my dear, but your influence does extend well beyond Little Barlow."

Grampapa smiled. "I'll remember that, my dear." He slapped Owen's shoulder. "Shall we?" And then to Eva, "Don't worry, this will all turn out right."

Eva nodded but her worried look persisted, as did the apprehension churning in Phoebe's stomach. Apparently, Grams decided her role should be to distract them.

"Come, dears. We'll adjourn to the Petit Salon and await their return. Mr. Fairfax, come."

Grams led them upstairs. Eva positively didn't know what to do with herself when they reached the Petit Salon. It had taken her years to feel comfortable sitting in Phoebe's presence. Doing so in Grams's seemed impossible for her, until Grams herself drew Eva to the table and gestured for her to sit. Grams sat beside her, while Phoebe sat across from them.

"We shan't stand on ceremony tonight," Grams said in her matter-of-fact way. "And Eva, you needn't put on a brave face for our sakes. We understand how distraught you are. Although, I do know from experience that putting on a brave face is often the best way to meet adversity. Chin up, shoulders straight, and all that."

Phoebe wanted to hop up and hug Grams. For a woman of the old school who most often *did* stand on ceremony, her generosity toward Eva brought a lump to Phoebe's throat. Vernon and Douglas arrived with more tea, and after they left, Grams asked if Eva might rather have something a bit stronger. Phoebe nearly fell off her chair at such uncharacteristic behavior, but she was grateful for it. Eva declined the offer, reaching instead for the lavender almond biscuits. She plunked an extra lump of sugar into her tea. No matter the crisis, there was always tea.

Julia appeared in the doorway. "I've just said good night to little Charles, and Theo is reading to him." She eyed them all quizzically. "There's something terribly wrong, isn't there?"

"Come in, Julia." Phoebe tapped the back of the chair beside her. "We'll fill you in. It's about Constable Brannock."

Julia immediately took on a concerned look and shifted her attention to Eva. "What happened? He's not hurt or . . ."

Eva shook her head. Mr. Fairfax came up beside her and

she absently stroked his head. "No, my lady. Physically, he's fine, but he's been arrested."

"Arrested? Whatever for?"

When Eva looked about to choke on the answer, Phoebe replied, "For the murder of Isaac Perkins."

"That's absurd," Julia exclaimed.

"Yes, it is," Grams agreed. "And your grandfather and Owen are off to do something about it. Now then . . ."

Grams led the conversation away from their worries, focusing instead on proposed changes for the fall term at the nearby Haverleigh School for Young Ladies, where Grams sat on the board of directors. She asked Eva's opinion on several proposals for a new curriculum, as well as sporting activities. Again, Phoebe could have kissed her for so deftly keeping Eva's mind occupied. She knew Eva hadn't for an instant forgotten Constable Brannock's predicament, but Grams's chatter prevented her from dwelling on it.

Finally they heard voices from the Great Hall, and then footsteps in the corridor. Grampapa and Owen entered the Petit Salon smiling. Theo, who must have met them in the Great Hall, followed them in.

"He's been released," Grampapa announced, and Eva let out a cry of relief. They pulled out chairs and sat. Grampapa patted Eva's hand. "The magistrate agreed to release him on my recognizance. He's not to leave Little Barlow. In fact, he's more or less under house arrest, but at least he may sleep in the comfort of his own bed. And eat his own food."

"The charges are still pending," Owen cautioned. "But the magistrate agreed that while Miles might have had opportunity and even something of a motive, there is no physical evidence linking him to the crime. Burridge insists there is and that he'll find it." He smiled at Eva. "But he won't, will he?"

Eva shook her head. "No, he won't, because Miles is innocent. Oh, but I should go to him . . ."

Once again, Grampapa placed his hand over hers. "Not tonight, Eva. He's exhausted. Let him sleep and you may visit him tomorrow."

Tears, suppressed while they had waited for the men to return, filled her eyes. "Thank you, Lord Wroxly. And you, Lord Owen. I'm so grateful to you both. For Miles's sake, and my own. You've been so kind . . ."

"My dear." Grams leaned toward her as if confiding a secret. "You have been part of this family these many years. We look after our own."

Later that night, Phoebe and Owen returned alone to the hunting lodge. Eva came in the morning to help Phoebe prepare for her day, but she also brought news. "Miles has learned something. If you can spare me, I'd like to go directly to the village from here."

"Of course. I'll drive you."

CHAPTER 5

The moment Miles opened the door to his flat above Henderson's Haberdashery, Eva threw herself into his arms, nearly knocking the two of them to the floor. She wouldn't have cared. She didn't even care that she, a single woman, was visiting a man unaccompanied.

They broke apart rather awkwardly, as if both suddenly realized they might be engaging in an impropriety. Eva gave a laugh; Miles chuckled, shoved his hands into his trouser pockets, and gestured for her to have a seat on the nearby settee.

Having never been inside his flat before, she took in her surroundings. It didn't take long, as the main room wouldn't hold more than three or four visitors comfortably. A settee, chair, and hassock made up the parlor, while a small kitchen area occupied one of the far corners. A doorway led into another room—the bedroom, she surmised. A sensation fluttered inside her and she pulled her gaze back into the main room. A wide, tall window overlooking some trees and, beyond, the rooftops of several other village homes, prevented the room's tight dimensions from becoming oppressive.

"This is very nice," she murmured, noting that the furniture all looked to be secondhand—older than the amount of time Miles had been living in Little Barlow.

"You didn't come to admire my humble abode." He sat beside her. Eva nearly opened another inch or two between them, then realized there was no one else here to criticize.

"No, I didn't. You said you learned something . . ." Her pulse thumped in eagerness.

"I received a telegram from a friend at the Greater Gloucester Constabulary. There was a man released from Gloucester Prison recently, someone Isaac Perkins arrested some eight years ago, just as the war was starting."

"Good heavens, how recent?"

"About a fortnight ago."

Eva sucked in a breath. "And you think he might have wanted revenge for his incarceration?"

"Listen to this." Miles leaned forward, his elbows propped on his knees. "This man—his name is Ian McGowan—was arrested by Perkins in 1914 for horse theft. But because he should have reported to his regiment that morning, Perkins added desertion to the charges. There were extenuating circumstances. His son was ill and McGowan needed to find a doctor."

"His son must have been extremely ill for him to take such a risk with his own freedom."

"I don't have all the details yet. Givens—that's my acquaintance on the Gloucestershire force—has put it all in a letter and sent it off this morning."

"Perhaps we could telephone over and find out sooner."

Miles shrugged. "If we can manage to reach him. I doubt he has a telephone in his flat."

Eva considered a moment. "McGowan only served eight years. I should think the penalties for horse theft and desertion would be much more severe than that, especially

considering how the army dealt with deserters on the bat-
tlefield." She shuddered.

"I'm hoping we'll find an explanation for that as well in
the letter."

"Do you have any idea where this Ian McGowan lives?"

"Givens did include that information, at least for the
McGowan family." He paused as if for dramatic effect.
"They live just outside of Heathcombe."

"Why, that's barely five miles away." Eva started to rise.
"Miles, we need to speak to Detective Burridge about
this."

He grasped her hand and pulled her back down onto
the cushions. "I don't see what use that will be until we
have more information. We'll have to wait for the letter."

"That could take days . . ."

"I'm not going anywhere, and neither is Burridge."

She swatted his arm. "Don't make jokes."

He looked contrite. "You know, Eva, there's no guaran-
tee that McGowan has gone home. It's been eight long
years and much has happened since then."

"Where else would he go? I should think his wife and
family would be elated to have him home again."

"Perhaps."

Three days later, they had their answers. Eva had taken
to visiting Miles each morning after seeing to Amelia's and
Phoebe's needs. That both sisters had decided to dress as
simply as possible and had taken to "practicing with their
own hair" didn't fool Eva one bit. They were reducing her
daily tasks to allow her more time with Miles, and had she
not already loved them to pieces, she would have now.

But this morning Eva didn't go to see him alone as she
had been doing. She brought not only Phoebe, but Lord
Owen as well. Miles was waiting for them, letter in hand.

"I know the whole story," he said in greeting, and waved
them inside his tiny parlor. They all three squeezed onto

the settee, with Phoebe in the middle. Miles took the chair. "You already know what charges were filed against McGowan," he began. "As I initially told Eva, at the time he claimed his son's illness prompted his actions. When Perkins caught him with the stolen horse, McGowan begged him to let him go. His son had a raging fever and needed a doctor." Miles's gaze connected with Eva's. "It turns out the boy had scarlet fever. McGowan was desperate, enough to risk being hanged for desertion."

Eva let go a long breath, emptying her lungs.

"McGowan was initially sentenced to forty years but . . ." Miles paused again, his head bowed.

"Yes? What changed?" Lord Owen reached for the letter, which Miles placed in his hand. He made a sound in his throat, shaking his head. "Good grief."

"What?" Phoebe glanced over his shoulder, trying to read what was on the page.

"The son died," Miles said quietly. "Of scarlet fever, and McGowan's sentence was commuted to ten years. Apparently, he's been a model prisoner and was released early. The magistrate took pity on him."

"But Perkins didn't," Lord Owen concluded with another shake of his head. "Blasted man."

When he would have said more, Phoebe laid her hand on his. He compressed his lips. "This would certainly give Ian McGowan a motive," she said.

"It most certainly would." Eva pressed to her feet, eager to take action. "We need to speak with Detective Burridge immediately. Then he'll see that Miles is innocent."

"This doesn't prove anything." He remained sitting, looking up at her. Eva wanted to pull him out of his chair.

"It proves you're not the only suspect," she insisted. "This man has much more motive than you. Strike that. You had *no* motive."

Miles stood and took her hands. "That's true, I didn't.

But we don't yet know if Ian McGowan had opportunity. He may be nowhere near Little Barlow. I don't want you getting your hopes up."

"Of course my hopes are up. Why shouldn't they be?"

"I agree with Eva." Phoebe came to her feet as well. "We should at least speak to Mr. Burridge and alert him to the fact that there could be another suspect in this case. It might not immediately absolve Constable Brannock, but it's a new lead to follow. Owen, I think you and I should go."

"I agree." Lord Owen stood at her side. "Again, Eva, I think it would be best if you wait here. Let Phoebe and me speak with Burridge. It won't be as easy for him to put us off."

"If he does, I'll have my grandfather intervene again," Phoebe added with a shrewd grin. "But I'm hoping that won't be necessary."

Two days later, Phoebe decided Detective Burridge had had enough time to follow up on Ian McGowan. She was determined to find out what he had learned, and this time when Eva insisted on going with her, she didn't argue.

He wasn't in when they stopped at the police station, but that didn't deter them. Little Barlow's tearoom, opened a year ago and called Pippa's Delights after the proprietress, stood across the street and a few doors down. "If we sit near the window, we'll be able to catch him before he can give us the slip again," Phoebe said as they crossed the High Street.

The green door and window boxes teeming with fragrant lavender and rosemary beckoned cheerfully. As they approached, the door swung open forcefully, flung so hard from inside it hit the outer wall with a bang. The sound startled them both. A voice cried out, "Out with you, and don't come back."

Two women, somewhere between Phoebe's age and Eva's, came stumbling out and nearly collided with them. Behind them, the door slammed shut.

"Good heavens, what was that all about?" Phoebe looked the two women over. They were flushed, obviously upset. "Are you both all right?"

The taller of the two wrapped a paisley shawl tighter around her shoulders despite the warm breeze. Freckles dotted her light complexion; her eyes were green and sharp, her hair a light brown that would have been blond when she was a child. "We're quite fine, thank you. Just a misunderstanding."

Her accent spoke of northern England, Manchester or thereabouts. Considering how they had just been thrown out of the tearoom, it took Phoebe only another moment to realize these women were not villagers, nor were they likely to be welcomed at many places in Little Barlow. Despite the objections of many here, her grandfather had permitted a caravan of gypsies to set up a temporary camp in one of his outlying fields, and Phoebe was certain these women were part of that caravan.

The same caravan to which Serena Blackwell belonged.

"I'm Phoebe Renshaw," she said, and held out her hand. Both women stared as if it were some kind of trick.

"I'm Eva Huntford. Welcome to Little Barlow." Eva stuck out her hand, too. Again, the women didn't reciprocate. "Are we correct in assuming you're visiting our hamlet?"

When they remained mute, Phoebe felt compelled to add, "It's my grandfather's land you're staying on, I believe. Do I assume correctly?"

"What of it?" the shorter, darker-haired one asked. "His lordship said we can stay as long as we like. We're not hurting anyone."

"No, of course you're not," Phoebe exclaimed. "Do

you have everything you need? Is there anything we can do for you?"

"Why would you ask?" The taller one tilted her head as she assessed Phoebe and Eva from head to toe.

"Because you're my grandfather's guests, of course." Phoebe attempted to convey her reassurances with a smile. "I'll ask again. Do you have everything you need? Do your children have enough to eat? Because if you need assistance, I—"

"Our children are fine and healthy. They're not neglected," the dark-haired one said defensively.

"I apologize. I didn't mean to imply they were." Phoebe did her own quick, discreet assessment of the two women. Unlike many stories she had heard about Romany women, they were not dressed in flowing, colorful skirts with many strings of bead around their wrists and necks. Although one did wear a shawl, it was no different than the sort she might have seen on the women of Little Barlow. The other wore a knitted cardigan in a handsome shade of dark green. Their dresses were ordinary, if a bit worn-looking, and, again contrary to popular belief, both wore shoes—pumps to be exact. Certainly not new shoes, but made of serviceable leather, one pair black, the other brown.

"We don't mean to be rude, but we must be getting back," the darker-haired one said. They both turned, preparing to walk off.

"Ladies," Phoebe said, "I wish to apologize for the way you may have been treated here. I know our chief inspector was pressuring your group to leave. And . . . is a Mrs. Serena Blackwell among you? I understand she—"

"What about Serena?" the shorter one demanded, her expression growing stormy. Her eyes were black and fathomless, surrounded by thick, kohl-black lashes.

"Well . . ." Phoebe looked at Eva, who nodded. They both watched the women intently as Phoebe said, "We understand she was accused of stealing at one of our shops."

"She didn't do it."

"No, I expect not," Phoebe went on, seeing that they were once more turning to go. "It must have been dreadful for her to be accused that way. If she was innocent as she claims, it was grossly unfair—"

"She was more than falsely accused." The fair-haired woman spoke as if challenging Phoebe to refute her claim. "Someone put those goods in Serena's bag without her realizing it."

"I understand," Phoebe said. "She must be terribly angry about it."

"Wouldn't you be?" The black-haired woman scowled; her companion did likewise and added a funny little twist of her fingers. A gypsy curse? How angry were they over the incident involving their friend? Had the entire camp been enraged over the treatment of one of their own? Had Serena—or another among the group—taken revenge against the chief inspector?

"I hope you won't judge the entire village on the actions of a few," Phoebe began. "We—"

The fair-haired one cut her off. "We don't mean to be rude, but we've things to attend to."

"Yes, of course," Phoebe said.

They started off, but the dark-haired one stopped. "You needn't concern yourselves with us. Best if you minded your business. Meddling in other people's lives never reaps the sorts of rewards people expect."

"Goodness," Eva said on a release of breath once they'd gone. "If we hadn't been trying to take their measure, I'd have given them both a thorough dressing down for speaking to you that way. Of all the—"

"What reason do they have to show me any deference?

I'm not part of their world. People like me simply have no importance in their lives."

Eva harumphed. "There's such a thing as manners."

Phoebe had been watching the gypsy women retreat down the pavement. Now she turned to Eva. "What were your impressions?"

Eva's annoyance evaporated as she considered. "I think they're afraid. I think your questions unnerved them because they're simply not used to anyone outside their group taking an interest in them."

"I think so too. I don't believe they meant to be rude. We simply put them on their guard."

"I thought it was interesting when the taller one admitted that stolen items were found in Mrs. Blackwell's bag, rather than denying the whole matter."

Phoebe thought that over. "They want justice," she concluded. She gestured toward the tearoom. "Let's go in. I hope Detective Burridge hasn't slipped in and out of the station while we were engaged."

"Don't worry," Eva said. "I've kept an eye out the entire time."

The tearoom's interior offered subdued lighting that brought a warm glow to an array of toile, moiré and other silks, and light, feminine furnishings. There were several tables occupied, but luckily one by the front window was vacant. The owner, Pippa Young, saw them from across the room, waved, and hurried over.

"My goodness, Lady Phoebe, I didn't expect to see you again so soon. I'd have thought you and that handsome husband of yours would have left on your honeymoon by now."

Phoebe, her sisters, and her grandmother had come for tea accompanied by Lucille Leighton, Lady Cecily, and Owen's mother three days before the wedding. Phoebe hadn't expected to be back this soon.

"We'll be leaving shortly," she replied, and left it at that.

"In the meantime, might Eva and I sit there?" She pointed to the empty table by the window.

"Most certainly. Will you be having afternoon tea?"

"Cream tea, please. With a pot of Darjeeling." Phoebe accepted the chair Miss Young held for her. Eva pulled out her own. "If you wouldn't mind my asking, who were those women who came out right before we came in?"

Miss Young made a clucking noise. "Gypsies." She nearly spat the word, prompting Phoebe and Eva both to wince.

"And you wouldn't serve them?" Eva tried to keep her voice steady and not imbue the question with every bit of outrage she felt.

"I most certainly would have served them had they been paying customers. I would not have liked it one bit, mind you, but I'd have suffered through." The woman rolled her eyes and tsked. "No, can you believe they came in asking if they could set up a table for fortune-telling in the back corner. Of all things. Can you imagine? Well, didn't I tell them to turn right back around and take their gypsy double-dealing elsewhere. I'll not have my customers swindled."

"But most people see fortune-telling as good fun," Eva said. "Nothing to be taken too seriously."

"That's true," Phoebe agreed. "My own sister once had her fortune told." Actually, Julia had taken the incident far more seriously than she should have, but she decided not to mention that to Miss Young.

"Be that as it may." Pippa Young smoothed the points of her lace collar. "I neither like nor trust their race, nor any foreigners, to be frank. Coming here and interfering with our traditions. Who do they think they are?"

"I don't believe this group are foreigners. Most gypsies in this country have been here for generations. Isn't that right, Eva?"

"I believe since the time of Henry VIII," she confirmed.

"Besides," Phoebe went on, "the women we spoke to outside sounded as though they're from Manchester, or thereabouts."

"*Hmph*. A shame the chief inspector died before he was able to run them out of town." Phoebe's eyes went wide at this statement, while Eva's mouth dropped open. Suddenly though, Miss Young's expression changed from annoyance to sympathy. "Forgive me, Miss Huntford. I know Constable Brannock has become entangled in this unhappy business. I refuse to believe he did anything wrong and he has my full support. And the support of just about everyone in the village. You may tell him I said that." She leaned down to whisper, "It was more than likely one of those traveling heathens that did it. Well, I shall go and prepare your tea."

Her mouth still gaping, Eva watched her go, then leaned toward Phoebe. "Good heavens, the past several minutes have quite shocked me."

"And me as well, Eva. I think our Miss Young could use a strong cup of tea and a good lesson or two in compassion."

CHAPTER 6

"Eva, there he is!" Phoebe's blurted declaration startled Eva. She pointed out the tearoom window, then opened her handbag and counted out the money to pay for their tea.

Eva drained her cup, as much to fortify herself as to not waste the rest. The two of them hurried outside. Just as Phoebe was about to lead the way across the High Street, a farm lorry carrying cages of chickens rumbled past. Eva grabbed her arm and held her back.

"Goodness. Thank you, Eva. But let's hurry." She rounded the back of the lorry, looking in either direction to make sure nothing else might be barreling toward them. Eva saw several handcarts, a wagon loaded with beer kegs, and a motorcar driven by someone she didn't recognize moving slowly along the street, probably looking for a particular shop. They saw their chance and ran across.

"Detective Burridge," Phoebe blurted out upon opening the door to the police station. "We'd like to speak with you."

The man, sitting at Miles's desk as though it belonged to him, looked up with no hint of interest. "Ah, Lady Phoebe." He said her name as if it heralded some stroke of misfortune. "And Miss Huntford."

He didn't ask what he might do for them but that didn't deter Phoebe as she demanded, "Have you discovered anything about Ian McGowan? Have you found him?"

"No, I have not."

Phoebe and Eva exchanged exasperated looks. It was Eva's turn to demand, "Have you been to the family's farm?"

"I have. He wasn't there. His wife says she hasn't seen him. In fact, she says they've gone their separate ways. Can't blame her." He turned the chair and stretched out his legs in front of him, crossing them at the ankles in the most insolent way. Eva wanted to box his ears.

"He could have been hiding somewhere. Did you poke about?" She wasn't about to skulk away quietly. This was Miles's fate at stake, and she had as much right as anyone to know how the case was proceeding.

"I looked about the place, yes." He stared at his fingernails. "Saw no sign of him. Saw no sign that his wife and family need him, actually. They're doing well enough on their own. Four children in all, each in their teens, and fully capable of managing the farm. I say it's a blessing he's not come back."

"From what we understand, there were five children originally," Eva pressed stubbornly on. "One died as a result of Mr. McGowan's arrest. That certainly gives him a motive to want to take revenge against Isaac Perkins."

"Perhaps. Perhaps not. I can't question someone I can't find, can I, Miss Huntford? Besides, no one I questioned in Little Barlow remembered seeing a stranger about on the morning the chief inspector died."

"Just because no one noticed him doesn't mean he wasn't here." Phoebe stopped just short of raising her voice, but Eva heard the anger in her tone.

"I understand you're both just trying to help." The detective uncrossed his ankles and sat up straighter. "But I'm afraid it's not looking good for your constable, Miss Hunt-ford."

She wanted to snap that Miles was not *her* constable, but that wouldn't have been true. And this man knew it. If he hadn't walked in at the most inopportune time that first day, he might not have known of the affections between them and might not have decided Miles had a perfect motive for doing away with Isaac Perkins.

But he did know, and there was no changing it. It only made Eva more determined to prove Detective Burridge wrong. She couldn't do that standing where she was.

She turned about and headed for the door, Phoebe following at her heels as though their roles had suddenly been reversed. Once the door had shut behind them, Phoebe said, "I have serious doubts about Mrs. McGowan's claims."

"So do I." Eva strode at a brisk clip along the High Street toward the lane where Lady Phoebe had parked her Vauxhall. Only when she reached the corner did she remember to slow her pace and not make Phoebe practically trot to keep up.

"Years apart could certainly damage a marriage, and it's possible Mr. McGowan hasn't been home," Phoebe said a little breathlessly. "But it's just as possible his wife is hiding him, as you said. I think we should pay a visit to the McGowans."

Here, Eva stopped short and turned to regard her mistress. "I was hoping you would say that. Although . . ."

"Yes?"

Eva blew out a breath. "I don't wish to put you in danger. Not for my sake."

Phoebe smiled. "It's not for your sake. It's for the sake of Little Barlow's constable, without whom this village would suffer. Come, let's drive back to Foxwood Hall and devise a plan."

"If you wouldn't mind, I'd like to stop in on Miles first. I'll make my own way back. But I'll walk you to the motorcar."

As the little green Vauxhall came into view, Eva saw immediately that something was wrong. The windscreen looked as though a spider had spun its web across the glass, but that was merely an illusion.

"The windscreen is cracked," Phoebe cried out. "How on earth could that have happened?" She gazed upwards, inspecting the branches of the oak tree crowded between the lane and the nearest building front. The acorns were small and green and not at all ready to drop.

Eva inspected the crack, almost dead center in the glass, and saw where the lines spread outward from a single hole about an inch in diameter. About the size of a pebble kicked up by the motor's wheels—except that they would have noticed if such an event had occurred while they were driving. The hole could also have been caused by the head of a hammer or other striking implement. "This was no accident."

"What do you mean?"

"I think someone did this intentionally, perhaps as a message."

Phoebe stopped inspecting the tree and came over to stand beside Eva in front of the motor's bonnet. "To mind our business, perhaps?"

Eva nodded, remembering the gypsy woman's words to them outside the tearoom. "Meddling in other people's lives never reaps the rewards people expect," she repeated. A chill went through her. "On second thought, I will come back to Foxwood Hall with you. I don't want you driving alone. Perhaps Douglas can run me back to the village to see Miles later this afternoon, before you need me to dress for dinner."

"I can dress myself tonight, Eva. You visit with the constable and remind him again that we all believe in his innocence."

After seeing Eva off, Phoebe joined her family and guests in the drawing room. They were all there, sitting or standing in small groups like characters on a stage. Even Mr. Fairfax. Phoebe smiled as she remembered a time, before the war, when Grampapa had kept hunting dogs, when Grams had strictly forbidden any animal to enter the drawing room. *My, how that rule had fallen by the wayside.* Not to mention revealing how much of a softy Grams had become in recent years—though she would choke before ever admitting it.

Phoebe scanned each grouping of her family. In front of the French doors, Uncle Bert and Uncle Greville stood with their heads together, murmuring at a frantic rate. Phoebe heard their voices but couldn't make out the words. Julia and Theo sat together at the piano, Julia tapping out the tune of a brand-new song from America by the showgirl Fanny Brice. Julia loved American music.

Across the room, seated beside the fireplace, Grams pursed her lips, quirked an eyebrow, and sipped from her glass of sherry. Grams did *not* care for American music, or American anything, for that matter. But today at least, she refrained from asking Julia to play something else. Grampapa, a snifter in hand, sat across from her, while, facing the fireplace, Amelia, Lucille, and Aunt Cecily occupied the settee. Aunt Cecily had a ball of soft yellow yarn beside her. Her knitting needles clicked a lively tune while she kept up a steady if quiet stream of chatter. Lucille nodded frequently, pretending to listen.

Phoebe coveted a seat beside Aunt Cecily for herself. Although Amelia possessed the patience of a saint and wouldn't likely move away, perhaps Lucille would grow tired of the elderly woman's ceaseless prattle and seek refuge in another part of the room. If she did, Phoebe planned to take her place beside the octogenarian. She wished to try to spark Aunt Cecily's memory again about the morning of the chief inspector's murder.

While she waited, her gaze landed on Owen and Fox, seated on either side of the chess table, their shoulders hunched as they each leaned over in deep concentration. A smile grew on her face. During Fox's earlier teenage years, when no one else could engage him in a civilized conversation, he and Owen had bonded over chess. Owen had always been able to bring out Fox's more serious, responsible side, the side necessary for him to one day assume the responsibilities as Earl of Wroxly.

She went over to them and set her hand on Owen's shoulder as he considered his next move. He turned to look up at her, his eyes suddenly filling with a depth of feeling, with the knowledge of all they had shared since the moment they had said *I will.*

Her hand tightened on his shoulder. She watched as their game resumed. Fox had the advantage, she saw. She hoped he would win—without Owen letting him. But no, she knew Owen wouldn't do that. He never treated Fox, or anyone, with condescension, but gave each individual in his acquaintance the opportunity to prove their own potential to themselves.

It was that trust in other people, in their abilities, that had led Phoebe to fall in love with him. Among other, more intimate qualities, of course.

After several minutes she drifted toward her uncles. Their conversation stopped the instant they noticed her, and they greeted her, each kissing her cheek. It was then she realized Giovanna was missing.

"Where is your wife?" she asked Uncle Greville, keeping her tone light. Yet, part of her couldn't help acknowledging the woman's presence would only bring tension to the room.

"She'll be along any moment." Uncle Greville glanced at the doorway. He shrugged. "You know women."

She frowned but changed the subject. "You two were deep in conversation when I came in. What was so interesting?"

"Were we?" Uncle Bert swirled the drink he was holding, something amber in a glass tumbler. Whiskey? He, too, shrugged. "Ah yes, yesterday's racing results. My horse lost."

She studied him, not believing a word. "I hope you didn't wager too much, then."

"Nothing catastrophic." He chortled, absently setting a hand at his trim waist.

"Did you place a bet, Uncle Greville?"

"Me? No, gave it up years ago." His gaze darted to Grampapa, his father. Physically, the two were similar, or were, before Grampapa's physician had ordered him to shed some extra weight. Uncle Greville looked as though he'd had no such advice. Quite the opposite.

As with Uncle Bert, she doubted Uncle Greville's sincerity. Why did neither of them seem capable of speaking the simple truth?

She knew why. Because they were hiding something—whatever it was she had overheard.

Once again keeping her tone light, half disinterested, she asked, "What brought you back to England, Uncle Greville?"

"Why, your wedding of course." He reached out as if to tweak her nose as he used to do when she was small, but at the last moment his hand dropped to his side. "Such a goose you are, Phoebe."

"But Julia got married and you didn't come then," she challenged.

"That was different. Too soon after the war. Traveling from Italy was still too difficult then."

Hm. Not an unreasonable excuse, yet something about the way he said it, the way his eyes continued to dart from person to person, only to land again on Grampapa, set Phoebe on her guard. There was a time she had loved this man unconditionally, but as she matured she had begun to see his flaws in all their glaring certainty. She began to see Greville through Papa's eyes—and through Grampapa's eyes, on those rare occasions during the war when Greville's name came up. And she had begun to wonder why he hadn't returned to England to buy a commission and join a regiment; why his name had sometimes been spoken in whispers that fell silent when she or any of her siblings entered a room. And how, eventually, his name ceased to be heard in the house at all.

Finally Phoebe's chance to speak with Aunt Cecily came. With a gusty sigh, Lucille rose from the settee and sauntered down the room toward the piano. She made a request of Julia, who switched songs in mid-note. Amelia, too, rose and followed her, and when she reached the piano she began singing in her lovely voice. That drew Grams and Grampapa to the piano as well.

Phoebe crossed the room and sat beside Aunt Cecily. She fingered the ball of yarn, a soft angora wool. "What are you knitting?"

"A little jacket for Julia's baby. I think I'll make a blanket to go with it, too."

"How darling." Phoebe regarded the rows growing from Aunt Cecily's knitting needles. "Perhaps when Owen and I have a child, I could persuade you to make something for him or her?"

"I'd most certainly love to, my dear. Knitting keeps my hands limber and my mind sharp. One mustn't lose track of the stitches, you know, or your garment will come out all higgledy-piggledy."

"We wouldn't want that." Phoebe chuckled and reflected on Aunt Cecily seeming rather lucid tonight.

"I could teach you, if you like," the elderly lady offered.

"I might take you up on that. Although . . ." She fingered Aunt Cecily's fine work. "I doubt I'd ever be as good at it as you. My rows would never be so perfectly straight."

"Oh, you might surprise yourself, my dear."

"You do have such a fine eye for detail, Aunt Cecily. I've been wondering if you remembered anything from the morning of my wedding. When you went for your walk," she added. "I know you said you didn't see anyone but . . ."

"As a matter of fact, I did." Aunt Cecily kept Phoebe in suspense as she focused the whole of her attention on her knit-purl-purl for a long moment. Phoebe refrained from nudging her to continue, but only just. Finally, "I remember the farmers being up and about. I could see them, though they were rather far from the road. Still, they made a picturesque scene, with the morning sun slanting over their fields."

"Anyone else? Anyone visiting at one of the homes, perhaps?"

Aunt Cecily lowered her knitting to her lap. "Visiting? I don't recall . . . Oh, wait. There was someone. Now, who was it?" Aunt Cecily pondered, staring at the brass fan covering the unlit hearth, her brows converging. She shook her head. "Well, all I can say is I was not invited to tea."

That again. Phoebe held in the sigh bursting to escape. But then an idea flashed in her mind. "Aunt Cecily, thank you. You've been a great help."

"Have I?" The woman blinked. "Goodness, I'm glad."

Phoebe came to her feet as Lucille returned. "It's almost

dinnertime, Aunt," Lucille said. "You might want to put your knitting aside now."

Phoebe hurried down the room to the piano, where Julia continued to play while Amelia, Theo, and her grandparents talked quietly. "Amelia, Julia, I'd like your help with something."

"What's that?" Julia asked without missing a note. She had lapsed into another favorite American style, ragtime, her hands traveling languidly up and down the keys in a sultry rhythm.

She addressed a question to Grams. "It's our tradition to bring the local farmers gifts when the ladies of the family marry, isn't it?"

"It is." Grams took on a look of mild surprise. "With all that's happened since, we've quite forgotten about it, haven't we?"

Julia nodded. "And you want help making up the parcels?"

"I do," Phoebe admitted. This was a task traditionally not left for the servants to accomplish. "Would you mind terribly?"

"I suppose not," Julia murmured noncommittedly, but Phoebe didn't doubt she would help. Her next words proved her correct. "If we start tomorrow, we'll have everything ready in a day or so."

"Yes, we'll get right to work in the morning," Amelia said brightly. "It sounds like jolly fun to me."

Theo, on the other hand, regarded Phoebe with eyes that narrowed the longer he looked. Phoebe began to feel self-conscious.

"What?" she asked him when the others once again began talking amongst themselves.

"You're planning to ask questions, aren't you? About what people might have seen right before the chief inspector was murdered."

Phoebe compressed her lips. She had known Theo Leighton all her life. Their families were close, and their estates practically bordered each other. Apparently, he knew her all too well. "Someone *had* to have seen something that morning, even if they don't realize it. Besides, the gifts *are* a tradition, and I wouldn't want to be neglectful."

"Then we'd all better get to work tomorrow morning," Amelia whispered at Phoebe's ear. Phoebe hadn't realized she'd been listening in. "Or you'll have nothing to hand out and no excuse to ask your questions."

"What are the lot of you conspiring about?" Grams rejoined their circle, eyeing each of them as she had done when they were children. Then she harrumphed and shrugged. "Never mind, here's Giles to announce dinner. Come, everyone."

Douglas returned Eva to Foxwood Hall before the family had finished dinner. Her time with Miles had felt almost normal, except that she had visited him unaccompanied at his flat. Had anyone noticed her arrival? Would the villagers begin gossiping? What would her parents think?

She couldn't worry about that. With Miles under house arrest, she had no other choice if she wished to see him. And she *did* wish to see him. The thought of him having to bear the burden of his arrest and its possible consequences alone was intolerable to her. She had brought a simple dinner of sandwiches prepared by Mrs. Ellison, the cook, and a bottle of wine slipped into the basket by Mr. Giles. It hadn't been one of Lord Wroxly's costly vintages, but rather something set aside for Mr. Giles's own use—and Eva would have kissed him for it if she hadn't known how embarrassed he would be.

It had been all too soon that Douglas returned for her, but she had work to catch up on. She had just brought up some of Lady Amelia's fine linens, all of which Eva had hand-washed earlier, and was letting herself out of the bedroom when a sight across the gallery stopped her in her tracks.

She thought the family and guests were all still in the dining room, but she had been mistaken. Despite the low lighting from the wall sconces, she could make out Lady Cecily's plump figure, so unlike Lady Wroxly's tall, lean form, hovering in front of the door to Lord Wroxly's study.

Had Lady Cecily become lost? By the time Eva crossed the gallery, the woman had disappeared inside. Lord Wroxly was not a man to forbid others entry into his study—in fact, Phoebe and her siblings had spent a good amount of time there as children—but what could Lady Cecily possibly want in an empty room?

And a dark one at that, for she hadn't switched on a light. Even so, Eva saw her standing a few feet in front of Lord Wroxly's wall-mounted gun case, where he kept several hunting and target-shooting rifles. As Eva looked on, dumbfounded, Lady Cecily stepped closer to the case and ran her hands around its edges as if searching for the latch. Lord Wroxly kept the case securely locked at all times. Even Fox had to consult his grandfather whenever he wished to use one of the weapons. Lady Cecily gripped either side of the frame and tugged. As Eva expected, nothing happened.

She stepped into the room. Quietly, so as not to startle the elderly woman, she asked, "My lady, may I help you with something?"

Lady Cecily dropped her hands to her sides and spun about. "Oh! Goodness. I didn't see you there. It's . . . it's Miss Huntford, isn't it?"

"Yes, my lady. Are you looking for something? May I fetch something for you?"

"Well . . . I . . . er . . ." She turned her head to glance

over her shoulder at the gun case. "It's a . . . er . . . fortunate thing that his lordship keeps this case locked."

"Yes, it is, my lady."

Lady Cecily frowned in a look of perplexity. She compressed her lips and clutched her hands together. "Well, then, I'll be going . . ." She ambled past Eva and into the corridor.

Eva followed her. "Everyone is still downstairs, my lady. Perhaps you'd care to rejoin them?" From the voices rising from the Great Hall, it sounded as though the family and guests were now moving into the drawing room.

Lady Cecily hesitated at the top of the staircase. Eva joined her there.

"I'll walk you down, if you like, my lady."

"Yes, that would be most obliging of you, Miss . . ."

"Huntford, ma'am."

At the bottom of the stairs, Eva gently took Lady Cecily's elbow and guided her toward the drawing room. "Thank you, dear," the woman said. "I know the way from here."

"You're quite welcome, my lady." Eva again followed, making sure Lady Cecily didn't take another detour.

"There you are, Aunt Cecily!" The dowager Marchioness of Allerton stood up from her chair and drew her aunt into the room.

"Why Cecily," Lady Wroxly said, "we thought you'd gotten lost."

"That nice Miss Huntford showed me the way . . ."

Eva lingered, hoping to catch Phoebe's eye. She didn't have long to wait. Phoebe excused herself and came out, and the two of them moved to the bottom of the stairs, out of hearing range of the others.

"What happened up there?" Phoebe pointed above to the first floor.

"I found Lady Cecily in your grandfather's study, trying to open the gun case."

"What? Good heavens!" Phoebe pressed a hand to her lips before continuing, "Not that she would have any success, but why? What could she have wanted?"

"A rifle?"

"To my knowledge Aunt Cecily hasn't hunted in decades, and even then she never carried a weapon, and certainly she's never been interested in skeet shooting. How odd. Well, I'll have to speak with my grandfather. With everyone, come to think of it. We all need to keep a keener eye on her, don't we?"

"I think that would be best."

"Poor Aunt Cecily. She's growing more and more confused by the day, it seems."

The next morning, Eva arrived belowstairs to a hullabaloo and the presence of Lord Wroxly and Lord Allerton. She quickly learned they had come to recruit Vernon and Douglas and were preparing to leave the house within the next few moments. Eva spied another unexpected individual: one of the Romany women, the dark-haired one with the turbulent black eyes, whom she and Phoebe had encountered outside the tearoom, the same woman who issued a subtle threat that Eva and Phoebe should mind their business. Nonetheless, Eva quickly went up to her.

"Is there trouble for your people?"

The woman's eyes sparked. "Do you care?"

"I do, as a matter of fact." Eva gestured at the men preparing to depart. "And so does Lord Wroxly and my mistress. What's happened?"

"Your detective is trying to evict us." Her chin jutted defiantly. "He's a fool, and if he doesn't listen to reason our men might resort to violence. I'm trying to prevent that."

"For one thing, he's not *our* detective. He's here from London to find whoever murdered Chief Inspector Perkins."

The woman huffed. "Yet another fool who wanted us gone."

The hairs on Eva's nape bristled to attention. Perhaps Serena Blackwell, arrested for shoplifting, hadn't had enough reason to murder Mr. Perkins, but what about another member of the caravan? Someone who resented Mr. Perkins's intentions to evict them enough to want him out of the way?

"I'm Eva Huntford," she said, holding out her hand.

"I remember." But for the squaring of her chin, she exhibited a complete lack of interest.

Eva let her hand drop. "Won't you tell me your name?"

After a roll of her eyes and another huff, she said, "Fiona."

Eva didn't press for more. "I'm happy to meet you, Fiona. I'll see you at your campsite."

"Why would you go? There could be trouble."

"I realize that. But I know that once my mistress hears of this, she'll go, and if she goes, I go."

Fiona scoffed. "I suppose she doesn't give you much choice."

"There you're wrong. In matters such as these, I have all the choice in the world, and I'll be there."

CHAPTER 7

Eva's arrival at the hunting lodge, flushed and out of breath, gave Phoebe a fright. Her first thought was that someone up at the house had taken ill. Before she hazarded a guess, however, Eva explained what she had witnessed belowstairs.

Owen had his boots on before she had finished the tale. "You say Lord Wroxly and Lord Allerton have already gone to the encampment?"

"Yes, with Vernon and Douglas." Eva clutched her hands together, mirroring Phoebe's own anxiety.

"I'm glad Grampapa didn't go alone." She drained the last of her coffee and stood. "I'm coming with you," she said to Owen.

"I wish you'd wait here. Especially after what happened in the village yesterday with the Vauxhall."

She issued him a stern glare. "I seriously doubt anyone will come at me with a hammer at the gypsy encampment."

"Perhaps not, yet things could become violent," he tried again.

She raised an eyebrow, her gaze continuing to issue a caution.

He exhaled. "Fine. But you and Eva stay back." He spoke as if issuing an order, but he and Phoebe both knew it was a request, one she would grant if only to ease his mind and those of Grampapa and the other men.

With Eva's help, she, too, donned a pair of sturdy boots. They would be traipsing well off the road into a field, surely no place for fashionable pumps.

They drove in Owen's Rover along the estate roads, which took them beyond the tenant farms to the forested hillsides that bordered them. The camp nestled between the slopes of two rolling hills, awash in the rich creams, golds, and violets of pennycress, cowslip, and bluebells. When they arrived, Grampapa and the others were already deep in conversation with Detective Burridge. The camp was smaller than Phoebe had imagined, only five caravans where she had pictured at least a dozen. They were brightly painted with intricate designs and trimmed in carved woodwork. Phoebe had also imagined they would have formed a circle, but each caravan stood at least a dozen yards from the next, providing a modicum of privacy. Tents had been pitched beside three of the caravans, and the horses were tethered nearby.

Just as Grampapa hadn't come alone, neither had the detective. He had apparently recruited several men from the village whom Phoebe recognized. Perhaps he had deputized them, for they were presently searching the caravans and tents as well as dousing cookfires. The women stood with their arms crossed in front of them and murderous expressions on their faces, with frightened-looking children peeking out from behind their skirts. Some of them were unkempt and in various states of dress, but no wonder; Burridge and his men had obviously disrupted their morning.

But it was the gypsy men who worried Phoebe most. Their scowls suggested more than murderous sentiments, but rather murderous intentions. They shadowed the intruders, some of them gripping lengths of firewood, while another wielded what appeared to be a wagon axel. For now, they held their ground, but Phoebe felt the rumblings of an impending explosion.

Owen hopped out of the vehicle and turned to address Phoebe through the open window. "Perhaps you might wait here, in the motor?"

She was already opening her door, while Eva climbed out of the backseat. Owen sighed loudly and strode over to the other men. "Don't let anything happen to my grandfather," Phoebe called after him. As she watched him go, two of the gypsy men, leaders perhaps, approached the group surrounding Detective Burridge. She studied them for signs of impending violence.

"Things seem fairly calm at the moment," she concluded. She linked her arm through Eva's. "Let's see if we can speak with some of the women."

There were several of them watching the activity, standing in a group. Once again, they were clad in ordinary frocks, some wearing colorful shawls, others in brightly knitted jackets or cardigans. Phoebe also noticed that they wore beaded necklaces and painted wooden bracelets that looked to be handcrafted. Some of the children were barefoot, while others wore soft leather shoes that might have been handmade.

Eva gestured at one of the women. "That's Fiona, who was at Foxwood Hall earlier."

"Yes, I remember her from outside the tearoom. Let's see if she can tell us anything more."

"They're searching for stolen goods," the black-haired Fiona told them, indicating the village men rummaging through the caravans. "Looking for a reason to arrest us, or at the least drive us out of the area."

"How dastardly," Phoebe blurted out. "Searching with no good reason? My grandfather will put a stop to it." At least, she hoped he would be able to. She stole another peek at the negotiations. Another gypsy man, younger than the first two, joined them, striding over with a stern expression on his stony features. Like Fiona, he possessed raven's black hair, which he wore loose and flowing to his shoulders. Her brother, perhaps?

Fiona recaptured her attention when she muttered, "They don't need a reason." The other three women nodded.

"But they won't find anything, will they?" Eva spoke with confidence, and Phoebe hoped she was right.

The women traded looks. One with a buxom figure and hair the color of dark fire, thickly braided and falling over one shoulder, said, "If they can't find anything, they'll likely plant something they've brought with them. It's what they did to me."

Ah. The woman accused of stealing from the dry goods store. Phoebe and Eva traded a glance, and Phoebe said, "You're Serena Blackwell, aren't you?"

The woman's mouth flattened and her chin came up. But at the same moment, Phoebe heard a sound she had rarely heard in her life: Grampapa raising his voice.

"Now see here, Burridge. This is my land and these people are here with my permission. They'll leave when they're ready."

"And actually, Burridge, we don't see why this is any of your business." Owen pulled himself to full height, dwarfing the detective. "You're here to investigate the chief inspector's death, not decide who may and may not visit Little Barlow."

"As a matter of fact, my lord, I've been put in charge of

the village's constabulary until a permanent replacement can be assigned." The man's mustache twitched.

"This is *our* village and we don't want gypsies here," one of the village men shouted. Phoebe gasped. She recognized him as a farmer who also worked at the village gristmill. A few of his fellows nodded their agreement. Others, however, stood back, looking ill at ease.

The three Romany men standing with Grampapa turned toward the farmer, issuing scowls that could freeze an ember of coal. To their credit, they took their anger no further. For now.

The detective leered with a self-satisfied *I told you so* expression.

Grampapa stepped closer to him, his voice low and steady, calm to the casual observer, but Phoebe recognized his simmering fury. "This stops now or I shall contact your superiors in London. You may be temporarily in charge, but that doesn't give you the right to harass people who are simply going about their business. I'm sure Scotland Yard would be interested to know how you're wasting your time here . . . and ours."

A surge of pride filled Phoebe. Grampapa had never been a man to suffer an injustice, whether directed at himself or others, nor one to cower from an argument, provided it was a fair one. She turned back to the women, surprised that the defiance on their faces had turned to admiration.

"You see," she said, "my family cares what happens to you. My grandfather isn't about to let anyone run you off his land."

"Perhaps we were wrong about some of you." Fiona offered something approaching a smile, which brought an exotic beauty to her face. "But we're rarely given the benefit of the doubt."

"Perhaps, if I may . . ." Eva paused, allowing her gaze to travel over each woman. "You're all wearing such lovely jewelry. Did you make the pieces yourselves?"

"Serena and Juliana make most of the jewelry we wear," Fiona said. Serena and an older woman each gave a nod. "We also weave the scarves and shawls we wear."

"And do you sell these items?" Eva continued, and suddenly Phoebe understood what she was getting at.

"It's one of the ways we make money." Serena sounded almost defensive. With her fingers she combed back a lock of coppery hair that had come loose from her braid. "We travel to market towns and fairs to sell our handicrafts."

"Little Barlow is but a stopover for us," Fiona explained, "to give the horses a chance to rest and the children time to run and play."

"Why not invite the villagers here to see your wares?" Eva suggested. "It might help them to see that you're not very different from the rest of us. It might change their minds about you."

"I think you should," Phoebe agreed eagerly. "You could tell fortunes as well, and there would be no one to tell you you can't."

The women conferred in murmurs. The one named Juliana, older than Fiona and Serena by a couple of decades, said, "Our men could entertain the villagers with music and games of chance. We could demonstrate our dances. But do you think your grandfather will mind?"

"I don't believe he would, but I'll speak with him."

Fiona held out a hand, her finger pointing. "Look, they're leaving."

Phoebe turned to see Detective Burridge walking back to his motorcar. The village men piled into a farm lorry. The engines puttered to life, and the vehicles pulled slowly away, maneuvering carefully over rocks and hillocks.

That left Grampapa, Owen, and Theo still speaking

with the gypsy men. More joined them, accompanied by some of the women. Fiona and her group nodded to Phoebe and Eva and began making their way over as well. Phoebe and Eva followed.

"That was a brilliant suggestion," she whispered to Eva.

Eva grinned and nodded. "But more out of self-interest, I must admit. I'm so curious about them. I would love to spend a couple of hours in their company, learning more about their lives."

"I would as well. And some real good may come of it. I realize they're not here to stay, but they might return, might make Little Barlow a regular stopover on their travels. And perhaps then they would be welcome here."

"It would be lovely to think so," Eva agreed.

Miles let Eva into his flat with a concerned look that raised Eva's fears.

"What is it? Has Detective Burridge been to see you?"

"No, it's not that." He took the sack she carried, set it aside, and took her in his arms. "I'm worried about your being seen coming here so often."

Relief drew a laugh. "Is that all?"

" 'Is that all?' " He held her at arm's length. "We're talking about your reputation, and that of your family. I can't have you risking—"

"It's my choice to be here, to see you. My family will understand." Would they? Eva could only hope they continued in the unconditional support they had shown her all her life. "And Lord Wroxly and the rest of the Renshaws certainly understand. Who else matters?"

He stared at the floor, obviously unconvinced. "I suppose."

She framed his face with her hands, not roughly, but not gently either. "The only person doing wrong here is Detective Burridge. I believe he and Chief Inspector Perkins would have gotten on famously." She pursed her lips and shook her head. "I'm sorry, there I go again, speaking ill of a man who can no longer defend himself."

Miles chuckled, then laughed outright. After a moment, Eva joined in his merriment, as much because it had become a rare treat as because she found humor in the situation. As long as Miles kept up his spirits . . .

He retrieved the sack from the side table. "What have you brought?"

"Let's take it to the kitchen." She led the way to the counter. To term the cramped corner of Miles's flat a kitchen was to overstate the case, as it contained merely a stove, sink, an open cupboard, a tiny icebox, and just enough space to set out a plate or two. A table and two chairs separated the kitchen area from the parlor. She opened the sack and emptied it of its contents.

"Mrs. Ellison made you a pork pie, some bread pudding, and there are some scones and hot cross buns." She took out each package and placed it on the counter. "Oh, also some jams and a bit of brandy butter."

"Bless Mrs. Ellison." He came up beside her and wrapped an arm around her waist. "Hungry?"

"I've eaten, but you go ahead." She had made a point of eating back at Foxwood Hall. The food had been meant for Miles, and she wanted it to last until her next visit.

After he had eaten his fill and they had each enjoyed a splash of Mr. Giles's wine, they moved to the sofa. Though Eva tried to distract him with happier subjects, the case inevitably came up.

"I've been thinking." Miles slung his arm across Eva's shoulders. "The lack of clues as well as the killer having entered the cottage without any signs of a struggle suggests two things."

"One being that Mr. Perkins knew his assailant?"

"Yes, that, but more. Perhaps he'd been drugged or otherwise incapacitated before the actual murder. The killer had to have gotten hold of Perkins's gun and then managed to shoot him while he was sitting in his own chair."

"Had he been himself he would have fought back and tried to reclaim the gun," Eva said, following his train of thought.

"Exactly. He wouldn't have obligingly sat there waiting to die."

"Did the coroner find any other wounds on him? Such as a head wound that might explain his being such a passive victim?"

"No, that's just it. There weren't any other wounds." Miles was silent a moment. "I think someone must have drugged him, either in his coffee or his breakfast. There were the remains of a Cornish pasty on his plate."

"Yes, I remember. But how could someone have . . ." Eva raised her eyebrows in surprise. "You mean this wasn't a spur-of-the-moment opportunity. Someone planned this in advance."

"*Well* in advance, if I'm correct."

"You said you found a bottle of whiskey beside his coffee." When Miles nodded, Eva continued, "Could that have made him tipsy enough to render him helpless?"

"I don't believe so." Miles gave a firm shake of his head. "The chief inspector was often tipsy, but rarely drunk. If anything, his morning tipple steadied him. It wasn't until later in the evening that he was ever blathered."

"Have you discussed this with Detective Burridge?"

Miles chuckled, this time without humor. "He doesn't exactly pop by to chat."

"Then I'll tell him." Eva slid out from beneath Miles's

arm—and immediately missed the reassuring weight of it. She pushed to her feet. "I'll go right now."

"Eva, no." He rose and grasped her hands. "I don't want you dealing with that man."

"I'm not afraid of him." She straightened her spine. "I'm only afraid of his not finding the truth and letting you suffer for it."

"Then wait until someone can go with you. Lady Phoebe or someone."

She shook her head, then leaned in to kiss him. "I'll be back soon." She hurried to let herself out of the flat before Miles could protest again.

Detective Burridge was outside the post office when she reached the High Street. Their gazes met, though he quickly cast his away and pretended he hadn't seen her. With a slight hunch to his shoulders as if to avoid imaginary rain-drops, he strode briskly toward the police station. Unde-terred, Eva followed in pursuit.

"Detective Burridge . . . Detective!" she called after him, knowing full well he heard her though he continued to pretend oblivion to his surroundings. He disappeared through the police station door. "Good," Eva murmured aloud to herself. "Now he's trapped and can't escape me."

She pretended not to notice his groan when she stepped inside. "Hello, Detective. How lucky to catch you in."

"Hmm. I'm terribly busy, Miss Huntford."

"Are you? But you only just set foot inside a moment before I did." She scanned his messy desktop. "Surely you haven't had time yet to bury yourself in your work."

"As a matter of fact, I—"

"Good," she said, and after scraping the other desk chair closer, she sat with an air of having no intention of rising until she was good and ready. "There's an urgent matter I'd like to discuss with you. It concerns Constable Brannock's case. Or, I should say, it concerns Chief Inspector Perkins's murder, which had nothing whatsoever to do with Constable Brannock."

"Did it not, now?" the man mumbled, which Eva also ignored.

"Was the chief inspector's breakfast analyzed at the police laboratory in Gloucester?"

"Say what?"

"I'm sure you heard me quite clearly. Was it analyzed?"

The man's features scrunched with perplexity. "Why would it have been?"

"To see if he'd been drugged."

"My dear Miss Huntford, the man was shot to death. Why would his killer need to drug him?"

"Don't you find it strange that he was shot in his own chair, beside his breakfast? That whoever pulled the trigger met with no resistance from him at all?"

A little spark of . . . surprise? . . . lit the detective's eyes. He *hadn't* considered it, had he?

"Of course I thought of that, Miss Huntford."

Liar.

"And? Did you have the remnants of his plate and cup analyzed?"

"The lab is quite busy. Backlogged, you see. They'll get to it when they can."

Eva would have wagered her best fabric shears that he had *not* sent the evidence to Gloucester. And now it was probably too late. "What about the coroner? Did he check for signs of the chief inspector having been drugged?"

Detective Burridge blinked. His nostrils flared. "Now see here, Miss Huntford, I know how to conduct an investigation. And as I said, I'm terribly busy. I must ask you to leave at once."

"All right. But do speak with the coroner." She went to

the door, turning before she opened it and assuming her most appreciative expression. "Thank you, Detective. Good day."

Outside on the pavement, she heaved a deep sigh. Had she gotten through to him? Planted the seed of what needed to be done next? Or had she simply wasted his time and hers?

It had been worth a try.

CHAPTER 8

"I believe it's high time to visit the McGowans' farm," Phoebe said to Owen over breakfast the next morning.

"I could ask Theo to come with me," he offered without meeting her gaze.

"We can go together, while the windscreen on the Vauxhall is being repaired." Douglas had driven the motor at first light to the nearest repair shop two villages over.

She expected a protest, but she received none. They finished their meal and prepared for the day.

With the brisk spring breeze flowing in through the Rover's open windows, Phoebe felt a sense of relief as they left Little Barlow behind. She hadn't realized how oppressive matters there had become. This should have been one of the happiest times of her life, but with Constable Brannock under suspicion of murder and Eva's future shredding before her very eyes, Phoebe simply couldn't be happy.

"We may meet with no more success than Detective Burridge." Owen changed gears and gunned the motor along a straightaway bordered by hedgerows and open fields.

"Perhaps not, but even if we find no sign of Ian McGowan, I would at least like to speak to his wife. Gauge her responses to questions about her husband, and see for myself whether the marriage is over or if she's protecting him."

Owen nodded his agreement, keeping his eyes on the road ahead and slowing their pace once it began to twist and turn again. Clouds threatened rain, but Owen's sedan offered better shelter than Phoebe's canvas-topped Vauxhall.

The McGowans lived some five miles from Little Barlow, in a rural hamlet called Heathcombe, which boasted little more than a church, a village hall, and a post office–cum–general store. Here the road presented an obstacle course of deep holes and ruts, sudden turns, steep hills, and dangerous descents. It took them nearly an hour to reach the village precincts. But once there, it didn't take them long to find the McGowans' farm. Owen pulled the car onto the verge outside the fence.

A stone, two-story cottage with yellow shutters and a matching door stood nestled beneath old-growth pines and oaks. A picturesque covered well stood out front, and several stone outbuildings were ranged behind the house. All appeared in good repair.

"It would seem the family has been maintaining the property." Phoebe craned her neck to see into the distance. "See the neatly plowed fields beyond the farmyard. Perhaps Mr. McGowan *hasn't* been missed, at least not as the family provider."

"Appearances can be deceiving." Owen set his hand on the door latch. "But the homestead does appear neat and tidy, if not outright prosperous." He climbed out of the car and came around to Phoebe's side to help her just as she was about to step out. She took his hand, smiling up at him.

"Ready?"

He quirked an eyebrow and offered his arm. They walked

up the short front path from the road. At their knock, a young teenage girl answered the door. She gazed at them expectantly, showing no fear or timidity. She wore a boy's coveralls, her hair hidden beneath a kerchief.

"May I help you? If it's my mother you're looking for, she's tending the chickens." The savory scents of cooking wafted through the open door. Phoebe's mouth watered at the warm aromas of beef, sausage, onions, and rich pastry crust.

She half wished to invite herself in for a meal. Instead, she smiled. "We would like to speak with your mother if she isn't too busy. Would you mind showing us the way?"

The girl stepped outside and closed the door behind her, cutting off the enticing aromas. "Follow me."

"Is your father at home?" Owen asked offhandedly.

The girl missed a step, not hard to do with so many tree roots pushing up into the front garden. Or had Owen's question brought on a bout of nerves? "My dad's been away for many years now," she said cryptically.

"I see." Owen cast a glance around him. "Your family runs a fine farm, from the looks of it."

"My brothers and I all pitch in to help our mother. She's a cracking farmer. It's hard work, but I enjoy it. Better than school."

"School is important, too," Phoebe couldn't stop herself from saying. "Someday you might not want to farm, and an education will allow you choices."

"I'll never not want to farm," the girl declared. As they came around the house onto flatter ground, she walked faster, prompting Phoebe and Owen to do the same to keep up. A long, low stone building, enclosed by a knee-high wire fence, sat off to the side of a larger barn. She led them to it. "Mum! Some people here to see you."

Amid clucks and cackles coming from inside the low building, a voice called out. "Who?"

"Don't know." The girl turned back to them, her head tilted in query.

"I'm Phoebe Renshaw—excuse me, Phoebe Seabright—and this is my husband, Owen."

The girl shrugged, their names meaning nothing to her. From the end of the coop, a figure appeared, obviously the girl's mother. Wearing overalls like her daughter, she cast them a curious glance. "Hello. I'm Mrs. McGowan. What can I do for you? But mind, I've plenty of work yet and not much time to chat."

She came toward them and handed a basket filled with eggs to her daughter. The girl tipped a nod at them and set off back to the house. The mother waited for either Phoebe or Owen to explain the reason for their visit. Suddenly Phoebe realized how awkward a conversation this would be.

She cleared her throat. "You've a lovely farm here." She glanced out toward the fields. "You grow wheat as your main crop?"

"That and rapeseed, yes. And there are the eggs, of course. I do a good business in eggs. But I'm supposing you're not here to ask about my yields." She took on a wary expression, edged with anger. "If you're here to try to buy my land, you can turn right around and go back where you came from."

"No, Mrs. McGowan," Phoebe hastily said. "We're not here for your land. We have a question or two about . . ." She glanced up at Owen.

"Out with it," the woman demanded. "I've morning chores to complete and my ledger to attend to. Farming isn't all about the ground. There's business—and figures that must add up. I've also a batch of meat pies to take out of the oven."

"Sorry, yes." Phoebe swallowed and hoped she didn't anger the woman so much she marched away. "Mrs. Mc-

Gowan, we understand your husband was recently released from prison. Have you seen him?"

Her eyebrows knitted. "There was a detective here asking the same question about a week ago. I don't know why
it should concern you. You're obviously not with the police." She surveyed them up and down. "But I suppose I
can tell you what I told him. I haven't seen my husband in
years. We've gone our separate ways. Eight years apart
will do that."

Owen, who had been gazing out over the fields, turned
back, looking unconvinced. "He hasn't even been by to see
the children?"

"What can I say?" Mrs. McGowan held up her hands
and didn't offer anything more.

Not quite a denial. Nor did she ask why they were
searching for her husband. A boy, nearly a man, came out
of the barn and ambled over to them. He took up position
beside his mother and folded his arms, looking none too
friendly. "Is there a problem, Ma?"

"No, no problem, Gideon."

"You asked about my dad," he said in accusation. "I
heard you."

"It's all right, Gideon." His mother prodded his side.
"Best get back to work."

He gave Phoebe and Owen what he probably believed
was a fierce look, but only made him appear more child
than man.

"We've bothered you long enough." Phoebe slipped her
arm through Owen's. "By the way, your meat pies smell
heavenly. You must be a splendid cook. Your family is
very lucky."

"Thank you. But most of my pies are spoken for. I supply several inns and restaurants in the area. My son deliv-
ers them. Yet another way we've found to stay afloat."

They said their goodbyes and retraced their steps to the Rover. Once there, Owen asked, "Where to next?"

"The church."

"Feeling the need to say a prayer?"

"No. I'm feeling the need to speak with the vicar. I'd like to learn more about Mr. and Mrs. McGowan, and he might be the perfect source of information.

Eva and Amelia spent the better part of an hour below-stairs making up the parcels to be dispersed to local families in honor of Phoebe's marriage. They had set up in the servants' hall, as lunch had already been served and no one would be using the room until later that evening. Mrs. Ellison and Dora had worked overtime the night before, and an array of goods covered the table, including baked treats, savory pies, homemade candies, and small jars of spices and teas. Lady Amelia hummed as they worked, making occasional comments or sharing bits of harmless gossip concerning her circle of friends and acquaintances. Eva enjoyed their companionable industry and with a not unpleasant jolt realized her days ahead would be very much like this, with her being Amelia's maid rather than Phoebe's.

She had been dreading the day Phoebe moved away with her new husband, but now the prospect of a quieter life with Amelia seemed not only pleasant, but rewarding. Being a lady's maid had always meant much more to her than simply keeping wardrobes in shape and helping her ladies look their best. She had often been like a surrogate mother to them, and since Phoebe no longer needed her in that way, it was now time to support Amelia as she ventured further into the adult world.

"Isn't it just like Phoebe to request our help and then not be here herself." Lady Julia came into the room, holding little Charles's hand as he toddled beside her. His already large eyes widened and an eager smile blossomed when he saw the goodies spread out on the table.

"Chaws wan eat," he exclaimed, which Eva knew translated to *Charles wants a treat*.

Eva plucked up a chocolate bonbon with raspberry filling and questioned his mother with a quirk of an eyebrow.

"Just the one," she replied, then shook her head. "Let's cut it in half." She looked about for a knife and found one near Amelia's elbow. After handing her son the chocolate and popping the other half into her mouth, she asked, "Now then, where on earth is Phoebe, and why are we working when she is not?"

"Technically speaking, Julia," her sister calmly pointed out, "you haven't been working either. It's been Eva and me. But you're welcome to stay and help us now."

"That doesn't answer my question, dearest." Lady Julia sat at the table and drew Charles into her lap, against her growing belly. The boy chomped his candy noisily, the chocolate and jam coating his lips and threatening to do the same to his chin. Eva hurried to a sideboard, found a checked serviette, and pressed it to the boy's mouth.

"Your sister and Lord Owen have gone to see if they can find Ian McGowan," she explained as she carefully wiped away all traces of chocolate from Charles's face. He grinned up at her, his tiny teeth still working the sweet, and suddenly something inside Eva twisted with longing.

"You really ought to wait until he's finished chewing," Lady Julia advised with a laugh, "or you'll be doing it again." She took the serviette from Eva. She was almost reluctant to give over the wiping of Charles's mouth to his mother. "What do they hope to accomplish that Detective Burridge didn't?"

"They're hoping to catch Mr. McGowan at home."

Amelia wrapped a completed bundle in packing paper and tied it with ribbon. "They don't believe his family hasn't seen him since he was released from prison."

Lady Julia shrugged a shoulder. "Even if they find him there, what do they hope to accomplish? He'll simply deny being in Little Barlow the morning of the chief inspector's murder, and how will they prove otherwise if his family corroborates his claim?"

"Julia, you're such a skeptic." Amelia began gathering items for another bundle. "Why don't you let Eva hold Charles awhile and lend me a hand here?"

"Oh, all right." Without ceremony Julia rose and thrust Charles into Eva's arms. Eva stood with him, finding herself rocking side to side and chuckling at his half-toothed grins.

"Chaws wan maw!" *Charles wants more.* Eva glanced at Lady Julia, who shook her head.

"That's all for now, Charles. Treats are only for sometimes."

"Maw time." *More times.* But when Eva worried that he might whine or cry, he simply laughed and tugged on the collar of her dress.

A moment later Hetta, Lady Julia's Swiss lady's maid, came into the room. She stretched out her arms. "I take him," she said in her German accent.

Without thought, Eva turned aside, putting the boy out of Hetta's reach. "That's all right. I don't mind."

Hetta frowned slightly but let her arms fall to her sides. She glanced at the table. "I come to help then."

While the others continued tying up small bundles, Eva strolled around the room, pointing out items to Charles. He seemed particularly interested in the call bells on the wall behind Mr. Giles's chair at the head of the table. He stretched his arm and pointed.

"Those are the bells," Eva explained, and he launched

into a repetition of *ding, ding, ding.* "That's right, that's how the people upstairs call us when they need us. Each bell is linked to a particular room upstairs, so we always know where we're wanted." She knew Charles didn't understand what she was telling him, but his face took on an interested look all the same.

"Ding, ding."

"Right you are." She brought him over to the long sideboard. "And this is where we keep our dishes and cutlery, oh, and serviettes, as you now know."

"Charles, dear," Lady Julia called, "are you tiring out our poor Miss Huntford?"

"Not in the least, my lady." All the same, Charles *was* becoming heavy in her arms. Eva used her foot to move a chair out from the table and sat, placing the boy on her lap. He leaned comfortably against her, his head level with her chin, and she leaned her cheek gently against his hair. The warm weight of him felt heavenly, in a way Eva had never noticed before.

"I think Phoebe owes us all a treat when she gets back." Lady Julia tied a neat bow around the bundle she had just wrapped. "What shall we ask of her? How about if she agrees to hold down the fort while the rest of us take a turn in town. We can have tea at Pippa Young's shop, all of us—Eva and Hetta included—while Phoebe takes care of Charles and keeps the adults from killing one another in our absence."

"Killing one another?" Amelia sounded outraged at the very notion. "Everyone has been getting on splendidly."

"Splendidly?" Lady Julia leaned an elbow on the table and dropped her chin in her palm as she regarded her younger sister. "Lucille is going mad trying to keep Aunt Cecily in check; Grampapa and Grams cannot *stand* Giovanna—truly they cannot, though they're doing their best to hide it—and they're both walking on eggshells around

Uncle Greville, wondering what he's up to being back in England. Meanwhile, Uncle Bert is trying to be diplomatic with everyone but it's beginning to wear thin."

"You didn't mention Theo and Owen," Amelia reminded her.

"No one need worry about *them*." Lady Julia gave a wry chuckle. "They know how to make themselves scarce when needs must. The same for Fox."

They talked on, but Eva barely heard the rest. She was too fascinated with Charles—with his curious little hands reaching for the goodies on the table, his downy hair, his soft babbling, and the powdery smell of him.

An ember burned beneath her breastbone, and she blinked away sudden tears. She turned her head as if she, too, found the call bells fascinating, but in actuality she didn't want the others to witness the emotion that welled within her.

A child of her own . . . would she ever have one? She certainly wasn't getting any younger. What if . . . what if Miles wasn't exonerated? If the charges stood and he was convicted, he would . . . hang. And with him would go Eva's heart and her hopes and her entire future. And this . . . this promise of a new life that would someday come from their love.

"Eva, are you quite all right?"

Amelia's question startled her out of her reverie. Eva turned to discover all three women staring at her in concern. "I'm . . . yes . . . I'm fine. Perfectly. Of course."

Lady Julia narrowed her dark blue eyes, her gaze sharp. "No, you're not and you needn't pretend. We all know how worried you are about Constable Brannock."

"Yes. But I'm all right." She blew out a breath and drew herself up. "I have faith that an innocent man will not pay for another's crime." Did she? Her doubts persisted like tiny pinpricks, each one stinging and drawing a spot of blood. In her lap, Charles began to fuss. Had he sensed the change in her mood?

Hetta came to her feet. "I take him now. Time for nap." Eva relinquished the child to Hetta's arms, the loss of his warmth leaving her chilled.

Phoebe and Owen retraced their route through Heathcombe proper and pulled up beside the churchyard. Like most of the other structures that made up the village, a façade of golden Cotswold stone presented a warm welcome to both the church and the vicarage next door. The church stood silently amid overhanging trees and the graveyard that sprawled beside it. Owen opened the wrought iron gate and they proceeded up a slate-lined path to the vicarage's front door.

An elderly man, bald but for tufts of gray hair that stuck out around his ears, answered their knock. "Good heavens, you're early. I wasn't expecting you for another half hour at least."

Phoebe stole a glance up at Owen. "I'm sorry? I don't believe—"

"Well, come in, come in. My housekeeper has already put the kettle on low. I'll tell her to turn up the flame." He paused to regard them, his eyes crinkling with merriment. "Do you like crumpets? She makes fine crumpets, my housekeeper does."

"Thank you, but no, we don't wish to impose," Owen said.

Phoebe took up where he left off. "Sir, we'd like but a moment of your time . . ."

"Of course, of course. We'll talk in the parlor. So much less stuffy than my office. I'd like you to feel at home while we discuss the ceremony."

"Ceremony?" Phoebe allowed the man to lead them into a pleasant parlor that looked and smelled as if it had just been thoroughly cleaned. The mahogany furnishings gleamed with a recent polishing. "I believe there's been a mistake."

Here the man stopped midway across the room. "Aren't you Mr. Commish and Miss Jenkinson? Aren't you here to discuss your upcoming nuptials?"

Phoebe stifled a laugh of surprise.

"No, sir, we're already married." Owen put out his hand. "I'm Owen Seabright and this is my wife, Phoebe. We were recently wed in Little Barlow."

"Good heavens, my mistake. Then are you here to discuss a baptismal, perhaps?"

"What?" Phoebe's hand flew to her belly. "My goodness, no. I'm not . . . we're not . . . I mean . . ."

"We're here about a different matter entirely, sir. May we sit?" Owen gestured toward a comfortably worn settee whose down cushions bore the permanent imprints of the many individuals who had come to visit the vicar.

"Please do. And let's begin again. I'm Mr. Abbott, and I've presided over St. Lawrence parish some twenty-five years." His eyes twinkled. "Which could explain the rather addled state in which I greeted you. You'll have to forgive me, I'm not as young as I used to be."

"Nonsense, sir." Phoebe smiled a reassurance. "We're actually here to discuss one of your parishioners, or a former one, perhaps I should say. Ian McGowan?"

"Ah . . . yes, Mr. McGowan. A tragic story there. Quite tragic."

Owen settled back against the settee. "What can you tell us about him?"

The man's silver brows converged. "May I ask first what your interest in Ian McGowan is?"

Phoebe sighed and said to Owen, "I think we should be honest." He nodded, and she turned back to Mr. Abbott.

"Have you heard about the recent troubles in Little Barlow? Our chief inspector himself was the victim of a violent crime. He was murdered."

"Yes, I read about it." The vicar nodded his grizzled head. "His own assistant has been charged with the crime. A most regrettable business."

"We don't think the constable had anything to do with the chief inspector's murder, sir." Owen's hand found Phoebe's and closed around it. "You see, it was Chief Inspector Isaac Perkins who arrested Ian McGowan all those years ago. We know McGowan tried to reason with him, told him about his ill son, but Perkins followed the letter of the law. McGowan was recently released from prison."

"And you think he murdered the chief inspector out of revenge?" Phoebe heard the skepticism in the vicar's voice. "I don't know . . . I can't see it. The Ian McGowan I knew was not a violent man. Not in any sense of the word."

"Prison can change a person," Phoebe suggested.

"True, true, but I'd be surprised all the same."

"What was he like before he went to prison?" she asked.

The housekeeper, a middle-aged woman of average proportions and a pleasant countenance, entered the room. "Tea for your guests, sir?"

The vicar cast a glance at Phoebe and Owen. They shook their heads no. "Nothing for now, Mrs. Garr." Then he turned his attention to Phoebe's question. "I knew Ian McGowan to be an even-tempered man, devoted to his family, and quite fond of his wife. They attended church every Sunday, rain or shine, and whenever anyone in the village needed a hand, he was there to help. Rarely argued with anyone that I know of." He folded his hands together and leaned forward. "His arrest was wrong, plain and simple. Yes, perhaps he broke the law, but only fear for his son's life would have compelled a man like Ian McGowan to do such a thing. Those years he spent behind bars were a waste of a good life, in my opinion."

A short silence followed. Phoebe met the vicar's gaze. "And have you seen him since his release?"

"I have not, and that is the truth."

"Would you tell us if you had?" Owen pressed.

The vicar sighed again. "I suppose I would, given the circumstances. Not that I believe for a moment he could have had anything to do with the chief inspector's death, but I'm a man of God, sworn to uphold the truth."

A knock on the door brought their discussion to an end. Mr. Abbott came to his feet. "That will be Mr. Commish and Miss Jenkinson."

"Yes, of course." Owen stood and helped Phoebe to her feet.

"Thank you, Mr. Abbott."

"I don't know that I've been any help, really."

"You've given us a lot to think about," she said, and they took their leave, wishing the engaged couple well as they passed them in the front hall.

Once more in the Rover and heading back to Little Barlow, Phoebe fell to contemplating what they had learned. "It doesn't add up, not by half."

"How do you mean?" Owen drove with a look of deep concentration, more so than was necessary on the stretch of road they presently traveled. Phoebe guessed he was as baffled as she.

"If Ian McGowan was as saintly as Mr. Abbott described, why *wouldn't* his wife want him back?"

"Eight years is a long time. And the couple also suffered the death of their son. Perhaps Mrs. McGowan blamed her husband for not bringing back a doctor."

"That wouldn't have been his fault. He was arrested."

"Yes, but a grieving parent isn't always the most rational.

Phoebe agreed, but doubts about the state of the McGowans' marriage persisted. "I think she knows exactly where he is. I think she's protecting him."

Owen took his eyes off the road long enough to angle a glance at her. "Because he's guilty of murder?"

"Or because he's not, but they're afraid he'll be accused and condemned, just as he was eight years ago. Which leaves us with a gaping question and no clear path to an answer."

"Except finding Ian McGowan."

"Yes. We must find Ian McGowan."

CHAPTER 9

"Phoebe, come with us," Uncle Greville urged the following morning as he, Giovanna, and Theo prepared to go for a ride in Theo's Silver Ghost motorcar, another item he'd inherited from his brother.

"Where are you all off to?" As if she didn't know. The plan between her, Theo, and Owen had been well formed, and now she was pleased to see Theo's part progressing smoothly.

"Just a ride round the estate and the farms," Uncle Greville replied. Giovanna slipped her sleek arm through his in a proprietary manner, staring darkly at Phoebe as she did so. Phoebe couldn't fathom why, but before she could wonder about it, Greville spoke again. "It's been ages since I've seen it all, and I'm curious to see what kind of shape the place is in."

Phoebe joined them at the front door as Mr. Giles handed them their dusters. Giovanna also covered her abundant hair with a silk scarf and tied it beneath her chin—all the while continuing to stare at Phoebe. Phoebe ignored her. To Uncle Greville she said, "I think you'll find it's all shipshape these days. The tenants, and indeed the entire vil-

lage, have been working to repair everything that went un-
done during the war."

"Really?" Uncle Greville looked skeptical. "A thorough
renovation? Must be costing the estate a pretty penny. I
can't imagine the locals are funding the work themselves."

It was Phoebe's turn to stare. What was his point? That
Grampapa was squandering the entailed fortune? "Don't
you worry," she told him, "there's been a plan laid out and
it's being followed to the letter."

"What kind of plan?"

This, too, Phoebe ignored. She turned to Theo. "So,
where will you take them first?"

"I thought we'd see the cultivated fields first, then the
livestock and grazing pastures."

"I'd like to see the other houses in the area." Giovanna
gave her free hand a careless flick. "A field is a field—what
good is it to anyone but a farmer? I want to see where people live, what other grand houses there are in the region."
She appealed to her husband. "Couldn't we do that instead?"

"Well, now, darling, I'd like to see the old homestead.
As I said, it's been years." She pouted, and he quickly
added, "After that we'll go house hunting."

Phoebe's spine went rigid. Were they considering a permanent move to England? And would they expect Grampapa to fund their purchase of a home?

"Let's be off, then," Theo said, and Mr. Giles moved to
open the front door for them. "We'll see you later, Phoebe."
At the last instant, he gave a little wink for her benefit
alone. She half smiled in response, then flattened her mouth
when she noticed Giovanna eyeing her speculatively from
over her shoulder. What bee had gotten into that woman's
bonnet today?

When they had gone, Phoebe turned to Mr. Giles. "Have
you seen my husband lately?"

"In the garden room, my lady."

"Good," she murmured and, again half smiling, started back up the stairs. Owen was where he had planned to be, and what he needed to do, he must do without her. Though she wished she could be a fly on the wall.

She spent the next hour in the nursery with Julia, Amelia, and little Charles, sitting on the floor and playing. The child was fussy, alternating between whining and burrowing against his mother, until she grew tired of it and handed him off to Amelia.

"Come to your godmother, darling." Amelia gathered Charles and his favorite stuffed bear into her arms. He seemed contented for a few minutes, but then began to squirm. Amelia stood him on his feet, holding his hands for balance.

"He's teething again," Julia said with a sigh. "It's so wearisome. I can only hope he's finished with it before the next one arrives." She patted her belly.

"You know I'll come to Allerton Place to help you." Amelia released one of Charles's hands and wiggled the bear against his stomach, eliciting something between a whine and a laugh. He stomped his feet and grabbed hold of the bear. "I wouldn't miss it."

"I do have Nurse at home," Julia reminded her, "and Hetta. Not to mention Lucille. And Aunt Cecily, too. I must admit that even on her most confused days, she's good with Charles."

"You're very lucky in that respect," Phoebe said.

Amelia reached over and laid a hand on hers. "We'll be there to help you, too, when the time comes."

"Speaking of help." Julia spoke as if just remembering an important detail. "Your packages are ready to be delivered. You're welcome."

"I *am* sorry. It was terrible of me to run off and leave you to do the work. Thank you, both of you."

"It was our pleasure," Amelia said, and tossed a glance at Julia. "Wasn't it?"

"*Hmm.*" Julia made a bored face. "Well, if you think we'll deliver them as well, you've got another thing coming."

"I wouldn't presume." Phoebe watched as Charles pulled away from Amelia and took several tottering steps on his own. They were not his first, but they were still tentative. He plopped down on his well-padded bottom. "Besides, it was *my* wedding. I should be the one delivering them."

Amelia compressed her lips in a secretive smile. "Not to mention the questions you wish to ask them. Are you any closer to finding out who killed the chief inspector?"

Phoebe shook her head. Scooting forward, she reached out to run her fingertips through Charles's hair. "Not yet. We tried to find Ian McGowan yesterday, but according to his wife he hasn't been home since he was released from prison."

"Do you believe her?" Amelia moved forward, too, and adjusted the ruffled sleeve of Charles's cotton shirt. He pressed his hands flat to the floor and pushed his bottom into the air, then straightened once more into a standing position.

"I don't know," Phoebe mused.

"You want someone other than Constable Brannock to be guilty." Julia tilted her head knowingly. "For Eva's sake."

"Yes," Phoebe readily agreed. "For the constable's sake, too. He's a good man, and I firmly believe he didn't do this."

"So do I," Amelia said forcefully.

"Didn't do what?"

All three—no, make that four, for Charles turned his face toward the door as well—watched as Grams came into the room, skirts sweeping over the floor. Despite the steady rise of women's hems in recent years, she insisted on the floor-length frocks she had worn all her life.

"What are the three of you talking about? Does it have anything to do with Chief Inspector Perkins's murder?" She spoke as if only casually interested, but Phoebe suspected Grams knew exactly what they had been discussing. Then Grams surprised her further. "And does it also have to do with Theo getting Greville out of the house and Owen holing up in the garden room with Bert?"

Phoebe, Amelia, and Julia darted glances at one another while Grams dragged a Windsor chair away from the wall, brought it closer, and sat. She watched each one in turn, waiting for an answer.

Phoebe chose her words carefully. "Grams, doesn't it seem awfully strange that after ten years, Uncle Greville and Uncle Bert should be spending so much time together, as if they have always been the best of friends?"

Grams took her time considering this. Finally she nodded. "You're right, they never seemed particularly chummy in the old days. Perhaps they've found common ground in their reminiscences. After all, with your father gone, along with so many others . . ." Grams's breath hitched. She pressed her lips together, frowned, and gave her shoulders a brisk shake. "I'd like to hold my great-grandson now. Put him on my lap, Amelia."

Phoebe's throat tightened. Grams rarely spoke of Papa, and never mentioned his death. As stoic a front as she showed the world, Phoebe recognized the depth of hurt that still lodged at Grams's core over the loss of her eldest son. Perhaps that meant she could not, or would not, allow that her younger son might have something to hide, whether it had to do with Chief Inspector Perkins or not.

But perhaps Owen had learned something. "If you'll all excuse me, I . . . er . . . need to talk to Eva about when we might deliver the bundles."

She did have to speak with Eva, but first she made her way down the two flights of stairs to the ground floor, and along the corridor off the Great Hall to the garden room. As she got close, she quieted her steps and listened for voices. She heard nothing, so she kept going. She found Owen sitting alone at the garden table, his chin raised as he contemplated the mosaics that wrapped around the room above the French doors. Two snifters and a bottle of brandy sat on the tabletop.

"I see Bert is gone," Phoebe said as she entered the room, her heels tapping on the tiled floor. "Or was he ever here?"

"He was here all right." Owen stood and pulled out a chair for her, sliding it closer to his own. "I have a lot to tell you, though none of it is conclusive."

"Why did I think it would be?" She glanced up at the ceiling, at murals of half-dressed gods and goddesses. "Tell me what you learned. I see that bottle is well on its way to being empty. I trust it played an important part in your intrigue."

"It certainly helped." He picked up the bottle, but before he poured any into his snifter, he questioned her with a look.

She shook her head. "You know it's too strong for me. But are you saying I'll need a drink?"

He gave a laugh. "Perhaps. We could ring for something else."

"No, just tell me what you know."

"I felt like a spider inviting Bert into my web . . ." As Owen vividly related the details, Phoebe found herself picturing their discussion as if she had witnessed it herself . . .

Owen refilled Bert's snifter, not for the first time, and leaned back in the garden chair with a half smile. "That

Greville is something, isn't he? Back after all these years. Say, does the earl have any idea about . . . ?"

Bert glanced over at him, looking startled. "About what?"

"You know. The reason he left in the first place."

"You know about that?" Clearly disconcerted, Bert took a deep draft of his brandy, compressing his lips and shuddering slightly as the liquid went down. "How?"

"Look, old man, it doesn't matter what I know or how. Don't worry about that. What's important is the earl and countess haven't gotten wind of it. Or have they?" He played a hunch. "No, they couldn't. It would blasted near kill them."

"It would at that." Bert hissed air through his teeth. "That's why I stepped in. For them, and for my sister's sake. Yes, she'd passed on by then, but her children . . . Phoebe, Julia, Amelia, and Fox. They didn't need to grow up with such a stain on the family reputation."

"No indeed. It was good of you to help. Above and beyond." Owen searched Bert's features while the other man stared through the glass at the garden outside. He burned to ask outright what had happened, but that would be admitting he had no idea what they were talking about. He needed to get Bert talking again, find a way to induce him to spill the details, without digging himself in so deep he risked revealing his intentions. He thought a moment, then asked, "Why you, though? You're only a brother-in-law. Why not his own brother?"

Bert flipped a hand in dismissal. "You know how it was with them. Never really got on, even as lads. Besides, Grev couldn't risk the old boy going to their father. And anyway, I was closer at hand. I was living in Gloucester at the time, which is where it happened."

"Ah, right. I can only imagine what was going through *your* mind at the time."

"Good God . . ." Bert took another big swallow and reached for the bottle. After pouring another healthy dose, he cleared his throat. "I mean, finding Grev blind drunk and the girl . . ." He released another loud breath. His eyes closed and a shiver went through him. "They hadn't even closed her eyes yet when I arrived."

Shock riveted through Owen. His own eyes went wide before he could school his features. He hoped Bert hadn't noticed. He didn't seem to, too caught up in his memories. What girl did he mean? Did she die? She must have, or Bert wouldn't look so pale now, so shaken. He must not have related these details in years. Perhaps ever. He almost seemed relieved to be talking about it.

"It happened late, if I remember correctly," Owen ventured, hoping he guessed right.

"Middle of the night. They'd been to a house party and were on their way back to Grev's flat in town. When I got there, he told me the stone wall came out of nowhere." Bert laughed softly. "As if stone walls do that, jump in the way of motorcars with no warning. Like I said, blind drunk. The bloody idiot."

"What about the girl's family?"

Bert shrugged, not a cavalier gesture, but rather one filled with regret. "She had none, as far as anyone knew. She wasn't some nice, respectable girl he met through mutual acquaintances. Picked her up at a tavern and brought her with him. I suspect she was a prostitute. Of course, that doesn't mean she deserved what happened to her. Not much more than a kid, really, from the looks of her." He shook his head remorsefully.

"So Greville telephoned you . . ."

"From a nearby inn, yes."

"And the police?"

"Already there when I arrived. That's where I came in. It took quite a heated debate and all the cash I had on hand at the time. Got the copper to agree the motor had been stolen and crashed by the perpetrator. Then I took Greville home and got him in bed. Like nothing ever happened." Bert swore softly under his breath.

Once again, shock made Owen rigid. A crash. A death. And bribery. Bert indicated only one copper on the scene. Phoebe had wondered how this secret might relate to present-day events. A sudden suspicion crawled up Owen's spine. "Bert, the policeman—who was he?"

Bert's snifter halted halfway to his lips. Without moving a muscle, he shifted his gaze to Owen. He hesitated. Compressed his lips. "I . . . er . . . don't remember his name. Just a flatfoot out of Gloucester."

"Surely you must—"

Bert pushed to his feet, startling Owen with his abruptness. "You never did tell me how you found out about this." He didn't wait for a reply. He set his snifter on the table and teetered out of the room, smacking his shoulder against the jamb as he went.

When Owen had finished his story, Phoebe remained silent for a long moment. The truth had sent her mind careening. She felt almost dizzy. Uncle Greville had committed manslaughter, and Uncle Bert had helped him get away with it. Yes, perhaps Bert had wished to spare the family from the repercussions, but he had also allowed Uncle Greville to spend the past decade free of all responsibility for what he had done. And a young woman . . .

"What about the others at the house party," she finally asked. "Didn't anyone there remember seeing the pair together? Wouldn't they have known she had been with Uncle Greville?"

"I have a feeling it was one of those parties where no one remembers much of anything." Owen's mouth slanted in disdain. "And if they do, they have no wish to be involved."

She nodded. She had never attended such a party herself, but she knew about them. The kinds of affairs thrown by the Prince of Wales's set or London's avant-garde, people who cared nothing for the old ways, who had more money than they knew what to do with, and who pushed all boundaries in the name of diversion. Sometimes, Phoebe knew, it went too far.

"Could the officer on the scene that night have been Isaac Perkins? Do you think it's possible?" She half hoped Owen would say no, that it would be too much of a coincidence. That Isaac Perkins had been nowhere near the area that night.

"He *was* a member of the Greater Gloucester Constabulary back then, a constable himself at the time. He hadn't yet been assigned to Little Barlow."

Her heart froze. "Then it's also possible that Uncle Greville . . ."

Owen nodded, his gaze connecting with Phoebe's. "Feared the truth coming out. That upon his return to Little Barlow he panicked at discovering that the only other man besides Bert who knew his secret lived less than a mile from Foxwood Hall."

Another thought struck Phoebe. "I wonder if Giovanna knows about Uncle Greville's past."

"I very much doubt he would have shared something like this with her."

"Do you? Because if she did, she might have helped Uncle Greville make sure the chief inspector stayed silent on the subject." A wave of queasiness rolled in her stomach at the thought of two murderers under the same roof as the rest of the family.

"This would have been a couple of years before Perkins

arrested Ian McGowan." He lifted his snifter, then placed it back down with a shake of his head. "I've had enough."

"Both men had reasons for wanting Mr. Perkins out of the way, one in revenge, the other out of an abundance of caution." She stood up from the chair. "Then it's our job to discover which reason proved lethal enough to drive a man to murder."

Although Eva and Lady Phoebe had intended to deliver the wedding parcels to the tenant families the next morning, a missive arrived belowstairs that put their plan on hold. Eva used the house telephone to call over to the hunting lodge.

"The gypsies are holding a fete today," Eva told her. "It'll be at their encampment. It seems they took our idea to heart."

"*Your* idea," Phoebe said, "and it was a brilliant one. This will put off my plan to deliver the parcels this morning, but it's no use knocking on doors if people are at the fair. Do let everyone there know, upstairs and down, and I'll meet you at the house in a little while. I'll drive. The Vauxhall has a brand new windscreen."

"Let's hope it stays that way. Wear comfortable shoes. Perhaps your sturdy boots."

Eva spread the word, and before long Lord Wroxly had given his permission for the servants to attend the fete in shifts. Eva and several of the others were among the first to go. Eva waited for Phoebe in the service courtyard, her own feet encased in the boots she wore when helping out at her parents' farm.

They arrived at the encampment to find a good crowd of villagers milling about. "I'm glad to see it," Phoebe commented as she pulled the Vauxhall off the road and onto the edge of the field. "I was afraid that business the other day with Detective Burridge might keep people away."

"It's good to know the majority of our villagers have open minds and good hearts." Eva adjusted the scarf she had tied over her hair as she surveyed the scene before them. In addition to the brightly painted caravans and tents they had seen the last time they were here, there were festooned tables and booths, each offering an array of goods. There was also a low wooden stage, and, judging by the lovely aromas carried by the breeze, the several campfires served as cookstoves for savory treats.

In the very middle of the proceedings, six musicians sat or stood with their instruments: a violin, a mandolin, fiddle, an accordion, a wooden flute, and a set of drums made from inverted wooden buckets. Eva couldn't keep the smile from her face as she took in the festive atmosphere.

The lorry from home pulled up near where Phoebe had parked the Vauxhall, and as Dora, Douglas, Josh, and a few others climbed out, Phoebe issued a friendly warning.

"Spend your money wisely and sparingly. Don't let yourself be talked into buying anything you truly don't need."

They made their promises to be prudent and set off, dispersing in twos and threes. Eva watched as Douglas and Josh made their way over to a table where one of the gypsy men was demonstrating what appeared to be card tricks. Phoebe's brother Fox stood among them as well. Greville Renshaw hovered beside him.

Eva shook her head and chortled. "I hope they all didn't bring much to lose."

"Speaking of which." Eva followed as Phoebe strode across the way to the card table and set a hand on her brother's shoulder. "And what are *you* doing?"

He turned with a start, then grinned. "Phoebe, about time you got here. Isn't it brilliant? These people know how to throw a party. Hello, Eva," he added congenially, obviously in high spirits.

Phoebe flashed a stern expression, one that included her uncle. "You're not wagering, are you?"

"I might toss down a bob or two." Fox shrugged.

"You'll lose it," she warned.

He balked as though highly insulted, making Eva hide a chuckle. "Says you. I'll have you know I've a sixth sense when it comes to betting."

Phoebe grinned even as she shook her head. "You think so, do you?"

"I do."

"Well, prepare to be proven wrong." Phoebe turned away from her brother. "Come, Eva, let's find my sisters. We'll leave Fox to his own devices. He's got a bit of a lesson to learn. Oh, look there." She pointed to where several village women, including Mrs. Hershel, the vicar's wife, were perusing colorful goods laid out along a table. Every now and again, they could hear their *oohs* and *ahs*. Mrs. Hershel appeared to be making a purchase. "Let's go see what's captured their attention."

"Something smells wonderful." As they walked through the encampment, Eva lifted her nose and sniffed the air. "Roasting nuts. And some kind of spiced meat. I'll be having some of that before we leave." She noticed some of the attendees held small pasties wrapped in paper, nibbling them as they walked through the fete.

They reached the tables, where they discovered hand-painted wooden bangles and beaded necklaces. There were also hair combs in the shapes of butterflies, dragonflies, and various flowers. Yet another table held woven potholders and dish towels, each with a distinctive pattern in an array of colors.

"So much for gypsies only selling clothes pegs," Eva

whispered. "That's something I've heard, that clothes pegs are their major source of income."

"Along with thieving," Phoebe whispered back, and Eva heard the sardonic note in her voice, aimed, not at the gypsies, but at those who had spread such rumors.

"Phoebe! Eva!" Amelia, with Lady Julia in tow, came running over, holding on to her hat to keep it from tumbling off. "Isn't this fun? Have you seen what's for sale? The most darling things."

Phoebe reached out and flicked a crumb from the side of her sister's mouth. "And baked treats, too, I see."

Amelia laughed and twirled about. "I'm going to go over to the table selling linens. I noticed some lovely Irish-style lace. I'm told the women here make it themselves." With that, she was gone.

Julia shook her head. "Sometimes it's hard to believe she's basically an adult. Then again, I hope she never loses her enthusiasm."

"Did you leave Charles at home?" Phoebe craned her neck to see through gaps in the crowd. "Or is he here somewhere with Theo?"

"No, neither of them is here. I left Charles with Hetta and Theo had something else to do. With Owen, apparently."

"With Owen?" Phoebe seemed surprised to learn this.

"I'm sure we'll hear about it later." Julia adjusted the cashmere jacket that matched her skirt. "I'll going to catch up with Amelia. Have fun, you two."

Eva noticed some commotion over by the stage. "Look there. Those girls are going to dance."

Five young women stepped up onto the makeshift stage. They wore wide, circular skirts with red backgrounds emblazoned with colorful paisley patterns. Their loose, wide-sleeved blouses were embroidered, and each wore a bright scarf. Two of the five held tambourines. The other three wore bells on their fingers and on their chain belts. Eva recognized two of the younger women, one of them being the black-haired Fiona, whom they had met the morning Detective Burridge had tried to run them off the property.

The fete attendees gathered in front of the stage. The musicians switched to a lively rhythm, and the dancers began to whirl and move their feet so fast Eva could hardly see them beneath their swirling skirts. Her heart beat faster, and she held her breath at the spectacle.

"Isn't it thrilling?"

"They're highly skilled dancers," Phoebe said. "But watching them almost makes me dizzy."

"I know what you mean." Eva blinked and gave a laugh. One dance ended and a slower one began, the music dramatic and romantic. Eva realized the women's clothing was as much a part of the dance as their limbs, their skirts and sleeves billowing and swaying in time to the music. "Honestly, this is how I thought Romany women always dressed, silly me."

"We're learning a lot about these people that we didn't know before," Phoebe agreed. "They're full of surprises."

They watched for a while longer. Then they began milling through the crowd and viewing the goods again. As they neared the outer perimeter of the encampment, angry voices from behind a caravan brought them to a halt. "Phoebe, do you hear that?"

A man and a woman were quarreling. Or, rather, the man was quarreling. The woman seemed to be pleading with him to stop.

Phoebe stood with her ears pricked. "I most certainly do. And . . . her voice sounds familiar."

"It sounds like Serena Blackwell, doesn't it?"

They conferred with a silent look and, nodding, they rounded the caravan. Sure enough, Serena Blackwell stood toe to toe with a man they also remembered from the other morning, with the long, raven's black hair and chiseled features. As handsome as he might have been under ordinary circumstances, today his mottled complexion and steel-sharp gaze rendered him almost ugly. The guttural rumbling of his deep voice didn't help. He bellowed something at Serena, and she flinched back a step.

"Now see here." Phoebe strode into the fray, with Eva quickly following. "That's no way to treat anyone."

The young man rounded on her, and for a moment Eva feared for her lady's welfare. Phoebe held her ground. Eva moved closer to her, ready to strike if need be.

His nose and lips pinched, his jaw rigidly square, the man seethed a moment longer, then stomped away. Not once did he look back. Serena wrapped her arms around herself. Her head was down, her breathing hard.

"Are you quite all right?" Eva moved to the woman and put a hand on her shoulder. "Did he hurt you?"

Serena Blackwell shook her head. Her fiery-colored hair, plaited into a single braid, swung slightly where it rested over her shoulder. "He wouldn't hit me."

"Are you sure of that?" Phoebe came to stand beside Eva. "I'm sorry if we were intruding on something that's none of our business, but we feared for your safety."

"We most certainly did." Her indignation rising, Eva removed her hand from Serena's shoulder and propped both on her hips. "A man shouldn't speak to anyone like that, much less a woman. Who does he think he is?"

"Peregrin Blackwell," Serena mumbled. "My husband."

CHAPTER 10

Still looking cowed, Serena blinked back tears. "He gets like this sometimes. He doesn't mean anything by it."

"That's no way to look at it." Eva fished in her handbag and drew out a clean handkerchief. She handed it to Serena, who hesitated before taking it. "No matter the source of his anger, his behavior was disrespectful, not to mention frightening. You say he doesn't mean anything by it, and that he wouldn't hit you. But you looked and still look afraid, Serena."

"You don't understand," she whispered. "It's my fault."

"How?" Phoebe shook her head. "He was bullying you. There's no excuse for it."

Serena grabbed hold of her braid as if it were a lifeline. "He blames me for what happened in the village, and for bringing the detective out here to clear the field."

Eva exchanged a glance with Phoebe and said, "You claim you're innocent, that someone planted the stolen items in your bag."

"It's true." Her features tightened in anger. "I did nothing wrong, but Peregrin says I shouldn't have gone into the village at all. If I had stayed here where he says I belong, the trouble wouldn't have happened."

For the first time, Eva noticed that Serena was dressed like the dancers onstage. "Did you mean to perform today?"

Serena shrugged.

"He wouldn't let you," Phoebe ventured. Her query was rewarded with another shrug, one that confirmed her hunch. "Has your husband not considered that if you hadn't gone into the village that day, someone else might have been framed for shoplifting?"

Serena's head swung up, and she gasped in surprise. "I hadn't thought of that. But you're probably right. It could have been anyone."

"Exactly." Eva smiled. "Now, is there anything we can do for you? If you need help in any way . . ."

"Thank you, but no. I'll be fine. As I told you, my husband can be like this. He's got a hot temper and trouble controlling it sometimes. But he's not a violent man."

Eva had trouble believing her, especially given that Serena had planned to dance with the other women, but her husband wouldn't allow it. Why not? To punish her for what he perceived as her wrongdoing? Or was he the jealous sort, not wanting his wife to be up on display, as some men would see it. Goose bumps rose on her forearms as she considered the dangers a woman could face at the hands of a hot-tempered man.

"Blimy, take it back!"

The shouts drew Eva's and Phoebe's attention to the center of the fete.

"I bloody well won't!"

The outburst was followed by a crash, the cries of women, and more shouts from the other men. Eva and Phoebe went running, not stopping until they could see the source of the commotion. Peregrin and another man about his own age had fallen to fisticuffs.

Eva whisked a hand to her bosom as she attempted to catch her breath. "Good heavens, is he always like this?"

"Not violent, she said?" Phoebe caught hold of Eva's hand. "I beg to differ."

A table had gone over, spilling pasties, a small barrel of pickles, a container of roasted nuts. As they watched, another table, this one holding jewelry and scarves, was knocked a good foot from its position and threatened to topple until one of the women grabbed hold and steadied it.

The two men in the middle of the ruckus traded blows and curses with equal force. Mothers—Romany and villager alike—grabbed their children and tugged them to safety. The music ceased. The dancers stood frozen on the stage.

Although the village men stood back as well, several of the gypsy men rushed in to stop the fighting. Eva compressed her lips at the sight of the blood running down their faces, until one of them wiped it way on his sleeve and she saw it originated from a minor cut above his eyes. Peregrin Blackwell was bleeding from his nose. The other men restrained them by the arms from behind. Peregrin continued cursing, while the other man held up a hand and curled his fingers in a *come and get me* manner.

Finally, though still heaving, both men appeared to calm down. Their fellow gypsies eased their grips, and when the pair didn't charge at each other, they were released. Serena went to her husband's side and tried to wipe away his blood with Eva's handkerchief. He waved her away and stalked off.

One of the men who had been holding the other brawler demanded to know what started the fight.

"I ribbed him, is all. About not keeping Serena under

control. I didn't mean it. But he came at me like a raging bull."

"Did you hear that, Eva?"

"I did." A chill of foreboding passed through Eva. "It would seem Peregrin Blackwell is completely unreasonable when it comes to his wife."

"Completely irrational, you mean."

The crowd began to thin, prompting two older men, the leaders Eva recognized from the other morning, to hold up their hands. "Please, everyone, we apologize for the bad behavior of two of our own, but it's over now and it won't be repeated." He glared at the man with whom Peregrin had fought. He looked appropriately sheepish, clasped his hands behind his back, and nodded.

"And to make up for the disruption," the other leader said, "the next round of ale is on us!" He held out an arm as if to invite the fete-goers to the booth where the ale was being served. That did the trick, with most of the villagers remaining.

"What do you think," Phoebe asked Eva. "Is it safe? Or should I advise our people to return to Foxwood Hall?"

Eva glanced around the now peaceful encampment. The musicians took up a new tune. After a moment's conversation, the dancers retrieved their tambourines and bells and resumed their performance. "I think it's all right now. The storm has receded."

"But for how long?" Phoebe's gaze followed Serena Blackwell as she joined another woman selling household goods behind a table. "He's trouble, that husband of hers, and I don't trust him."

Eva nodded. "How much don't you trust him? Serena Blackwell might not have enough motive to have killed Chief Inspector Perkins, but what about the hot-blooded Peregrin? The *irrational* Peregrin, who attacks other men for little cause?"

"My thoughts exactly, Eva. I believe we have a third suspect firmly on our list."

Phoebe was all too happy to linger at the fete, observing and asking questions. As she examined wares for sale and made some small purchases, she engaged the women in conversation.

"How much longer do you think you'll be here" she asked one who was selling hand-painted boxes just the right size for storing hairpins. The edges were gilded, as were the birds carved into the lids. The gilding wouldn't be real, of course, but they were pretty all the same. Phoebe picked out one each for Grams, Julia, and Amelia, and hoped the latter two hadn't already bought one for themselves.

"We're waiting for another group to join us here before moving on," the woman replied, "although your detective might force us out before that happens."

"I think my grandfather has stilled his hand, at least for now."

"I hope so. He's nearly as bad as your former chief inspector." The woman grimaced at her own words. "I'm sorry to speak ill of the dead, but he was no friend to us, that's certain."

A second gypsy woman sidled up to the table. "The incident with Serena didn't help matters. It gave people an excuse to say we're no good."

"Serena insists she was innocent." At the end of the table was an assortment of pincushions covered in gaily printed fabrics. Phoebe inspected them and chose one for Eva and another for Hetta, Julia's maid.

"She *probably* didn't do it," the first woman said.

"Or maybe she did," the other murmured. "It wouldn't be the first time. Serena has, on occasion, been known to have sticky fingers."

Phoebe's eyes widened at this disclosure. Had she been foolish to believe Serena's story? If she lied about that, had she also lied about what happened between her and her husband today?

"You can hardly blame her," the first one scolded. "That husband of hers is difficult, always trying to control her. No wonder she consoles herself with the occasional treat she can't afford to buy."

"Oh, dear." Phoebe handed the pincushions to the first woman to add to her other purchases. "I understand the chief inspector threatened her with incarceration."

"He threatened the lot of us with incarceration," the first woman said with a twist of her lips.

Phoebe played a hunch. "Did he threaten Serena's husband?"

"Peregrin?" The second shrugged. "He did indeed, but only after he stormed into your little police station and demanded his wife be set free."

"He's got quite a temper, from what we saw here today." Phoebe watched as the first woman wrapped her purchases in brown paper and tied the bundle with twine.

"Yes, but he really is mostly bluster, that one," she said.

Phoebe resisted the urge to chortle. "The blood flowing on both men says differently."

"Bah. That was nothing. They're brothers. Half brothers, actually, but they grew up together. They're always tussling. They'll make up before suppertime, see if they don't."

"Tell me," Phoebe ventured, "on the morning the chief inspector died, did you happen to notice anyone leaving the encampment?"

The first woman eyed her shrewdly. "By anyone, do you mean Serena or Peregrin? Is that why you're asking these questions about them?"

"Well . . . yes."

The two women regarded each other, looked back at Phoebe, raised their chins, and compressed their lips. Duly chastised, Phoebe paid for her purchases, gathered up her bundle, and moved on. Back at the jewelry table, she tried the same tactic of engaging the proprietor in conversation, gradually steering their talk to the chief inspector's death. She never mentioned Serena or Peregrin, but she did ask whether the woman behind this table had seen anyone leaving the encampment that morning.

"Now that you mention it, I did."

"And?"

Like the other two, this woman compressed her lips, but she also held out her hand. Phoebe understood. She fished in her handbag for a coin and placed it in the woman's palm. "Will this do?"

"Nicely, thank you. Now then, I happened to see one of our young men walking toward the road just before sunup, but it still dark and misty, so it was hard to be sure who it was." Once again, she held out her hand, her fingers curling.

Good heavens. Dipping her fingers back into her handbag, Phoebe extracted another coin.

"As I said, it was hard to be certain, but it certainly looked like Peregrin Blackwell with that midnight hair of his." She considered a moment. "He might have been trailing after his wife."

"His wife? Did you also see Serena Blackwell leaving camp?"

"No, but she typically does of a morning. Goes foraging for herbs and such. She supplies all of us with such niceties for our cooking. Knows which plants and mushrooms are safe and all that."

Phoebe thanked her, bought a necklace and a bracelet, and went in search of Eva. She found her in an unlikely place: inside a small striped tent, its flap partially closed.

Hearing voices and recognizing Eva's, Phoebe peeked in. A table with two chairs opposite each other occupied the center of the tent, and atop the table sat a crystal ball. At least, Phoebe assumed it to be a crystal ball. A candle in a brass holder burned beside it, the flame reflected in the glass orb.

Eva sat at the table across from an older woman dressed in similar fashion to the dancers, but also sporting a turban and a silk shawl. She had laid out a line of cards in front of her. Just as she was about to flip the first one over, she went still and stared straight at Phoebe.

"I see I should have closed the tent flap all the way." One eyebrow lifted in admonishment. "Not everyone respects the sanctity of the fortune teller's tent."

"I'm so sorry . . . I didn't mean to interrupt . . ." Phoebe started to back out of the tent.

"No, it's perfectly all right." Eva beckoned Phoebe inside and turned to the fortune teller. "I don't mind if Lady Phoebe listens in. I have no secrets from her."

The woman frowned, prompting her turban to slip slightly forward onto her brow. She shoved it back into place and shrugged. "It's up to you." She raised her gaze to Phoebe. "But you must be completely still and silent. Make no comments, no matter what you hear."

For some inexplicable reason, the woman's somber tone raised the hairs on Phoebe's nape. With no other chairs in the tent, she moved off to one side, feeling chastised for no good reason. "I promise."

"Now then." The fortune teller flipped over each card in a methodical fashion, pausing several seconds over each and making noises such as *hmmm*, and *ah*, and *mmm*. . . . Then she consulted her crystal ball, staring hard and long into its lustrous depths, until Phoebe felt her mouth twitch with the urge to ask what the woman saw.

She hunched farther over the table and reached for Eva's hand. After a brief hesitation, Eva surrendered it to her, and the woman turned her palm upward. As with her crystal ball, she studied it closely, her lips skewing first to the right, then to the left. Finally she raised her face to Eva's.

"I see that your future is at a crossroads. There is the promise of great happiness. But also the threat of great sorrow. You have the power to avoid sorrow, but in so doing you will never quite know joy, either. You have an important decision to make. Live for yourself, or live for others."

Eva's pulse jolted. Obviously, the fortune teller spoke of Miles and the possibility of his being convicted of murder, but what was this decision Eva had to make?

"What does it mean," she asked, "that I either live for myself or live for others?"

The fortune teller's lips curled in a slight smile. "You know exactly what it means."

Eva suspected she did. These many years she had lived for her ladies, or very nearly so, but how could that affect Miles's future? "Which is the right choice if I wish to avoid tragedy?"

"Only you can decide that," the woman said, an answer both tantalizing and frustrating.

"Tell me more. Perhaps you can help me decide." Though couched as a request, Eva had issued a challenge to the woman. Could she truly divine another person's fate, or did she merely tell them what they already knew?

"I don't see how I can. It's not for me to interfere with your free will," the fortune teller replied, as Eva suspected she might.

Eva leaned closer to her over the table. "You can tell me if you know anything about the murder of Chief Inspector Perkins. I know you're referring to Constable Brannock when you talk about a promise of happiness or the threat of sorrow. For the record, none of that is any secret, so I'm not awed that you should know of it. And my decision concerning the matter is to do everything I can to prove his innocence. You seem to be a woman with her finger on the pulse of . . . well . . . everything. You would need to be in order to tell fortunes." Eva said this last with sardonic emphasis.

The fortune teller pushed her chair away from the table and sprang to her feet. "What are you saying? That I'm a charlatan?"

"No, not at all. I consider you an entertainer and a rather good one. The cards, the crystal ball . . . the air of mystery that hangs about you. It's all quite beguiling." When this didn't wipe the scowl from the fortune teller's brow, Eva chuckled. "Don't be angry. I admire your trade. But aren't I correct in assuming you keep abreast of all the news wherever you are?"

The woman slowly sank back into her chair. "It is necessary that I do so."

"Of course. That's why I wonder if you can help me."

Phoebe walked to the table and stood beside Eva's chair. "Help *us*, she means. We're both determined to prove the constable innocent."

Eva raised a look of gratitude to her lady, then turned back to the fortune teller. "On the day the chief inspector was murdered, did you see anything unusual here, such as anyone leaving the encampment at odd hours, or trying to sneak back without being noticed?"

Would she mention the Blackwells? Eva held her breath.

"What do you mean by 'odd hours'?" The woman held up her palms. "Our people come and go as they please. We're not beholden to the same strictures as you."

"Come now. You know exactly what I mean." Eva folded her arms and cocked her head. "Did you see anyone leaving in the early morning, say, before dawn, and hurrying back shortly after sunup?"

Beside Eva, Phoebe tucked her package under her arm and opened her handbag. She placed a coin on the table and with one finger slid it across.

The fortune teller stared at it, then looked up at Phoebe. "Do you think I'm bribable?"

"Forgive me, but if you truly can't use it . . ." Phoebe leaned down to retrieve it, but the woman moved faster, scooping the coin up in her hand.

"Serena Blackwell goes out at dawn most mornings," she said. "If she did that day, it's nothing new."

"She collects herbs from the forest and fields," Phoebe supplied, surprising Eva. "And her husband?"

The fortune teller raised an eyebrow. "Sometimes he follows her. I think he doesn't trust her, suspects she's meeting someone." She huffed. "As if any self-respecting woman would tryst in a field. Peregrin can be a fool."

Phoebe sighed. "Come on, Eva. We're getting nowhere here."

But Eva stayed where she was, leveling her gaze at the fortune teller until the older woman began to squirm.

"All right," she burst out as if Eva held a gun to her head. "That morning, at about eight o'clock, Peregrin came to me. I'm also a healer."

Eva placed her hands on the table and craned forward. "Peregrin needed healing?"

"He'd hurt his wrist and asked for some of my liniment."

"Did he say how he hurt his wrist?" Phoebe asked, taking the words out of Eva's mouth. "And which one?"

"His left," she replied, though the point of the question clearly puzzled her. "He said he was collecting firewood in the forest, lost his footing, and came down hard on it."

"The injury certainly hasn't limited his ability to fight, has it?" Phoebe snapped her handbag closed.

Eva stood up from the table, realizing they had gotten all they would out of the woman. "Thank you. For the fortune and the information."

Outside, they walked together through the crowd, which had swelled in the past half hour or so. Eva was glad the villagers had turned up, whether it was to support the gypsy group or simply out of curiosity. It didn't matter. What did matter was these people had themselves and their children to support, and today's proceeds would help.

"Interesting about Peregrin's injury," Eva said as they dodged a child here, greeted a villager there.

"Yes. It could have happened during a scuffle with Chief Inspector Perkins."

"Miles found him as though sitting comfortably in his chair, though," Eva pointed out. "Except with a bullet in his heart."

Phoebe appeared to consider this. "True, but just because he was in the chair when the constable found him doesn't mean he died there. He could have been placed there afterwards. Or forced into the chair first and then shot."

"I don't recall Miles saying there was any blood found on the floor or anywhere else."

"It could have been wiped up. And anything used to wipe up could have been disposed of. Burned or buried."

Eva nodded. "Burned in one of these campfires, for example."

"Exactly." Phoebe glanced out over the surrounding hillsides. "Or buried in the forest, where herbs and mushrooms are found."

CHAPTER 11

"All told, Fox, how much did you lose at the fete?" Phoebe couldn't resist teasing her brother. He was presently slumped in a wingback chair in the drawing room, his coat unbuttoned, his necktie askew. Without looking at her, he flicked a hand as if to shoo her away. "That much, huh?"

He *tsked* and rolled his eyes. "Only a pound or two."

"Only a pound?" Phoebe crossed her arms and cocked her hip.

"All right, four. Not the end of the world. And don't say 'I told you so.'"

"I wouldn't dream of it, little brother." She glanced downward to hide her gratified smile. Not that she was glad her brother had been fleeced of four pounds, but she *had* warned him. "Games of chance aren't like wagering on horses."

"You mean they're fixed," he murmured.

"Not necessarily, but they *are* engineered to make money for the house—or in this case, the tents and caravans."

"*Hmph.*"

"Phoebe." Her heels clacking, Julia turned into the room.

She looked harried. And annoyed. "You're wanted below-stairs."

"Is everything all right?" Her first thought was that Eva had heard something concerning Constable Brannock. "I'm needed by whom?"

"By me." Julia reached out to grasp Phoebe's hand and practically dragged her into the Great Hall. "It's Owen and Theo. They're in a state."

"A state?"

But Julia wouldn't answer her questions. Her jaws were clamped too tightly to allow for speech. What had made her so angry?

Phoebe found out when they reached the bottom of the service staircase and Julia led her into Mr. Giles's pantry. Owen stood off to one side while Theo sat in Mr. Giles's large desk chair. He was being tended to by Vernon, who was pressing wads of cotton to several cuts and scrapes on his face while Mr. Giles looked on and gave directions. Owen sported several sticking plasters on his own face, as well as a bandaged hand.

"A bit of iodine on that one, Vernon," Mr. Giles advised, raising a finger to point, "or it'll fester."

"Yes, Mr. Giles." Vernon tipped a drop or two of iodine onto a fresh bit of cotton gauze and touched it to Theo's chin. Theo winced. Owen winced in sympathy. His and Theo's clothes hung about them in wrinkles. Dirt clung to the elbows of their jackets and the knees of their trousers.

"Good heavens," Phoebe cried. "What on earth hap-pened to the two of you?"

"They've been brawling," Julia snapped, and tossed her hands in the air. "Like a pair of ill-disciplined schoolboys. Thought they'd sneak in and have their wounds tended, with you and I none the wiser, much less Grams and Gram-papa."

"Now, my love." Theo held up a hand. "That's not how it is at all. We merely wished to spare you and Phoebe the worst of it until we cleaned up. Can't see how you found out anyway."

Phoebe had an idea that Hetta had probably been the culprit, but for now it didn't matter. She confronted her husband. "What happened?"

"We found Ian McGowan."

"What?" she exclaimed with a gasp. "And he did *this* to you?"

"It's all right, we're fine." He put his arms around her for a reassuring hug, then released her, as mindful as she that Vernon and Mr. Giles were watching. "We found the elusive Mr. McGowan at home, in the bosom of his family, just as you suspected, my dear."

"I *knew* it." She felt a surge of triumph, though a short-lived one. "Obviously, the man is dangerous."

Julia scoffed. "You realize you easily could have—no, make that *should* have—alerted Detective Burridge rather than take on this man yourselves. Just look at the results." She thrust out a hand toward her husband. "I don't see why you went out there in the first place."

"Because, Julia," Phoebe said with a sigh, "Detective Burridge had already been there. He believed Mrs. Mc-Gowan's story of not having seen her husband since his release from prison and likely would have found no reason to make a repeat visit." She met Owen's gaze. "I'm sorry you were hurt, my love, but I'm so proud of you. Of both of you."

"Oh, please." Julia blew out a breath of impatience. But when Theo reached out a hand to her, she went readily, snaked her arms around his neck, and gave him a squeeze. Which prompted Mr. Giles and Vernon to excuse themselves and leave the room.

"Tell us what happened," Phoebe urged them.

"When we knocked at the McGowans' door," Owen began, "we could hear muffled voices and scuffling inside. Then a door opening and slamming shut—the kitchen door at the rear—and feet thudding over the ground out back. We didn't wait to ask questions. We rounded the house."

"At which point," Theo took up, "we could see the back of a man racing away. He disappeared behind one of the outbuildings. We managed to catch up to him, but good Lord, he's strong. The three of us ended up tussling on the ground, and even with two of us attempting to restrain him, he managed to break away."

"He made straight for a forested stretch of acreage, at which point we knew we had lost him," Owen concluded with a shake of his head.

"And he managed to inflict this much damage on the pair of you?" Julia demanded.

"Not really." Theo's expression turned sheepish. "But the property around the house is rocky. That's what did most of the damage."

"It certainly sounds as though he's guilty, doesn't it?" They all turned to see Fox hovering in the doorway. Phoebe hadn't realized he'd followed them down. With his hands in his trouser pockets, he sauntered into the room. "He wouldn't have run off like that if he were innocent. The detective *has* to bring him in after this."

"Not so fast, Fox," Owen cautioned. "We have to remember who this man is. Someone who spent eight years in jail when he shouldn't have."

"But he *did* steal that horse, didn't he?" Despite Fox's voice having deepened in recent years, he sounded almost childlike as he asked the question. "And what about failing to report to his regiment when he should have? That doesn't sound innocent to me."

"I agree with Fox," Julia said in that way she had of viewing things in black and white.

"His son was gravely ill," Phoebe reminded them. "And that should have been taken into consideration. He might have run today because he simply feared being treated unfairly again."

"Or, because he's guilty of murdering the chief inspector." Julia raised her eyebrows as if this should be obvious to all.

"We did come away having learned something." Theo touched his raw chin and grimaced. "Mrs. McGowan *was* lying when she said she and her husband had gone their separate ways."

"Did you confront her?" Julia asked.

Theo shook his head. "Not confront. But we did go back to the house and explain ourselves, and why it's important for her and her husband to be honest. He's only making himself look guilty by running away."

"And how did she respond?" Phoebe asked.

"She shut the door in our faces," Owen told her.

That evening Eva went to Lady Amelia's room to lay out her clothes for dinner and run a bath for her. Phoebe and Lord Owen had returned to the hunting lodge for much needed rest. Lord and Lady Allerton stole the opportunity for a respite as well. But Amelia seemed filled with energy. She chattered on about today's events, first the gypsy fete with both its delights and its scuffle, and then the developments with Ian McGowan.

"Life's become so exciting suddenly, hasn't it?"

"Today certainly was full of activity." Eva could use a rest herself, but as soon as she finished her duties for the evening she planned to go into the village and tell Miles all that had happened.

"I'm glad no one was hurt in either case," Amelia continued. "But goodness, such a lot of blood! Oh, I am sorry, Eva, perhaps I shouldn't say it so bluntly. But it was the bluntest sort of day, wasn't it?" Eva nodded, and Amelia went on chattering. "Do you think Mr. McGowan is guilty? I do so want him *not* to be, not after what happened to him in the past. I'd much rather believe he'll have a new lease on life now, with his wife and family. How utterly devastating not only to lose one's freedom, but one's child at the same time. I'd like to wish him happiness." She met Eva's gaze with a sorrowful look. "But *not* if he's guilty and has put Constable Brannock in such a lamentable position."

Eva wrapped her in a hug. "Thank you for caring so much. You always have everyone's best interests at heart. I hope things turn out exactly as you wish them to be."

With all solemnity, Amelia said, "The only person I wish ill upon is the chief inspector's murderer."

"I couldn't agree more—" Eva broke off at the sound of sharp report coming from somewhere beyond the gardens. It was distant, muffled, but still close enough that it must have come from somewhere on the estate. Another crack reverberated through the air. "Is that gunfire?"

Odd, that, for this time of the evening. She went to the window and scanned the garden and the lawns beyond. Twilight had not yet descended, but she saw no one, not even at the very base of the grounds where the park met the woodland. "What on earth? That sounded too close to be coming from any of the farms. In fact, it sounded closer than the riding trails."

Amelia joined her at the window, shoulder to shoulder. "I don't see anyone. It sounded like gunfire, but could it have been something else? A lorry backfiring, perhaps? I know of no plans for Grampapa and our guests to shoot tonight."

"Anyway, they wouldn't go this time of day, would they?"

Eva strained her eyes as she continued scrutinizing the distance. "Shooting is a morning activity."

"You're right. Still, I wonder if it might be Uncle Greville and Uncle Bert . . ."

Another shot reverberated. Eva turned from the window, a sudden misgiving sending her across the room and into the corridor. "I'll be back."

"I'm coming with you." Together they hurried along the corridor, across the gallery, and into the guest wing. "Eva, where are we going?"

"To see if Lady Cecily is in the house."

"Where else would she . . . Goodness! Do you think that's *her* out there shooting?"

"I hope not."

They reached the dowager marchioness's bedroom first and knocked. Receiving no answer, Eva tried the door. It opened upon an empty room. From there an adjoining door led into Lady Cecily's room—again, empty. Eva about-faced. Before reaching the gallery she ducked into Lord Wroxly's office and went straight to the gun case. She gave the glass door a tug and was relieved when it stuck fast. "It wouldn't have been Lady Cecily."

"Thank goodness. But I must alert my grandfather that someone is shooting near the house, if he doesn't already know."

"And I'd like to make certain Lady Cecily is somewhere safe." Despite the evidence that the woman hadn't gotten ahold of one of Lord Wroxly's rifles, Eva continued to fret over Lady Cecily's whereabouts. The niggling sensation had yet to fade. She followed Amelia downstairs.

In the Great Hall, Amelia pricked her ears. "Where is everyone?"

"Maybe they're still at the fete."

"No, Grams wouldn't have gone. She said she didn't intend to, although the others might have." Amelia crossed the hall to the drawing room. With a shake of her head, she continued to the library at the end of the corridor. "Uncle Greville?"

Eva peered over Amelia's shoulder to see her uncle sleeping in Lord Wroxly's favorite wingback chair near the fireplace. Light snores emanated from his open mouth. Amelia went up to him and gave his shoulder a nudge.

"Uncle Greville? Please wake up."

With one last, ripping snore, he stirred, blinked his eyes, and squinted up at his niece. "Amelia? Is it dinnertime already?" As he spoke, Amelia recoiled. Eva spotted a bottle of brandy and a half-empty snifter on the table beside hm.

"It's not dinnertime, Uncle Greville. But don't go back to sleep. Where is everyone? Where is Grampapa?"

He struggled to sit up straighter, meeting with limited success. "The Petit Salon, last time I saw them. Playing whist, I believe."

"That would account for how quiet it is." Amelia peeked at Eva over her shoulder. "Is Aunt Cecily with them?"

"Must be. She was in here with me for a spell . . ." Yawning, he shrugged and snuggled deeper into the chair.

Amelia led the way to the opposite end of the house. The Petit Salon, tucked into a corner facing the front forecourt, had always been one of Phoebe's favorite rooms, with its calming green walls, cheerful white wainscoting, and the half-round alcove that was part of Foxwood Hall's turret. Seated around the table at the center of the room, Lord and Lady Wroxly, the dowager Marchioness of Allerton, and Amelia's uncle Bert were intent on their game of cards. Mr. Fairfax lay snoozing by the fireplace.

"Grampapa," Amelia began, but her grandmother cut her off.

"Amelia, darling, I'd thought you'd gone up for your bath. There's still plenty of time before dinner. Come in and join us."

"Yes, Amelia, do." Waving the hand that held his cards, Lord Wroxly beckoned her closer.

Amelia didn't budge. "Grampapa, did you hear shots just now?"

"Shots? As in guns?" Frowning, he shook his head. "We heard nothing, my dear." He glanced at the others. "Did any of you?"

"I certainly didn't notice gunshots," Lady Wroxly said.

The other two nodded consensus. Perhaps the sounds hadn't traveled to the front of the house, Eva reasoned. But that didn't mean they hadn't occurred.

"Shots? I heard them from upstairs a few minutes ago." Giovanna Renshaw came up behind Eva and with a bored look nudged her aside. She did the same to Amelia before slinking—Eva decided that was the only word for the way the woman walked—into the Petit Salon. Approaching Bert Fletcher's chair from behind, she leaned with a hand on his shoulder and peered down at his cards. Her forefinger stroked the hair on his nape, while her snug skirts rode up, exposing shapely calves. Eva felt the urge to look away from what appeared to be a blatantly flirtatious act. The woman's Italian accent asserted itself as she said, "Bert, surely you heard something."

"Not I," he said impatiently, and shrank from beneath Giovanna's touch.

"I suppose we were concentrating so much on the game . . ." Lady Wroxly darted a puzzled look at her husband.

He came to his feet. "What direction did they come from?"

Eva went into the room. "From where the grounds meet the woodland, my lord. I'm also wondering, sir, where Lady Cecily is at the moment?"

"With the earl's son," Lady Lucille said. "In the library."

"Lucille, I'm afraid she isn't." Amelia wrung her hands

together. "We just checked. Only Uncle Greville is there. We also checked her room and yours."

"Are you saying Aunt Cecily is nowhere to be found?" With a cry, Lady Lucille sprang to her feet, her cards scattering. Her outburst drew Mr. Fairfax out of his slumber and to his feet. "Good heavens! We must find her at once. She could be out there, where bullets are flying. Who on earth could be firing at this time of day? Could it be poachers?"

Lord Wroxly glowered. "It had better not be."

"It is probably those gypsies," Giovanna said with a know-it-all expression. She remained standing behind Mr. Fletcher's chair, her hand again on his shoulder despite his effort to remove it. "Greville was right. You should not have trusted them on your land, Papa."

Eva winced at the Italian woman's familiarity with Lord Wroxly, and she noticed Amelia did, too. Perhaps he had given her permission to address him as such, but it nonetheless sounded forced and ingratiating.

Lady Lucille thrust a finger in Giovanna's direction. "You were supposed to be in the library with Greville, keeping an eye on Aunt Cecily. Where did you go?"

Giovanna Renshaw shrugged, her lips forming a pout. "Upstairs. I grew bored."

"Bored?" Lady Lucille's voice rose an octave. "Greville promised me the two of you would see that she came to no harm."

"Lucille, never mind that now. We'll find her." Lord Wroxly buttoned his suit coat as he made for the corridor. His face was grim as he passed Eva. He called for the dog, who trotted out after him.

Lady Wroxly had come to her feet as well. "We'll have the house searched. You mustn't worry, Lucille. I'm sure we'll find her."

Within minutes, Lord Wroxly set off across the gardens

with Vernon, Douglas, and the Staffordshire terrier, whom the earl led on a leash. Though Mr. Fairfax possessed the temperament of a kitten, his square jowls and muscular physique nonetheless posed a fearsome aspect, certain to make intruders, if in fact there were any, think twice before threatening the earl and the other men. Could the dog also sniff out the whereabouts of Lady Cecily?

Amelia had suggested rousing Lord Allerton to go with them, but then thought better of it after considering his and Lord Owen's experiences earlier in the day. Eva wondered if she should telephone Phoebe. Her instincts suggested her lady would be keen to know about this, but on the other hand, she loathed disturbing the newlyweds on those rare occasions when they were able to steal time alone together.

While the Renshaw women speculated, Lady Lucille fretted, and the servants mounted their search, Eva and Amelia watched from the terrace as Lord Wroxly and the footmen descended the tiered gardens to the expansive lawn below. From the elevation of the terrace, Eva could see all the way to the tree line.

Beside her, Amelia stood on tiptoe and craned forward, hands braced on the stone balustrade. Other than the men hurrying over the footbridge that crossed the stream, Eva saw no one, perceived no other movement at all but for the occasional swoop of a bird. Perhaps the shots had been fired from farther within the forest, with the culprits long gone by now.

Could it have been gypsies, perhaps poaching, as Giovanna Renshaw had suggested?

Eva didn't like to think it.

"Who is that over there?" Amelia pointed over the privet hedge separating the formal gardens from the service yard. Beyond it, a figure moved toward the house.

Eva narrowed her eyes to penetrate the slanting evening

shadows. With her hands braced on the balustrade, she leaned out, then gasped. "Good heavens, I think it's Lady Cecily."

She descended the terrace steps at a run. She had taken only a few strides when she realized Amelia had kept up with her, her skirts hoisted to allow her legs the freedom to run. When they reached the towering hedge, Eva fumbled with the gate latch until it clicked open, and they hurried through. As they skirted the hothouses, they discovered Lady Cecily some dozen yards away. Eva reached out, snatched Amelia's arm, and brought them to a halt. They nearly tripped over each other in their arrested momentum.

"Why did you stop?" Amelia panted from the exertion.

Eva pointed. A pistol dangled from Lady Cecily's hand as she tottered over the grass. She reached the stepping-stones that led to the closest hothouse, saw them, and smiled as if nothing were wrong. "Oh, hello, dearies."

"Aunt Cecily, what *have* you got there? Give that to me, please." Amelia started toward the woman but once again, Eva reached out to stop her. She took a cautious step forward.

"Lady Cecily, perhaps you might stop right there and allow me to come to you."

"Such an odd request." The woman chuckled but, much to Eva's relief, she stopped where she was.

Eva picked her way across the space between them, calmly and quietly. When she stood only a couple of yards from the elderly woman, she held out her hand. "Perhaps you'll hand that to me, Lady Cecily?"

"What? This?" Lady Cecily looked down at the weapon. It pointed toward the ground, but as she raised her arm, the barrel rose along with it until Eva found herself staring directly into its gaping blackness.

Behind her, Amelia spoke her name in a shaky whisper.

A sickening ball formed in the pit of Eva's stomach. How could she have let Amelia come along? Why hadn't she insisted the girl return to the house, where she would be safe?

Too late for that now. With no choice, she turned the entirety of her attention to the woman in front of her. She drew a breath and let it out slowly. "Lady Cecily, please take your finger off the trigger. That's a rather dangerous way to hold a firearm."

"Hmm, yes. I do see how that might be dangerous." Lady Cecily's hand quivered, her fingers trembling around the weapon.

With a fleeting, silent prayer, Eva braced herself. She reached out. Took another step forward. "If you'll lower it a bit and place it in my palm . . ."

Behind her, Amelia whimpered softly. Lady Cecily moved toward Eva. Her arm remained outstretched. At this angle, Eva couldn't judge whether or not her forefinger was positioned to put pressure on the trigger. She held up a hand. "Wait there. I'll come to you."

Eva moved forward until she could wrap her hand around the barrel of the weapon. For what seemed an eternity, they both held on. Then Lady Cecily's hand relaxed, her fingers opened, and her arm dropped to her side.

"There now, is that better, Eva?" Her pale lips curled into an innocent smile.

Eva lowered the firearm to her side. "Yes, Lady Cecily, that's much, much better. Thank you." Her knees gave way and she collapsed to the ground.

CHAPTER 12

"What hat were you thinking, Greville, leaving a weapon lying about where any innocent person could find it and come to irreparable harm?" Grampapa stormed up and down the library, alternately tugging at his thinning hair and waving his fist at his offending son. Phoebe couldn't remember ever seeing him so angry.

"I didn't leave it *lying about*, Father."

Had it been Phoebe or one of her siblings being taken to task, they would have been on their feet, rigid with attention. As it was, Uncle Greville slumped in Grampapa's wingback where Amelia and Eva had found him earlier, his shoulders hunched as if to shield himself. "It was tucked away in the drawer in my bedside table. What was she doing in my room anyway?"

Grampapa came to a halt in front of his errant son. The ire in his gaze made even Phoebe shrink slightly. "*She* has a name, and Cecily does not always understand the implications of her actions. I thought we all understood that. How the blazes did she even know you possessed a firearm?"

"Oh, that . . . well . . . we were browsing through a book

together. Lucille asked if Giovanna and I would look after her for a bit while she played cards with the others . . . and well . . . it was one of *your* books, Father. That one." Uncle Greville pointed at a volume lying on the sofa table. Phoebe read the title: *A History of Hand Weapons*. "Cecily picked it out. We came upon one that looked a good deal like mine and we discussed it."

"And you believed it a good idea to tell her not only that you'd brought one here, but where she might find it? Knowing she's already tried to open my gun case?" Fiery color flooded Grampapa's face, alarming Phoebe. She wished to caution him about his heart. For several years now, he'd been under the care of a physician—but she didn't dare interrupt.

"I told her we'd take a look at it later," Uncle Greville replied sheepishly. "Together. So no harm could come of it."

"No *harm*? Then how did she leave this room and get all the way upstairs, and then out of the house, without you being aware of it?"

At a sound behind her, Phoebe glanced over her shoulder to find Fox in the doorway, a look of disgust on his young face. For an instant she thought to shoo him away, but then realized this was no longer the pesky little brother who liked to make his sisters' lives difficult. This was a man nearly grown, preparing to take on responsibilities for the estate and the welfare of its inhabitants. The time to shield Fox from unpleasantness had long since passed. He met her gaze briefly, his features tightening grimly, before they both returned their attention to their elders.

Uncle Greville tugged at his necktie. "I . . . er . . . must have dozed off . . ." His brows drew together. "Wait. Giovanna should have been here . . ."

"She wasn't," Grampapa nearly shouted.

Eva and Amelia had said they'd found Uncle Greville fast asleep and that there'd been no sign of Giovanna, who showed up later in the Petit Salon. Uncle Greville had obviously been drinking heavily, seeing as the bottle on the table beside him was only a quarter full. Who knew how long Aunt Cecily had sat here contemplating that book, with Uncle Greville snoring away, before the thought entered her head to go upstairs and find the pistol. A deathly chill swept Phoebe from head to toe. Aunt Cecily might have accidentally shot herself. She might have shot someone else.

She might have *killed* Eva or Amelia, for that matter.

Phoebe knew she should feel relieved that the elderly lady hadn't hurt anyone, and perhaps in time she would, but right now the very notion of what might have happened filled her with an almost crippling trepidation. How close had Eva or Amelia come to being in the way of a stray bullet had Aunt Cecily inadvertently fired? Despite their protests that they were perfectly fine, they were both upstairs now in their respective rooms, ordered by Grams to lie down, each with a cold compress. Phoebe had agreed. Grams had brooked no argument, and the pallor of their faces had concurred. Julia was keeping Amelia company; Hetta volunteered to sit with Eva. Supper would be brought up to them.

Meanwhile, Grampapa had asked Phoebe to accompany him to the library to speak with Uncle Greville, and while she knew not to interrupt, she also knew she was there to prevent Grampapa from wringing Uncle Greville's neck. Yet, as the two men went back and forth, a dreadful possibility ran through her mind. Had Aunt Cecily, on her jaunt into the village the morning of the wedding, called on the chief inspector, gone inside, seen his gun, and fired it at him? Would Aunt Cecily remember doing such a thing?

Then again, why had Uncle Greville brought a weapon to Foxwood Hall—not a weapon used in hunting, but a handgun that had either of two purposes: defending one-self or purposely harming another individual.

In all the confusion of that morning, had *he* called upon the chief inspector? If Mr. Perkins had been the constable on the scene of Uncle Greville's accident all those years ago, had Uncle Greville gone there intending to silence him forever? It hadn't been Uncle Greville's gun that killed the chief inspector, but perhaps, seeing Mr. Perkins's own weapon had given Uncle Greville the idea to use the other man's gun, rather than his own.

"Really, Father, shouldn't we be having this discussion in private?" Uncle Greville's wheedling tone pulled Phoebe from her speculations.

"You're lucky my granddaughter is here, boy, or I don't know what I might do," Grampapa snapped in return. He did a double take as he noticed Fox. "And my grandson as well."

"Not to mention me." Owen surprised them all by squeezing past Fox and coming into the room. He went to Grampapa and murmured something in his ear. Grampapa listened, thought a moment, and nodded.

"Yes, perhaps you're right." Grampapa scowled at Uncle Greville. "We'll come back to this later." He strode from the room without another word, his hand clapping Fox's shoulder as he went. That brought a slight smile to Phoebe's face; it had been Grampapa's way of acknowledging, as Phoebe had, that Fox had a right to be there.

"Good grief, thank goodness that's over." Uncle Greville slumped lower in his chair and unbuttoned his collar. He grinned up at Owen. "I owe you one, old man."

"You don't owe me anything," Owen replied dryly, "because I didn't do you any favors." Owen took a seat across the low table from Uncle Greville and motioned for Phoebe to join him on the settee. Owen leaned forward and poured a generous measure of brandy into the snifter and pushed it toward the other man. Uncle Greville looked puzzled, but only for a moment. He snatched up the glass and took a healthy swig.

"I'd call *this* a favor." He took another sip, a less gluttonous one than the first. His nerves must have been steadying. Then he, too, noticed Fox. "Run along, boy. There's nothing of interest here."

"Isn't there?" Fox took several determined steps closer. "You stay away for a decade, without a thought for any of us, and now you come back and disrupt our lives this way?"

"It's none of your business." Uncle Greville regarded Fox with a steely gaze.

Fox didn't waver. "It's exactly my business."

"We'll see about that," Greville murmured.

Owen cleared his throat loudly. "Enough. Fox, you can stay." He gestured the boy to a chair and waited until he settled in. Then he returned his attention to Phoebe's uncle. "Greville, tell me about you and the chief inspector."

The request, spoken bluntly, drew a gasp from Uncle Greville. "Wh—what do you mean?"

Owen chuckled. "Come on, Grev. Let's be frank. What happened ten years ago?"

Even Phoebe was taken aback at such a direct approach. But poor Uncle Greville. He turned several shades of red until Phoebe feared he'd choke. Fox unsuccessfully tried to hide a smirk.

"Look," Owen went on, examining his fingernails, then smiling at Uncle Greville. "Before the war started you suddenly up and left the country." His gaze shifted briefly to Fox, then back again. "Why? Certainly it must have had something to do with that motorcar incident outside of Gloucester."

Uncle Greville, about to take another sip of his brandy, fell into a fit of coughing. He doubled over in his chair, the brandy in his snifter sloshing dangerously close to the rim.

Phoebe sprang to her feet. She took the glass from his hand and set it on the table beside him. Then she pounded on his back in hopes of alleviating his coughing. She also stared daggers at Fox when he showed signs of doubling over with laughter.

In a minute or two her uncle regained control of his lungs, breathing heavily but no longer sputtering. He raised his head, and the fierceness in his eyes sent Phoebe back to the settee—back to Owen. "I'll kill him."

"Who?" Phoebe guessed he meant Uncle Bert, for who else could have divulged the information?

"One shouldn't talk that way," Owen said evenly. "It might make people suspect you of violent tendencies."

"I didn't kill him. I didn't kill anyone." But the grimace clenching his features belied the second claim. A woman had died in the motor accident.

"Then it *was* Chief Inspector Perkins who was on hand that night?" Though Owen phrased it as a question, it sounded more like a statement.

Uncle Greville turned his head to stare at Fox. Phoebe guessed it was on his lips to try ordering the boy out again, but in the end he blew out a breath and nodded.

"And you and Uncle Bert paid him well to cover up what happened," Phoebe said.

With a look of consternation, Uncle Greville went still. "You're wrong. We didn't bribe him. It was his idea to let me go. But only *if* I paid dearly for the privilege. I had no choice. Perkins swore he'd bring down the entire Renshaw family in the scandal. That included you, Fox, by the way. That's when I knew I had to telephone Bert. I didn't have the kind of money Perkins wanted, and the only way to raise it would have been to go to my father. And you know I couldn't have done that."

"Perkins extorted *you*," Phoebe repeated, dumbfounded. Fox let out a whistle between his teeth.

Uncle Greville nodded. "And demanded payments every couple of years until near the end of the war. Suppose he found someone else to squeeze. Officer of the law? Don't make me laugh."

Phoebe caught Owen's eye. Was he thinking the same as she? Had the extortion ended years ago? Or not? Owen had rattled Uncle Greville into being honest. Perhaps Phoebe could further pry the truth out of him. Owen nodded subtly, leaving the next question to her.

"Did the chief inspector demand another payment when he discovered you were back in Little Barlow?"

Uncle Greville cradled his forehead in his palm. "I never would have come to Little Barlow had I known that fiend would be here. Why didn't I stay away?"

"My guess is you needed money, Uncle," Fox said softly.

He nodded without looking up. Leaning, he retrieved his snifter. "Giovanna's an expensive habit."

"And when Mr. Perkins saw you back in Little Barlow, he demanded more money?" Phoebe shook her head in disbelief. "Does Giovanna know anything about this?"

"God no." Uncle Greville finally moved his hand away from his face and met Phoebe's gaze. "She only knows my father has been less than generous over the years. Lucky for you, my girl, and for Fox and your sisters, that you're the children of the favorite son."

He said this without any particular rancor, yet it possessed a barb that stung. Phoebe and her siblings lucky? Had he forgotten that both their parents were dead? Then she realized he hadn't answered her question. "Did the inspector demand another payment?"

"Fine. Yes. But that doesn't mean I killed him. Good God, how can you even think it, Phoebe? I'm your uncle."

"I didn't say I thought you had, but even you must admit you had a motive. And, perhaps, an opportunity."

"I never left the house that day." His tone had changed, gone from plaintive to something cold, almost threatening. "You'll never find evidence to prove otherwise. Now, if you'll make my excuses to the others. I'm suddenly not hungry. I'll spend dinner in my room."

Fox came to his feet and watched Uncle Greville disappear through the doorway. "I don't know why Grandfather allowed him to come back."

Phoebe came to her feet, too. "Because he's Grampapa's son, and our father's brother."

"Well, he's neither son nor brother to me, and someday he won't be welcome at Foxwood Hall."

Eva finished her tea and carried her breakfast plate, cup, and saucer into the kitchen. Although Dora cleared the table in the servants' hall after meals, Eva liked to make as little work as possible for her. From the storeroom beside the larder, she took an empty basket and made her way outside and to the hothouses. The bundles for the farming families were ready, but she wanted to add a sprig of flowers to each. Phoebe would certainly approve of making the packages look more festive.

She went into the first glass-encased structure, its supporting woodwork painted crisply white, and went up and down the aisles, using potting shears to clip an assortment of blossoms in a mosaic of colors. No one else was about, although earlier one of the gardener's assistants had been in to water and trim. When she was satisfied she had enough flowers, she let herself out, carefully closed the door behind her, and found herself backed against the hothouse wall, a pair of stormy black eyes staring her down.

The basket of flowers dropped to her feet. Eva's heart pounded in her throat. She recognized the man immediately: Peregrin Blackwell. She stared back, unblinking, using every shred of her resolve to appear unafraid. "What do you want? You have no business being here."

Would he see her trembling?

"I have as much business being here as you do asking questions about me. You and that mistress of yours. What is it you want?"

"I want nothing from you," Eva declared with false bravado.

"No? I would have thought a cracked windscreen would have taught you both to mind your business."

"You did that!"

"You've been harassing my wife as well. I won't allow it."

"We've done no such thing. If anything, it was your boorish behavior at the fete that upset her. We only tried to offer our help if she wanted it."

"She doesn't." His eyes narrowed within a fringe of equally black lashes. "You'll tell me what you want, and you'll tell me now."

"If you'll kindly step away, perhaps we might have a civilized conversation." She drew a breath to steady herself. To her surprise, Peregrin Blackwell took a step backward. It popped into Eva's mind to shove him and run, but she didn't doubt he would chase her down, probably catching her well before she reached the service courtyard. Her gaze darted in that direction. She willed another of the servants—anyone—to come out.

No one did. Eva reached a decision. Lying to this man would only enflame his temper further. She couldn't risk that. No, better to simply come clean with the truth.

"All right. My lady and I are trying to discover the identity of Isaac Perkins's murderer."

His expression turned doubtful, then almost amused. "You can't be. You're women."

"I beg your pardon."

"Never mind." He waved away his perplexity. "And you think *I* did it? Why would I bother to kill some police inspector in a tiny village I'm stopping only briefly in?"

"Because he didn't want you here. Because he arrested your wife. And because . . ." She trailed off, having run out of reasons.

"And because I'm a gypsy? Because I'm lawless and uncivilized and a heathen?"

Her mouth dropped open in indignation. "I'll have you know I don't think any of those things. It's just that . . . Chief Inspector Perkins *did* try to make your lives miserable enough that you would leave Little Barlow, so I thought . . ."

"That we'd kill him so we could extend our stay? Do you know how often we encounter people like him? Villages like this that don't want us? Do you think it matters to us at all?" He shook his head adamantly. "We move on. That's all."

"Well . . . I . . . oh. I see. Yes, well . . ."

"Stay away from my wife." He lurched forward and pushed his face close to hers, prompting Eva to recoil. "Stay away from our people. Do not speak our names to anyone again. Do you hear? No questions, no more theories or speculations. Leave us alone."

Peregrin walked off, crossing the open lawn to a shortcut that led through the trees to the village road. Eva stood for some moments, how long she didn't know, with her back pressed against the cool glass of the hothouse. To her chagrin, she trembled all over, and she had half a mind to do as he said; that is, to do nothing from then on, mind her business, and leave well enough alone.

But that would never do. Could she believe his claims of having no motive for murdering the chief inspector? Certainly not—not with Miles's life at stake. No, she must simply be more careful. She mustn't allow herself to be alone in secluded parts of the estate or elsewhere, and she must ensure the same for Phoebe. With that resolve firmly in place, she bent to pick up her basket of flowers and hurried back to the house.

An hour later, she and Phoebe were walking along the village road to the tenant farms located in that part of Little Barlow. Josh, who had served as Foxwood Hall's hall boy since the age of fourteen, had only months ago been promoted to underfootman. Eva noted how, at the age of eighteen, he stood tall and strong, and filled out the shoulders of his livery coat as a proper footman should. She had little doubt that, should he choose to remain in service, he would move up in the ranks, perhaps all the way to butler someday. He followed along with them, pulling a cart filled with the bundles, never uttering a complaint about how recent rains had left the road pitted and bumpy, nor when Eva and Phoebe spent more time than needed at each stop they made.

"Then, you saw no one about that morning? Nothing unusual?" Phoebe asked each recipient of her gifts.

"No, my lady, not a soul. Of course, you know how busy we are here of a morning, what with chores and all."

"Yes, of course. If you do hear of anything odd that perhaps one of your neighbors saw, you'll let me know . . ."

"I will, my lady. Immediately."

And so it went, house after house, with Eva helping carry the little bundles up the walkways and Josh patiently waiting to move on to the next holding. With only two farms remaining, Phoebe sighed.

"It was worth a try," she said wistfully.

"Don't worry, we'll find another way to exonerate Miles. Besides, everyone is delighted with your gifts."

Phoebe smiled and nodded.

Once again, Eva knocked. Once again, the farmwife, in this case Mrs. Reynolds, somewhat nervously welcomed

Phoebe into her parlor, was delighted with the gift, and hadn't seen anything or anyone unusual the morning of the murder.

"But you know that detective from London has already been by. I told him what I told you. But thank you ever so much for these lovely treats, my lady. Many felicitations on your marriage."

"Thank you, and you're quite welcome, Mrs. Reynolds." Phoebe came to her feet. Eva was already on hers, having not sat down. They were both resigned to leaving when a youthful voice called down from the top of the stairs.

"I saw something!"

Eva and Phoebe exchanged startled glances then looked up at an elfin face framed by blond braids, much the same color as Phoebe's when she was a child.

"Annalise, have you been eavesdropping?"

"No, Mummy. Not on purpose." The girl, perhaps no more than six, bounced down the steps. "I couldn't help but hear you, and I *did* see someone that morning."

"Lady Phoebe," the mother said, "I'm sorry. She's got quite an imagination, this one. She's my youngest."

"I'm not playing pretend, Mummy. I really did see someone walking in the road. And he—" She stopped and wrinkled her freckled nose. "I *think* it was a man, but he had long hair like a girl's."

"Now, Annalise, you know you couldn't have," Mrs. Reynolds scolded. "Lady Phoebe was quite specific about the time, and you wouldn't have been up yet. If you saw anything, it was in your dreams."

"I wasn't dreaming, Mummy. I *was* up. I was excited about going into the village to watch Lady Phoebe arrive for her wedding." She stopped again and raised her chin high to look up at Phoebe, her expression filled with adoration. "So beautiful you were, like a princess."

"Thank you. You're pretty as a princess, too." Little

Annalise blushed with pleasure. Phoebe sank to her knees to be level with the child. "Please tell me what you saw when you woke up."

"Oh, really now." Mrs. Reynolds sounded as though her patience had worn thin. "She's only looking for attention."

"Please, Mrs. Reynolds," Eva intervened, "it can do no harm to let her speak, and it might be of great value."

With a sigh, Mrs. Reynolds held out a hand for her daughter to proceed.

"I woke up early. My sister Denise—we share a room—was still sleeping. I knew Mummy wouldn't want me about yet. She says I get un . . ."

"Underfoot," her mother murmured.

Annalise nodded. "So I stayed upstairs, but I sat on the window seat and looked out. And after a few minutes there he was. Or she was. Truly, it looked like a man with lady's hair. Long and dark. Black, I think, but it wasn't light out yet, so it was hard to know for sure."

"And which way was he going?" Phoebe asked. "Toward the village, or away?"

"Toward." The child sounded quite certain.

From here, Eva reckoned, he would have been walking toward the chief inspector's cottage.

"Thank you, Annalise." Phoebe smoothed a hand down one braid and got to her feet. "And thank you, Mrs. Reynolds, for allowing your daughter to speak to us. It *has* been a great help."

"Has it indeed?" Mrs. Reynolds turned to Eva. "I do hope so, Miss Huntford. I hope it all goes well with that nice Constable Brannock. Mr. Reynolds and I don't believe for a minute he's done anything wrong."

"Thank you, Mrs. Reynolds." Eva pressed a hand to the woman's forearm and blinked away a tear.

Outside on the road, Josh strolled behind them with the

now-nearly empty car. Eva glanced over his shoulder and saw he was paying them no attention. She couldn't contain her excitement, or her indignation. "No wonder that Peregrin Blackwell showed up and threatened me. He must have realized someone would turn up that saw him prowling along the road that morning."

Phoebe nodded. "But we must be careful, Eva. We don't want him finding out our witness is a child."

That had a sobering effect on Eva. "No indeed, you're quite right. Then . . . how do we bring this new evidence to Detective Burridge?"

"I'm not sure yet, but we must proceed with caution."

"This does corroborate the fortune teller's claim that Peregrin left the encampment early that morning and returned injured. Now it's more than her word against his." And that, Eva realized, meant they were finally getting somewhere.

Would it prove enough? And would the rest of the puzzle come together in time to save Miles?

CHAPTER 13

"And where might you be going at this time of night, Miss Huntford?"

With a startled gasp, Eva came to a halt on the pavement outside Little Barlow's haberdasher. She had heard the footsteps but hadn't thought much of them. There were other people about despite the time of evening, most of them on their way to the Houndstooth Inn for a meal or a pint.

Her first thought, of course, had been that Peregrin Blackwell had decided to waylay her again. But even before she turned, she discerned the identity of the speaker, and while he didn't frighten her, he did leave her perplexed and a bit angry merely by being who he was. She schooled her features to betray nothing. "Good evening, Detective Burridge. I trust you are well?"

"Well enough, Miss Huntford. You didn't answer my question. It's growing dark and the shops are closed. What brings you into the village?"

Her lips pinched and her nose flared; this time she didn't endeavor to conceal her ire. "Am I committing a crime by walking through the village at dusk? If so, arrest me. If not, I'll bid you good evening and be on my way."

"A spirited one, aren't you?" He quirked his mouth and snorted. "That's all right. I understand you have no love for me. But I have news for you, Miss Huntford, and for Constable Brannock. If you are on your way for an evening tryst, perhaps I should come along."

The alarm bells that had begun blaring in Eva's brain the moment he said he had news drowned out the last bit of whatever he said. Her bones became water and her breath lodged at the back of her throat. Was he about to declare he had all the evidence he needed to have Miles indicted?

She gathered her courage. "If you have something to tell me, Detective Burridge, you can say it now."

"No, not here. And it's something Brannock will want to hear as well. You're on your way there, no use denying it. It's all right. He's under house arrest. As long as he doesn't attempt to leave, he can entertain whomever he wishes." He leaned closer, the half smile on his lips making Eva want to back away. How she detested this man. "Once you hear me out, you might not think me such a useless sot after all."

She doubted that. She met his gaze, attempting to fill hers with all the contempt she felt for him. Yet something in his features gave her pause. A genuine desire to redeem himself? No, surely not.

In answer, she started walking again. He fell into place beside her, making no comment when she turned onto the side street that led to the entrance to Miles's flat. She opened the street door, typically left unlocked, and climbed the stairs. When Miles opened the door, his elated expression immediately turned wary.

"What's going on here? Eva, are you all right?"

Before she could reply, Detective Burridge shouldered

his way around her. "She's fine. No need to get your knickers in a knot."

"Now see here—"

Eva laid a hand on Miles's arm. "It's all right. He has something to tell us."

"That's right." The detective tossed his hat onto the sofa table and flopped down into Miles's easy chair. "And in exchange I expect you to tell me everything you've found out through your snooping, Miss Huntford. You and that Lady Phoebe of yours."

"That's not what you said outside." She had obviously been mistaken in bringing him here. If only she knew how to get rid of him.

"Did you think my information would come free?" He laughed softly, then addressed Miles. "Sit down. On second thought, before you do, have you got anything on hand? A whiskey perhaps?" He glanced around the room as if hoping to find what he sought.

Without a word Miles went to the kitchenette, took down three plain glasses, and brought them over to the table. Then he went back and took a bottle out of the cupboard.

Eva shook her head when he questioned her with a look. "None for me. I want my wits about me," she added wryly.

Detective Burridge took a sip. His eyes fell closed and he tipped his head back as he swallowed. He remained that way another moment, then regarded them both. "Now then, I'll come to the point. Although, first of all, the results from the coroner have come back. There was no evidence of any type of drug in the chief inspector's body. However, I've found something that sheds some doubt on your guilt, Brannock. But at this point, only *some*, mind you."

Eva sat up straighter, dismissing her reservations and giving the man every bit of her attention. "Well, what is it?"

"A pillow. *The* pillow."

"What pillow?" Miles scowled. "Don't be cryptic, Burridge."

The detective addressed this next question to Eva. "Did it never occur to you and your Lady Phoebe that in addition to no one seeing anything unusual that morning, no one heard the shot that killed Chief Inspector Perkins?"

Eva's brow drew tight. "We've been so focused on finding witnesses who might have seen something, we hadn't given any thought to what they might have heard—or not heard." How could they have been so slack?

"The killer used a pillow to muffle the sound of the shot," Miles concluded, his face filled with surprise. "I hadn't considered it either. But it makes sense, of course."

"Perkins's housekeeper came to me two mornings ago and said she thought she realized something, but she needed to see the house again." Burridge paused for another sip of his whiskey. He drank as a man well familiar with spirits, but not one dependent on them. That was to say, he sipped slowly, in small, measured drafts, and didn't hurry from one to the next. "She and I went over there, and I let her look around. That's when she told me a pillow from the sofa was missing. She said it looked as though someone had rearranged the other pillows so it wouldn't be noticeable, but being the housekeeper she knows exactly where every item in the house should be."

"I don't understand how this lessens my guilt." Miles shook his head. "I could have used the pillow and disposed of it."

"Miles!" Eva wanted to shake him. "Don't argue over this."

"No, he's right," Detective Burridge agreed. "And it's what I thought at first. Except, I think you'd have known better than to use something from the house itself. At least, I'd like to think any officer of the law would be clever enough to come prepared and not disturb anything that might be considered a clue."

"I'd like to think no officer of the law would ever commit such an act." Eva heard the self-righteous admonishment in her voice but didn't care. She still resented that Detective Burridge had ever accused Miles in the first place.

"There must be more to it." Miles held out a hand, beckoning the detective to continue.

"I spent the next two days searching roads and paths between the village and the chief inspector's house, as well as between the house and the gypsy encampment. And do you know what I found?"

"You already said you found the pillow," Eva reminded him impatiently.

"I did. A pillow with a cross-stitched design and a hole at its center. And I didn't find it half buried along a path or at the side of the road. I found it about a dozen yards from the encampment itself, where they've been putting their trash to eventually be buried before they go."

Eva's hand flew to press her lips. The gasp slipped out anyway. Miles's and the detective's eyes were upon her, expectant. She nodded. "I believe I know who murdered the chief inspector. There is other evidence pointing to this individual, including a child who saw him walking along the road toward the chief inspector's cottage that morning. This person paid me a visit only this morning, in a useless attempt to warn me off. It was Peregrin Blackwell."

Phoebe hated to dampen Eva's hopes, but she couldn't stop from speaking the truth. Eva had telephoned the hunting lodge when she returned to Foxwood Hall, saying she had just come from Miles's flat and had big news. Phoebe drove over to collect her, and now they were back at the lodge, where they could speak in complete privacy.

"Eva," she gently began, "would Chief Inspector Perkins have opened his door to Peregrin Blackwell and allowed him into his home?"

Eva's face immediately fell. "Miles said the same thing. But when taken with all the other evidence . . ."

"The pillow might have been planted near the encampment to make Mr. Blackwell, or any of them, for that matter, look guilty."

"But . . ."

"I wish to believe it too, for Constable Brannock's sake. But you know how important it is to proceed with caution. We wouldn't want an innocent man to be blamed."

"But again, the evidence. What about Mr. Blackwell's temper? He *says* Mr. Perkins didn't do anything the group hadn't encountered before in countless other villages, but we've seen how he can snap, even against his own brother."

"That's all worth considering, I agree." Seeing the desperation in Eva's expression, Phoebe's heart nearly broke. "Tell me what else the constable said."

Eva sighed and dropped her gaze to her feet. "For one, that it's doubtful Peregrin Blackwell could have gotten anywhere near Chief Inspector Perkins's parlor, but that the killer would have had to in order to grab the pillow to silence the shot."

"I'm afraid that does make sense." Owen came through the doorway. "Sorry, I couldn't help but overhear. But it's not as if Blackwell could have shot him at the front door and dragged the body inside afterward. There'd have been some evidence of it."

"No," Eva admitted. "There's little doubt the murder occurred in the parlor. Oh!" She suddenly sat taller. "Doesn't this rule out Lady Cecily? Surely if she picked up Mr. Perkins's gun and fired it, she would not have thought to use the pillow to deaden the noise, would she?"

"It's highly doubtful she would have." Owen took a

seat across from them, looking as relieved as Phoebe suddenly felt.

"Thank goodness!" The relief almost made her giddy. "But it doesn't mean there aren't other suspects. Uncle Greville for instance. Now, the chief inspector almost certainly would have let him in. After all, they had met previously, and the chief inspector had demanded another payment in exchange for his silence. He'd have thought Uncle Greville had come to make that payment."

"I certainly don't want it to be your uncle," Eva whispered, "if only because of what it would do to your grandparents."

"Indeed." A shiver skidded across Phoebe's shoulders at the thought of what such a shock might do to Grampapa in particular. Grams had the strength, both physical and mental, to persevere. But Grampapa, who had already had a scare or two concerning his heart . . . No, she did not *want* Uncle Greville to be guilty. "Let's not forget Ian McGowan. If anyone's actions are an indication of possible guilt, his are. He not only tried to evade Owen and Theo, he fought with them when they caught up to him. And did considerable damage, I might add." She tossed a pointed look at Owen, whose cuts and scrapes were still healing.

Owen offered a rueful smile. "Three men, one woman, all suspects. Lady Cecily we can pretty much rule out. But the men—all three had strong motives: in Greville's case, avoiding blackmail; in Blackwell's, anger over the ill-treatment of his people; and in McGowan's, revenge for the loss of eight years of his life."

"But which?" Phoebe asked. "Hasn't that been the problem all along?"

"Let's take another look, adding the pillow into the mix." Owen tapped his finger against the arm of his chair. "Would Ian McGowan have taken the time and the risk to hide the pillow among the gypsies' trash? I should think not. I believe he would have either left it there at the house, or he would have carried it with him on his way back to Heathcombe and disposed of it along the way."

"You're probably right." Phoebe nodded slowly as she thought it through. "The gypsy encampment is in quite the opposite direction. And would he even have known about the encampment? Even if he had heard gypsies were staying in Little Barlow, he wouldn't have known exactly where."

"And the other two?" Eva chewed her lip, then continued, "It would not have been out of the way for either Mr. Blackwell or Greville Renshaw to detour to the trash site." Her hand covered Phoebe's where it lay on the sofa cushion. "I'm sorry, Phoebe."

"Don't be. If my uncle *is* guilty, he deserves to be caught. And . . ." A thought took her aback. "Owen, you said Ian McGowan might have wanted revenge for the loss of eight years of his life. What if Uncle Greville never wished to leave England? What if he saw his exile as a prison sentence, so to speak, and sought not only to escape blackmail, but revenge for having to be away for so many years against his will?"

Owen nodded, this time with a pensive frown. "That's a compelling theory, my darling, which unfortunately shines a very guilty light on Greville. I agree he's become our prime suspect. Even so, I'm not yet ready to rule out anyone but Lady Cecily. When I think about it, McGowan *could* have learned about the gypsies, and used them to shield himself from guilt. Perhaps their arrival in Little Barlow provided him with the opportunity he'd hoped for."

Phoebe turned to Eva. "I'm sorry this isn't as easy as we'd like it to be, but we're getting closer. I feel it."

"I pray you're right."

* * *

In the laundry room the next day at midmorning, Eva and Hetta were handwashing their ladies' delicates when Vernon poked his head through the doorway. "Eva, someone to see you."

"Who is it?"

"I'm not sure. A woman. Says it's important."

"That's odd," she said to Hetta, and then to Vernon, "Tell her I'll be with her presently. Where is she?"

"Mrs. Sanders had her wait in her parlor."

"Perhaps it's Serena Blackwell," she confided in Hetta. Although the Swiss woman hadn't been involved in trying to determine who killed the chief inspector, she knew a good deal about the case. Lady Julia trusted in her discretion, and so did Eva.

"*Ja*, perhaps she has something important to tell you."

"Or she's come for help dealing with that husband of hers."

"Then she comes to the right place." Hetta took the damp shift from Eva's hands. "You don't worry, I finish here. Go, go! See what she wants. Then come back and tell me everything."

"Thanks. And I will." With a chuckle, Eva quickly dried her hands, smoothed her dress, and tucked a few stray hairs back into her coif. As she made her way up from the laundry basement, she silently rehearsed the comforting things she might say to the gypsy woman. She had already formulated a plan to help Serena leave the group if she wished to when she turned into Mrs. Sanders's parlor.

It wasn't Serena Blackwell sitting on the spindle-backed settee. Eva drew up short, unable to school the surprise from her features. "Mrs. McGowan."

The farmwife came to her feet at once. "Miss Huntford. Thank you for seeing me." She fidgeted with the strap of her handbag. "I'd hoped to speak with both you and your employer."

"She isn't here at the moment, but she should be arriving soon."

Mrs. McGowan gave a firm shake of her head. "I can't wait, so I'll say my piece now." She took a small step toward Eva. "Miss Huntford, I beg you to leave my family alone. We've done nothing, and my husband didn't kill that man. He couldn't have. He was home with me that morning."

Eva folded her hands at her waist and chose her words carefully. "Ma'am, you've already lied about your husband's whereabouts, to the police and to Lords Owen and Allerton. You claimed you hadn't seen him since his release from prison. Surely you can understand why we cannot simply take you at your word."

"That policeman from London believed me. *He* would have dropped the matter."

"But you lied to him, too. And your husband put up quite a fight when our gentlemen went to talk with him, and then he ran off. Surely, Mrs. McGowan, you realize how all that looks."

"What I don't understand is, if the detective was satisfied, why did *any* of you return asking questions?"

"Because, ma'am, my lady and her husband spoke with your vicar. His description of Mr. McGowan—a devoted family man, a fair-minded neighbor—was utterly at odds with the husband you claimed you no longer welcomed in your life. It didn't make sense."

"Eva?"

Phoebe's call sent Eva into the corridor. "I'm in here, my lady." She turned back to Mrs. McGowan. "You wished to speak with Lady Phoebe. Here she is."

As if on cue, Phoebe came into the room, the widening of her eyes declaring her as surprised as Eva to find Mrs. McGowan here. Eva relayed the conversation of the past few minutes while Mrs. McGowan shifted her weight, chewed her lip, and clutched the handle of her handbag as if her life depended on it.

Finally Phoebe said, "I'm sorry, Mrs. McGowan, but I concur with everything Eva told you. I'm sure this has been exceedingly upsetting, but I'm equally sure you can understand why we couldn't simply let it go. An innocent man's life is at stake."

"My husband is innocent. He was at home that morning."

"Perhaps," Eva said with a nod, "but Constable Brannock makes the same claim, that when the chief inspector died, he was at home. And so you see the problem."

The woman's lower lip trembled and her eyes filled. "I think you're both horrid. You want to blame someone—anyone—to save your constable. It isn't fair and I won't stand for it." She stamped her foot. "I'll go to Detective Burridge and tell him you've been harassing my family. That you . . . that you . . ." Her breath came in rapid heaves. Tears streaked her cheeks. She took a shaky step and her knees gave way beneath her. Eva sprang forward.

She caught the woman beneath the arms. Mrs. McGowan sagged against her, Eva bearing her full weight until Phoebe scampered over and supported the woman on one side. Together they maneuvered Mrs. McGowan the short distance to Mrs. Sanders's easy chair and lowered her into it. Eva rushed down to the kitchen for a glass of water.

When she returned to the parlor, Mrs. McGowan was conscious and quietly crying. "I'm sorry, I'm *so* sorry. I'm not typically like this. I don't normally go about saying dreadful things to people and causing a scene."

"We understand," Lady Phoebe said in a soothing voice. "And we also understand your desire to see your husband free of suspicion. It's what we want, too. We know his history, and yours, Mrs. McGowan. Please believe us when we say we hope you can go on with your lives in peace."

"But you must be certain." Mrs. McGowan accepted the glass from Eva. She thanked her and took a few sips.

"Would you like tea?" Eva asked her. "Something more bracing than water?"

"This is fine, thank you." Taking another sip and setting the glass on the table beside her, she opened her handbag and drew out a handkerchief. She dabbed at her eyes and blew her nose. "I'm sure you're not horrid at all. You're merely trying to find the truth."

"That's right." Eva dragged over Mrs. Sanders's small footstool and perched before the other woman. "That's why it's so important to be honest. Lying only draws suspicion upon oneself." Mrs. McGowan was about to reply, but Eva held up her hand. "We understand why you did, why what happened to Mr. McGowan in the past would influence your behavior now."

"Yes, we should have been honest when the detective came round that first time. I see that now, but I suppose I hoped the matter would be dropped, and we'd be left in peace."

"Matters such as these are never dropped," Eva reminded her.

"No, they are not." The woman blew out a long, weary breath. She came to her feet. "I've taken up enough of your time. I'll be going."

"We'll walk you out." Phoebe gestured for Mrs. Mc-Gowan to precede her.

Eva took up the rear. At the end of the hallway, she moved past the other two to open the door into the service yard. As they stepped outside, she asked, "How did you get here? Do you need a ride back into the village?"

"No, thank you." She gazed around the courtyard, taking in the two delivery wagons and the footmen helping to unload crates of potatoes, turnips, and parsnips. For their part, the workers ignored the women entirely, though Eva noticed a slight jolt from Josh when he realized Phoebe was standing only yards away. "Gideon, my eldest, drove me in our farm lorry," Mrs. McGowan said. "He's parked on the road."

"Mrs. McGowan," Lady Phoebe said, "rest assured we've no desire to clear the constable by shedding guilt on an innocent individual. That much I promise you."

"I believe you," the woman said, though she sounded no less frightened than when she had arrived.

"Well, I don't," a male voice said.

Mrs. McGowan gasped, and when Eva realized who this man must be, she let a cry of alarm.

CHAPTER 14

"Oy! Who're you?" Douglas, who had been helping unload the deliveries, came running as soon as he heard Eva's startled outcry. "You've got no business here."

He and Josh each grabbed an arm and pinned the newcomer up against the wall of the house. As they pressed him with questions, Phoebe took his measure.

Was this Ian McGowan? Judging by Mrs. McGowan's behavior now, as she demanded the footmen release him, he could only be her husband. Slightly taller than average and with a brawny build, he put up no resistance, as if he had grown used to such treatment. Which, of course, he had during his years in prison. A quick scan of his person revealed no weapon clutched in either of his large hands. His head down, his eyes averted, he appeared to pose no threat.

Then why had he come?

"Douglas, Josh," Phoebe said, "I believe it's all right if you release him. Mr. McGowan . . . you *are* Ian McGowan, aren't you?" At his nod, she went on, "Would you care to explain why you're here?"

"I would," he murmured, speaking half into his collar.

"Ian, how on earth did you get here?" his wife demanded. "And why did you come?"

"I hitched a ride with George Sanson. He wasn't coming this far but he agreed to bring me anyway."

Douglas and Josh had let go of the man's arms but stood on the balls of their feet, ready to spring back into action if needed. Mrs. McGowan went to her husband and framed his face with her hands. "Why?"

"Because when I saw you leave in such a hurry with Gideon, I guessed where you were going. After the way you were talking last night, saying someone had to reason with these people . . ." He poked his chin toward Phoebe and Eva. "You shouldn't have come here, Brenda."

"You shouldn't have either, you oaf. What if Detective Burridge had seen you? What if one of those gentlemen had?"

"If either my husband or my brother-in-law had seen you first," Phoebe said, "it would not have gone well. Not after you tussled with them out at your farm."

"No, I should say not." Mr. McGowan hung his head. "It was worth the risk to not let my Brenda come alone."

Phoebe traded a glance with Eva. In her eyes, she saw the evidence of her own thoughts, that Mr. McGowan certainly seemed to be a devoted husband and family man, and not someone given to murderous actions.

"Call them now," Mr. McGowan said, and in response to Phoebe's puzzled expression, he added, "Call your husband. Your brother-in-law. The police. Call everyone. I'll answer any questions anyone has. I didn't kill the inspector. That's all I know."

Ten minutes later, they were back in Mrs. Sanders's parlor, and had been joined by Owen and Theo. Douglas had gone back to work, but young Josh insisted on remaining, and no one ordered him away.

Phoebe and Eva sat together on Mrs. Sanders's settee,

while Mrs. McGowan took the easy chair. She had balked at first but Phoebe had insisted. The men had remained standing. Owen faced Ian McGowan from a few feet away. "Tell us everywhere you've been since being released from prison."

"Home," the man said. "I made my way from Gloucester over the course of two days, and ever since, I haven't strayed from our farm."

"Except to run off when my brother-in-law and I came calling." Theo turned his face toward the light streaming in from the high-set window. Though the cut from his brawl with Mr. McGowan had healed over, the scab hadn't yet fallen off and the bruises were still a faint yellow.

"Can you blame me for running?" The fingers of his right hand fidgeted with his trouser pocket. "After what happened to me years ago? Do you think I wanted to risk being drawn into a police affair?"

"Ian, please." His wife made a calming gesture with her hand. "They're only trying to help."

"Are they? You shouldn't have come here, Bren."

"Mr. McGowan," Phoebe said, "outside you said you were willing to answer any questions."

"And so I will." A hint of defiance entered his expression. "But you can't expect me to like it." He regarded Owen. "In answer to your question, I've been home. None of my neighbors knew I was there until today, when one of them drove me to the outskirts of this village. My wife knew, of course, as did our children. They can vouch for me, or will you call them liars?"

"Ian," his wife pleaded.

"No one is calling anyone anything." Owen shoved his hands into his suitcoat pockets. "Mr. McGowan, did you have any interaction with Chief Inspector Perkins once you were released from prison?"

"None whatsoever."

Phoebe watched his wife, who betrayed no emotion but interest in what was being said.

"And how did you feel about the chief inspector," Owen asked next.

"Feel?" Mr. McGowan scrunched his features. "I hated him. What do you expect? He ruined my life, and the lives of my family. Yes, they did well enough without me, I'll admit that. They worked the farm and they kept it profitable. But do you think it was easy for them, without a husband and father?"

"No, McGowan, I wouldn't think any such thing." Owen paused, his gaze finding Phoebe and settling on her for a long moment. His eyes filled with sadness, were almost apologetic. Was he putting himself in Mr. McGowan's place, pondering what it might be like for Phoebe if, at some future date, he simply vanished from her life? The notion filled her with a fear she had never felt before. Never considered. They were husband and wife now—could she go back to being only herself? Especially years from now, once they'd had children and had grown to depend on one another, what would it be like to have to carry on alone?

Her father had known. And Phoebe had known it had been hard for him, but only now did she come close to understanding the devastation of losing one's spouse—half of one's heart. Mrs. McGowan had a second chance, but for Papa there had only been the finality of living his life alone, until he, too, had been taken.

Such thoughts passed through her mind in seconds, the length of Owen's loving gaze before he turned back to Ian McGowan. "Your family is a credit to you."

"You needn't tell me that." Then the man shook his head. "It's not that I didn't dream of getting even with our chief inspector. I did. I laid awake some nights planning it."

A shock of surprise went through Phoebe at those words. Beside her, Eva gave a little startle.

"Even as I walked out of the prison gates," he went on, "I wondered how I might discover where he was living now and pay him a visit . . ." He compressed his lips and fisted his hands. Then he relaxed. "But I didn't. I had a chance to return home and stay there. I had no desire to be locked up again. Only I wouldn't be locked up this time, would I? For this, I'd hang."

Once Eva had completed her chores for the day, and before Amelia would need her help to dress for dinner, she approached Douglas about accompanying her somewhere before he was needed to serve in the dining room. He checked with Vernon, who released him for the next two hours.

Eva had chosen Douglas because of how he had comported himself in the service yard with Ian McGowan. He hadn't hesitated, but had swooped in to restrain the other man, who possessed no small physique of his own. Eva had been left with little doubt that had more force been necessary, Douglas would have had Mr. McGowan facedown on the ground. Call it physical strength combined with loyalty and sheer determination, much like a trained soldier.

She filled him in on her errand on the way. They walked along the main road toward the village before cutting across the fields to the gypsy encampment. As they got closer, she began to wonder if she should have had Douglas bring along a bat or some other means of self-defense. She said as much.

"Don't you worry, Miss Huntford." He held his hands up and curled them into fists. "These are all we'll need. My dad taught me and my brothers well."

"I hope those were friendly lessons and not his way of disciplining his boys."

"Now, that's the thing of it, Miss Huntford. My dad

rarely, if ever, raised his hand in anger. Said he'd had enough of violence in the Second Boer War. He just didn't want us falling prey to bullies." He pointed straight ahead. "Over there. I can see the tops of the caravans."

As they crested a hill, the rooftops of the brightly painted wagons came into view, then slipped away again as they descended. They circled the next hill and approached the encampment from the dirt road some twenty yards away.

No evidence of the fair remained, but Eva counted several more caravans and tents that hadn't been there previously. "One of the wives said they were waiting for others to join them here. That must mean they're planning to be on their way soon."

"Then it's a good thing we came now, isn't it, Miss Huntford?"

She nodded. As they entered the camp, they attracted a few looks but for the most part were ignored. Women were busily hanging laundry on makeshift lines, or minding children, or preparing to cook the evening meals in pots hanging above their cookfires. Meanwhile, men chopped wood, or hammered at whatever they might be making or fixing, and others tended to the horses.

Eva saw no sign of Peregrin Blackwell. But she did spot the very woman she had come to speak with.

Serena Blackwell tucked strands of fiery hair beneath a kerchief as she approached. "Miss Huntford. What are you doing here?" She looked, not at Eva as she asked her question, but darted her gaze around the camp. Was she looking to see where her husband was?

"I'm here to see you, Mrs. Blackwell. Is there somewhere we can speak privately?"

"Here to see me?" Wariness shuttered her expression. "Why?"

Eva, too, sent a glance around the encampment. They

were drawing more attention now. "Please, let's go where we can talk."

With a sigh, Serena Blackwell shrugged. "Follow me." She led them around a caravan and to the same area where Eva and Phoebe had first found her, by a smaller caravan with a tent set up beside it. Eva assumed this particular wagon was too small to move around in, so the Blackwells used the tent for sleeping.

"Is your husband here?" Eva asked.

"He's out collecting firewood with some of the other men." She jerked her chin at Douglas. "Who's he?"

"I'm no one," he replied genially, and moved a few yards farther away, where a rounded boulder provided a convenient place to sit and wait.

"I brought him for insurance," Eva confided.

Serena scoffed. "You still don't trust us, do you?"

"I don't trust a man who shows up unannounced, takes me to task, and basically threatens me." At Serena's puzzled look, Eva added, "Your husband paid me a visit at Foxwood Hall."

"He's impulsive like that." Her brow furrowed with worry. "He didn't hurt you, did he?"

"No, he didn't lay a hand on me."

Her expression eased. "What did he want?"

"He warned me to stay away from you. From all of you. But that doesn't matter, Mrs. Blackwell." Eva broke off when she thought she heard footsteps. When no one appeared, she relaxed and continued. "I'm here out of concern for you."

"Me?"

"Yes, I'm worried that you're married to a hothead who might one day snap and take his anger out on you. If he hasn't done so already."

"Peregrin wouldn't—" Fuming, Serena spun away.

Eva went closer and spoke to her back. "Are you certain

of that? And are you here because you wish to be, or because you have nowhere else to go?"

Serena slowly turned back around. Her angry look persisted. "Where *would* I go?"

"I could help you. You could come with me to Foxwood Hall, and we'll help you start a new life, if you want."

"You don't listen, do you, woman?" Peregrin Blackwell stepped from around the tent, his face contorted in anger. He carried an armload of cut tree branches, but now let them tumble to the ground. Eva recoiled and her breath lodged in her throat. She *had* heard footsteps. Peregrin must have heard their voices and decided to eavesdrop. His tone dropped to a growl. "I warned you to stay away. So what do you do? You sneak back here and try to persuade my wife to leave me."

Eva held her back straight, her head high. "First of all, I did not sneak. I came quite openly to speak with your wife, Mr. Blackwell. Your threats will not deter me, not when someone needs my help." Did he hear the tremor in her voice? She hoped not.

"No?" He strode closer, then whipped out a hand to seize Eva's wrist. He gave a yank that sent pain shooting up her arm. She cried out.

"Perry, stop it," his wife shouted.

Before Eva realized what was happening, Douglas was there, his fists swinging. He struck Peregrin's jaw, but the gypsy man barely winced. Still, such was his surprise that his hand opened, releasing Eva. At Douglas's command, she hurried out of the way. Douglas, continuing to use surprise to his advantage, wrestled Peregrin to the ground and perched with a knee on the man's chest, effectively pinning him in place.

By now, others had come running. Women and several children huddled around Serena, while the men encircled

Douglas and the fallen Peregrin. One Eva remembered as being a leader of the group stepped forward. "What's going on here?"

Eva couldn't help noting that the man hadn't ordered Douglas off Peregrin. Apparently, Peregrin's reputation as a firebrand was well established among these people.

Face up on the ground, Peregrin let out a string of curses.

"That's no answer," the gypsy leader said.

Douglas shifted his weight slightly but didn't let Peregrin up. "He got too ornery for his own good."

"It's because of me," Eva said, and walked toward the leader. "I came to speak with Mrs. Blackwell, and Mr. Blackwell obviously takes issue with that."

One of the women said, "Is that right, Serena?"

Serena nodded. "It is. Miss Huntford and I were speaking privately, and Peregrin came charging."

"Not the first time," someone muttered.

Peregrin cursed again, then demanded, "Someone get this buffoon off me. He's going break one of my ribs."

"Are you going to behave?" Douglas scowled down at the other man. Eva had been right to bring him along. Though she didn't like resorting to force, she didn't know how she would have managed the situation without him. He eased his weight off Peregrin's chest but remained poised to strike.

"Wait." Eva went to stand beside Peregrin and looked down at him. "On the morning the chief inspector died, you were seen walking along the road near his house. What were you doing?"

The man stared up at her with a murderous gleam. "None of your business."

"No? Perhaps I should let Douglas have a little more fun with you."

"Miss Huntford," Serena whispered to her back. Eva held out a hand to quiet her.

"Where were you going, Mr. Blackwell, so early in the morning?"

He clamped his lips shut, but in the next moment eased them apart. "To the Hobson farm. I've been doing some work for them. Repairs on the roof of their barn."

Serena moved beside Eva and spoke to her husband. "Why didn't you tell me?"

"I wanted the extra money to be a surprise," her husband replied after a hesitation.

She set her hands on her hips and scoffed. "Wanted to keep the money for yourself, more like. For ale and whatever else strikes your fancy." Serena turned away from him. "Let him up. The storm's over—no, wait." She turned back and crouched at Peregrin's side. "I'm going with Miss Huntford, Perry. Understand? You'd better not try to stop me. You brought this on with your temper and your thoughtlessness. I've had enough, I truly have. I've tried, but you've never met me halfway. And now, I'm leaving."

There were gasps through the crowd, especially among the women. When Serena pushed to her feet, several of them enveloped her and walked with her toward the small caravan, away from the others. Even so, Eva could hear their conversation.

"Serena, are you sure about this?"

"Are you really willing to leave us, leave the life?"

"Has it been as bad as all that, Serena? Really?"

"Yes, Serena, you know he does love you."

Though Eva understood their unwillingness to see their friend leave them, she feared they would convince Serena to stay and continue being the target of her husband's whims. She went to stand in their midst. "The decision is Mrs. Blackwell's to make, ladies. Please let her do what she feels is best for her."

"Serena, don't go." Peregrin was on his feet now. He hurried over and sidestepped into his wife's path. "I'm sorry. You know it's all bluster. I don't mean anything by it . . ."

She stood with her chin up, her eyes focused somewhere over his right shoulder, her features blank. Except that Eva could see the tensing of her jaws as she gritted her teeth. She tried to take a step away from him, but he moved too quickly for her to get around him.

"I'm an arse, Serena, I'll admit that, but you know I love you . . ."

"Do I?" Serena met his gaze. "Stand aside. I need to collect some of my things. I'll come for the rest later."

Eva had had enough. If Serena was going to be able to make any decisions about her future, she needed peace and quiet and freedom from the influence of others. She went to the woman's side and linked her arms through Serena's. "Do you wish to go?"

"I do," Serena replied without looking at her; without looking at anyone, her gaze adhering to some point in the distance.

"Then collect whatever you'll need. I'll wait right here for you."

Serena moved to the caravan, opened the small double doors at its rear, and climbed in. It took her only a few minutes to reappear, a tied bundle beneath her arm. "I'm ready."

"Serena . . ." Her husband hovered off to one side, looking despondent. "You can't mean this."

Serena made no reply.

"All right, then." Over her shoulder, Eva called, "Douglas? We're going."

Though dinner wasn't for another two hours, Phoebe went over to the main house early. She hoped to find out more about Uncle Greville's return to Little Barlow, but not from him.

After visiting with Grams, Amelia, Julia, and Baby Charles, she excused herself and searched the house. She found Giovanna in the garden room, little used by the rest of the family. Grams had once declared the room off-limits to Phoebe and her siblings, saying it was unsuitable for young eyes. That was because of the mosaics depicting mythological figures in rather a state of dishabille. The artwork had been accomplished more than two hundred years ago, well before Victorian sensibilities had deemed such displays risqué. When Phoebe had asked Grams why she had never had the room renovated, Grams had said, ironically, that art was art, and not to be destroyed.

She was not surprised to find Giovanna sitting at the garden table alone, a glass of wine before her, and her head tipped back as she perused the images splashed across the ceiling. At the sound of Phoebe's step, the Italian woman tilted her head to peer over her shoulder.

"Ah, it is you. I knew it couldn't be one of the men, your step is too light. But I didn't think the ladies ever came in here."

"Generally, we don't, but that's because my grandmother doesn't quite approve of this room."

Giovanna chuckled and glanced upward. "No, I shouldn't think so."

"What are you doing here all alone?" Phoebe went to the table, pulled out a chair, and sat. Manners dictated that she should first ask if Giovanna minded company, but she didn't wish to take the chance that the woman would tell her no.

Her uncle's wife emitted a long sigh. "How shall I put it?" She patted her lustrous hair, swept back in a cascade of glossy curls that touched her shoulders. "There is so little chance to be alone in this house. Until I discovered this room. Will your grandmother be angry with me?"

"Not at all. The room isn't forbidden. It's simply not

one she cares to frequent, and so the rest of us don't either."

"A compliant lot, aren't you?" She reached for a gold case sitting at her elbow that Phoebe hadn't noticed until now. She snapped it open and plucked out a cigarette. "Do you mind?"

As a matter of fact, Phoebe did mind. She hated having smoke in her face. It stung her eyes, burned her nose, and made her throat itchy. Thank goodness no one in the family smoked. Even Grampapa, who had always enjoyed his pipe and the occasional cigar, had never smoked anywhere in the house but his study, and he'd given it up recently on his doctor's orders. Julia had tried cigarettes for a while because she had believed the sleek holder she used made her look sophisticated, but eventually she had admitted that she loathed the taste of it. Theo's lung damage from the war made smoking painful for him, and while Owen occasionally smoked, he never did so in Phoebe's presence, something she vastly appreciated.

She nodded now to grant her permission. She wanted Giovanna relaxed and settled, not running outside to indulge in her habit. After placing the cigarette between her full, sensual lips, the woman procured a lighter, lit it, and drew the smoke deep into her lungs.

"Are you enjoying your stay?" Phoebe asked after Giovanna had breathed out a pearly-gray cloud. Phoebe tried not to squint as the smoke drifted past her.

"*Hmph.*"

Not an answer Phoebe expected. She watched as Giovanna took another drag, her lips pursing as tight as a rosebud. Then she said, "I hope there hasn't been anything troubling you while you've been here."

"Troubling me? No. Except perhaps being a fish out of water. I don't think your family knows what to make of me."

"That's not true—"

Giovanna laughed outright. "It is, and you know it. I am not like you. No one who is not English *can* be like you."

Once again, Phoebe started to deny this assertion, but she found she couldn't. There was truth in what Giovanna was saying, and, Phoebe suspected, in what she had been feeling here in household. Instead, she laughed and nodded. "We're an odd bunch, all of us. I'll grant you that."

"I'm grateful to have found the tearoom in town." She flicked the ash off her cigarette onto the tile floor.

Phoebe watched the ash fall, resisting the urge to spring up and find an ashtray. "I . . . er . . . hadn't realized you'd been there."

"A few times now. The owner, Signorina Young, has been gracious."

"You go alone?" This news surprised Phoebe. She hadn't noticed Giovanna's absences from the house, and no one else had mentioned them either. Is that how much attention the family had been paying their guest? Phoebe felt rather ashamed.

Giovanna shrugged and dragged on her cigarette. "I enjoy the walk. And I enjoy the company once I am there."

"I see . . ." Perhaps this woman, who had seemed impervious to the opinions of others, had been feeling slighted all along. "Tell me, this trip seems to have been very sudden. What prompted Uncle Greville to travel all the way to England? And don't say my wedding. My sister Julia got married and Uncle Greville didn't come for it."

Giovanna studied her intently, until Phoebe grew uncomfortable. "You want the truth?"

"Yes, I do." More than Giovanna could guess, Phoebe suspected.

"Well then, I'll tell you." She leaned forward, puffed on her cigarette, and as she blew out the smoke, the words came with it. "Your uncle Greville has been cheated out of his birthright, and he's come home to claim it." She tapped the cigarette, sending more ash falling.

"His birthright? But Fox is Grampapa's heir. Legally and otherwise. It can't be changed."

"Your little brother can have the title. And this house." Giovanna sat back, regarding the mythological images surrounding them. "We don't want any of this. What use is it to anyone? Times have changed. Places like this are a burden, not a blessing."

"Then you're talking about the money."

Giovanna raised an eyebrow. "Of course."

"You do realize, don't you, that the war greatly diminished this family's resources. That we're going to have to implement new farming practices and find other uses as well for the land around Foxwood Hall in order to ensure its viability in the coming years and decades. Fox will have his work cut out for him—with the help of the rest of us, of course—if he is to leave anything to his own heir someday."

"Heirs . . . estates . . . This is exactly how the money has been wasted, by putting it into the hands of the least skilled in such matters. Your grandfather should divide the money equally. That is the only fair way to do it."

"The title, estate, and the bulk of the money are legally entailed. It all goes to Fox. Even Grampapa can't change that."

"Bah! Excuses. No wonder Greville fled. Your grandfather always favored your father over him. A second son, a spare . . . disposable."

"That's not true." Phoebe meant this in more ways than one, for she knew quite well that it had been the car accident that drove her uncle out of the country. Forcefully she said, "My grandparents were crushed when Uncle Greville left England."

"Well, now he is back. They should make more effort to find out about his life in Italy. Our life. How hard it's been, especially since the war. We have very little, you know. We struggle. We only came back to—"

"To what, Giovanna?" To wheedle money out of Grampapa, only to be confronted by a greedy Chief Inspector Perkins, who wanted to take what little they had? Uncle Greville said Giovanna knew nothing of that, but what if he were wrong? Or lying? What if Giovanna had decided to do away with that one problem herself?

Phoebe's thoughts broke off when she noticed Giovanna staring at her through narrowed eyes, a speculative look sharpening her features. "Your sister Julia's marriage did nothing to help the family finances, has it? Her husband needed *her* money—the money her first husband left her. But *your* marriage . . . It has brought new income to the Renshaws, has it not? Your husband, he is rich, and his business is making him richer by the day."

"I don't see what that has to do with anything." This woman's audacity raised Phoebe's ire and set her pulse points thudding. "Surely you don't expect that you and Uncle Greville will profit off my marriage?"

"We'll see, won't we?"

Before Phoebe could react to that, Giovanna stood. She dropped her cigarette butt onto the tiled floor, crushed it beneath her heel, and plucked up her wineglass. After a sip, she strode off, her hips swaying beneath her tight skirts.

CHAPTER 15

"How are you getting on so far?" Eva asked Serena Blackwell the next morning, after she had helped Lady Amelia dress and had collected the clothing that needed to be laundered.

The gypsy woman had insisted on being put to work, so Mrs. Sanders had assigned her simple tasks. This morning it was putting away the washed dishes and cutlery the servants had used for their breakfast. Eva found her at one end of the servants' hall, stacking plates in the glass-fronted cabinets above the counter along the wall.

"I'm being of use," she said, unnecessarily.

"I can see that. Did you sleep well?"

She paused, a small stack of dishes in hand. "Well enough. I shared with two of the girls. They doubled up in one bed so I could have the other. I hope they didn't mind much."

"I believe you shared with Dora and Connie," Eva said. When Serena nodded, she added, "I'm sure they didn't mind. They're kindly girls, both of them."

"They seemed all right," Serena agreed. "And it won't be for long, I promise."

"No one is pushing you out. Especially with you so adamant about working for your keep."

"I know no other way." Her face took on a prideful
gleam. Then it faded. "But being inside these walls, beneath the ground like this . . . I feel trapped. Like I've
fallen into a well and can't get out."

Eva turned to the table, gathered a few clean glasses between her hands, and brought them to the bank of cabinets. Serena swung open the door so Eva could place them
on the shelf. "Have you never lived in a house?"

"For short times, I have. As a child. Though, never in a
house, exactly. In flats, usually one or two rooms, with
my parents and brothers and sisters. Only in the winter,
mind you."

Eva leaned with her hip against the counter. "Can you
join some of your family, if you wish?"

"I've written to my sister." She lifted the last stack of
dishes. "She's with her husband's family and I think they'd
let me travel with them, for a while at least."

"How do you find them if they're traveling?"

Serena smiled. She opened one of the drawers below
the counter and started to sort the clean silverware into
their proper slots. "We have our ways. The message will
reach her."

How mysterious. Eva was intrigued to know more but
didn't ask. If nothing else, she had learned that these people treasured their privacy and their way of life. And also
that her curiosity could be taken as an intrusion.

"My husband came by here last night," Serena surprised her by saying. "He swore to me he had nothing to
do with the inspector's murder."

"Do you believe him?"

Serena blew out a long breath. "I don't know. I want to.
But I sent him away. I told him I wasn't ready to talk to
him yet. Or should I have pressed him for the truth?"

"No, you did the right thing." The last thing Eva wanted was for this young woman to put herself in danger by confronting a murderer, whether it be her husband or someone else. "Good for you."

"He didn't like it."

"He doesn't have to. He only has to respect your wishes." Serena tilted her head as she regarded Eva. "Why do you care?"

She sounded merely curious, and not in any way cynical. Eva replied, "I don't like to see anyone being bullied. That's what he was doing, you know, and always will do, unless he's stopped."

"Well, you've certainly stopped him."

"No, Mrs. Blackwell, *you* stopped him, by leaving. It has to be you, or he'll never change."

"Call me Serena. May I call you Eva?"

"Of course."

The gypsy woman went quiet, her face turning solemn. She compressed her lips and raised a hand to her bosom as if to press her heart. "Do you think he can change?"

"I honestly don't know. I hope so."

"So do I," she whispered.

Eva finished her morning chores of handwashing delicates, ironing shirtwaists, and polishing shoes before leaving Foxwood Hall. This had become her routine since Miles had been arrested, accomplishing her work as quickly as possible that she might spend an hour or two with him during the day. Today they would have lunch together. Before climbing the stairs to his flat, she stopped in at the Houndstooth Inn and selected two savory pies and a crock of Scotch broth to share with him.

His happy look as he opened his door filled her with joy and made her glad she had been able to get her work done in record time. He relieved her of the items she carried, setting them on his tiny kitchen table, and gathered her in his arms.

"I'm glad you're here," he said against her hair.

"So am I."

"I wish you didn't have to go, ever."

"And what would people think of that?" she asked with a chuckle.

He pulled back until they could behold each other's faces. "I think you know what I'm saying. There wouldn't be talk, other than to wish us well."

A rush of warmth engulfed Eva's cheeks. This was as close to a proposal as he had uttered so far, yet, as the happiness dimmed from his features, she knew it was as close as he *would* get until his name had been cleared.

"Shall we eat?" she said to change the subject. It was no use being melancholy over what they couldn't change—at least not immediately. She unpacked the cloth bag she had used to carry their lunch, placing two Bedfordshire clangers— pastry stuffed with spicy pork and potatoes—on plates. Then she took down two bowls and ladled out the Scotch broth, thick with barley, lamb, and cabbage. The aromas made her stomach growl. They also brought a smile back to Miles's face.

He came to the table and inhaled. "You do know the way to my heart."

She swatted him with her napkin before placing it on her lap.

They both dug in with relish. But after a few moments, Miles went still. A pensive look crossed his features.

"What is it," she asked, setting her spoon down in her soup bowl.

"This . . ."

Eva stared down at her meal. "What about it? I think it's rather delicious."

"It isn't that . . ." He ran a hand through his hair, then beneath his chin. His eyes narrowed as he obviously thought something over. "Sausage pasty . . ."

"Miles, you're talking in riddles. This isn't sausage. They make sausage down at the pub on Saturday afternoons. And sometimes on Tuesdays. Today is . . ."

"No, it's what Perkins had for breakfast that morning. A sausage pasty."

"What of it?"

Miles met her puzzled gaze with one of his own. "Where'd he get it?"

"I don't know. His housekeeper made it for him, presumably."

"But she wasn't there yet. She always comes later, and Perkins does for himself first thing in the morning."

"Perhaps she made it the night before, and he heated it up in the morning."

"Perhaps . . ." He obviously wasn't satisfied. "Do we know if anyone asked her about it?"

"I haven't the foggiest, except that Lady Phoebe and I haven't. Honestly, it never occurred to me to question where his breakfast came from. And once we learned that no drugs were detected in the chief inspector's body, I never imagined it could have any bearing on the case."

He continued to brood even as he polished off the last of his soup and chewed absently on his clanger. "What if whoever killed him brought him breakfast that morning. It was a sure way to gain entry to his house, if you ask me."

Part of Eva wished the subject hadn't come up, that they could have enjoyed lunch together as if nothing was wrong; as if Miles's life didn't hang in the balance. But the other part of her, the part determined to clear his name, latched onto his logic.

"You're saying someone stopped by, pretending friendship, offering him something special for his breakfast . . ." She thought a moment. "I can't picture Greville Renshaw using such a ruse. Or Peregrin Blackwell. It's not something men tend to do for each other, is it?"

Miles shook his head. "No, not typically." He ruminated further while Eva ran through the list of suspects she and Lady Phoebe had compiled. Although Peregrin Blackwell and Greville Renshaw continued to be suspects, she now focused on the women.

"Last night, Phoebe told me about an encounter she had with her uncle's wife, Giovanna. She's greedy, that one, and determined for her husband to reap the benefits of being the Earl of Wroxly's son. Not the title or the estate, she made that quite clear. But the money. She admitted she and her husband had come seeking what they both consider his due."

"And Perkins had been blackmailing her husband," Miles said, suddenly more animated. "But would she think of something like this? Could she have gotten Mrs. Ellison at Foxwood Hall to make the pasty for her?"

Eva thought that over, then shook her head even as Miles did the same. She voiced the thought they were both having. "I don't think she would have wanted the pasty to be traced so close to home. She wouldn't want such a clear trail to herself."

Miles nodded his agreement. "Then could she have gone into the village to buy it?"

"Yes, in fact she could have. Phoebe told me Giovanna's been going into the village periodically to escape everyone at the house." She scoffed, and said with no small amount of sarcasm, "Poor thing, she feels out of place among the others."

"I'll wager." His mouth skewed. "Eva, will you ask at the pub if they remember her coming in to buy a Cornish pasty?"

"Of course. I'll need to be back at Foxwood Hall soon, but at the first opportunity, I'll ask."

"If she did, I'm certain they'll remember her. It's not every day we see Italians in Little Barlow." His eyebrows went up and he half smiled. "Especially not Italians who look like Giovanna Renshaw."

Eva swatted him again.

Phoebe drove into the village after lunching with the family at home. Owen had offered to come with her, but she didn't think his presence would help her cause, not if she hoped to find out more about Giovanna from Pippa Young. Instead, she had shooed him in Grampapa's direction. They needed to discuss the loss of two tenant farmers who had decided to move their families to the city. With no immediate prospects to replace them, the loss of income to the estate was a major concern.

When she arrived at Pippa's Delights, she was happy to find the place nearly empty. Had she come earlier, at the lunch hour, or later, when most people enjoyed their afternoon tea, such would not have been the case. After closing the door behind her, she hovered near the front of the restaurant. A moment later the woman she had come to see made her way out from the kitchen.

"Lady Phoebe! To what do I owe the pleasure?" Pippa Young peered over Phoebe's shoulder to the window overlooking the High Street. "Are there others coming? Your sisters, perhaps?"

"Not today, Miss Young. I'm in the village shopping," she half lied. "I thought I'd enjoy a bit of quiet time on my own."

The woman came closer and lowered her voice. "Nothing wrong at home, I trust? Forgive me, I don't mean to pry, but with you being a new bride and all . . . well, I do hope you aren't facing any difficulties this early on."

Phoebe smiled. "No, not in that respect, I assure you. I

couldn't be happier. But the house is rather crowded at the moment. You understand." Did Miss Young know that Phoebe and Owen enjoyed the use of the hunting lodge, where they could be away from the family and guests any time they wished?

If she did, she didn't remark on the fact. Instead, she said, "Follow me, please," and led her to a small table away from the other patrons. "Will this do?"

"Perfectly, thank you."

Miss Young held her chair for her. "What would you like today? Cream tea again?"

Phoebe thought a scone with clotted cream and jam might be consumed too quickly for her purpose. "What's on your savory menu today?"

"I have a lovely quiche Lorraine. Have you ever had it? It's eggs, cheese, and bacon, baked into a flaky pie crust."

"Sounds perfect. I'll have that and some fruit, please."

"Coming right up."

Phoebe waited patiently for her meal to arrive, rehearsing in her head the questions she wished to ask the woman. When Miss Young arrived, Phoebe commented, "It's very quiet in here. Very peaceful."

"It's our lull." She transferred Phoebe's plate, bowl of fruit, and a teapot from the tray she held to the table. "It happens every day at this time."

Yes, Phoebe had guessed correctly. "If you're not pressed to do other things, won't you grab a cup for yourself and join me for a few minutes?"

Miss Young's face took on a surprised and then pleased expression. She glanced at the other tables, as if to assure herself everyone was well taken care of. "Are you sure?"

"I wouldn't have asked otherwise," Phoebe replied with a smile.

"Then I'd enjoy that very much, thank you." She scooted off and returned a moment later with a cup and saucer.

She sat opposite Phoebe and, lifting the teapot, poured first into Phoebe's cup and then her own.

Phoebe cradled her teacup in her hands. "You've been here, what, a year now?"

"Almost, my lady."

"It seems to be a great success."

"I certainly can't complain. At first I feared I wouldn't find enough patronage in a small village like Little Barlow, but it seems people are coming from a wider area than our borders. I'm grateful for that."

"Word has certainly spread. You're quite popular with my family, and everyone I know. In fact, I understand my uncle's wife, Giovanna, enjoys coming here. I suppose I should call her my aunt," Phoebe added with a laugh. "It's just that we hadn't seen my uncle in so many years, and this is the first time I've met her."

"Yes, she comes in regularly." Miss Young raised her teacup to her lips, blowing first before sipping. "I was surprised at first that she came alone."

"Like me, she enjoys the quiet here, and the lovely surroundings. It's quite calming." She allowed her gaze to take in the soft colors and fabrics, the light wood furnishings.

"Thank you. While gentlemen are certainly welcome, I did my best to make this a woman's haven."

"Haven," Phoebe repeated. She ran her fingertip over the fine weave of the mauve linen tablecloth. When she spoke, she injected into her tone a hint of reluctance, as if it was a question she didn't wish to ask but felt compelled to. "Tell me, does Giovanna seem unhappy to you?" She reached out, grazing the other woman's hand with her own. "You don't have to answer that. It's just that . . . I'm a bit worried about her."

Miss Young compressed her lips as she considered her

reply. Like Phoebe, she spoke with the suggestion of reluctance. "As I'm sure you can see for yourself, coming to England hasn't been easy for her. For understandable reasons. We English are very different from the Italians. I believe she finds us a bit . . . cold. It's our reserve. It can be off-putting if one isn't used to it."

"I do understand that." Phoebe gave a rueful laugh and paused for a bite of quiche, a sip of tea. She expressed her appreciation of the egg dish with a moan of pleasure. Then she said, "I fear it might be more than that, though. Her unhappiness, I mean. I'd like to help if I can."

"I'm afraid there isn't much you can do, my lady, unless you have influence where your uncle is concerned."

"What do you mean?"

"I don't know the particulars, but . . ." She trailed off, looking uncertain.

"If you're afraid I'll go telling tales, I assure you, anything you tell me will remain between us. I only wish to help, not make matters worse."

With a look of relief, Miss Young continued. "She's disappointed, vastly so, in the marriage. I believe she went into it with overly high expectations. That perhaps your uncle led her to believe . . . well, you understand, I'm sure."

"That my uncle led her to believe there was a lot more money than there is."

Miss Young raised her teacup, let her eyes fall closed, and nodded. "They've had to scrounge, my lady."

"Are they very deeply in debt?"

Miss Young hesitated before nodding. "Mind you, she didn't confide these things all at once, nor did she express it in as exact terms as I have to you. These are my overall impressions, based on little comments here and there during the course of our conversations."

"She has found a friend in you," Phoebe said, but she wondered if that was true. Had Pippa Young been a true friend to Giovanna, she would not have broken her confidence now. Or did she think Phoebe could truly be of help? To put it to the test, Phoebe asked, "How far do you think Giovanna would go to right what she perceives as a wrong?"

Miss Young went still. "What are you asking me?"

"Is she, or are both she and my uncle, desperate enough to resort to extreme measures to obtain the cash they need?"

The indignant look on Miss Young's face made Phoebe fear she would spring up from her seat and stride away. The woman tensed as if she intended doing just that. But then she relaxed and sighed. "I can't speak for your uncle. But for Giovanna, simply coming to England was an extreme measure. She longs to go home."

Phoebe mulled these revelations concerning her uncle's wife on the ride back to Foxwood Hall. Once there, she collected Eva and brought her to the hunting lodge, where they could speak without being overheard.

"How is the constable?" she asked along the way.

"Frustrated," was Eva's succinct reply.

"But he hasn't given up."

"No, he hasn't. I think his mind is constantly working over the details. He's come up with a new theory."

"Wait until we reach the lodge." Phoebe increased the pressure of her foot on the accelerator. Once there, they made themselves comfortable in the salon.

"Is your husband at home?" Eva asked.

"I don't believe so." She got up from the settee and went into the hall. "Owen? Are you home?" When no answer came, she returned to the salon. "He doesn't appear so. Does it matter?"

"Certainly not. I merely thought if he were, he might want to join our discussion."

"I'll fill him in later. Now then, tell me all about your morning. How does Serena Blackwell seem today?"

"Strong," Eva said, and then explained, "leaving one's husband would tend to shake a woman's resolve. They often feel guilty and have second thoughts—at least, my sister did when she temporarily left her husband. She questioned whether she did the right thing. Serena didn't appear to be doing that when I saw her this morning. In fact, at her insistence, Mrs. Sanders has put her to work. Her plans are to join her sister, who is traveling round the country with her husband and his family."

Phoebe ran her hand back and forth along the edge of a velvet throw pillow. She pulled it onto her lap and hugged it. "And are you confident that she didn't murder the chief inspector?"

Eva hesitated, then said, "She did say one thing that might make one wonder. She said she felt trapped within the walls at Foxwood Hall, as if she'd fallen down a well and couldn't get out. Now, if she feared the chief inspector would see to it she went to prison for theft..." Eva shrugged.

Phoebe nodded, chewing the corner of her lip as she considered. "But her crime wasn't so severe that she would have gone to prison for any length of time. If anything, a fortnight in the village jail. Would her fear of being enclosed be so extreme she'd commit murder to avoid a week or two behind bars?"

"Probably not."

"Tell me about the constable's theory," Phoebe prompted.

"Oh, yes. It's about the chief inspector's breakfast the morning he died. Miles is wondering where it came from, seeing as the housekeeper hadn't arrived yet. The chief inspector wouldn't have cooked anything so elaborate for himself. It would have meant making the crust, stewing the meat and onions . . ."

"I see your point." Phoebe continued fidgeting with the edge of the pillow. "Someone had to have brought it to him, then."

"Exactly, unless the housekeeper made it the day before and left it for him to heat up in the morning. I don't know if she has been asked about this."

Phoebe sat up, casting the velvet pillow aside. "Then we must ask her."

CHAPTER 16

Cynthia Mathison, Isaac Perkins's housekeeper, lived two lanes over from Miles's flat, in a one up, one down stone cottage. Eva knocked at the front door, hoping they would find the woman at home. Then again, in a village this size, it shouldn't be too difficult to find her.

The door opened on a pleasant-looking woman dressed much as one might expect of a housekeeper, in black serge with a white lace collar, a matching square of lace pinned over her hair to form a cap. Having worked as a house-keeper for most of her life, she probably owned little else. "Oh, hello. I know you, don't I?"

"Sorry to disturb you, Mrs. Mathison. Yes, I'm Eva Huntford, and we know each other from church. We've both worked with Lady Phoebe sorting supplies for the RCVF," Eva replied, referring to the veterans' aid society Phoebe had established directly after the war.

"Why, of course. Do come in—oh! I see Lady Phoebe is with you. Please excuse my manners, my lady, I didn't see you there."

"That's quite all right, Mrs. Mathison," Phoebe said as she and Eva passed through the doorway into the cottage's downstairs room. The space extended back far enough to accommodate a small parlor area, a table and chairs, and, at the very back, a workable kitchen. Beyond, through a window above the sink, Eva spied a well-kept garden.

"Please, make yourselves at home." The woman folded her hands primly at her waist. "What may I get you? Tea? Lemonade? I made it only this morning . . ."

"No, thank you," Phoebe said. "We don't mean to take up too much of your time."

"Nonsense. I've nothing but time ever since . . . well, you know. Ever since my poor employer went to meet his maker."

Eva chose a seat on the wooden settee cushioned in a well-cared-for damask. "First of all, how are you, Mrs. Mathison? How are you getting along?"

"I'm well, thank you. I've too much time on my hands, mind you, although it's allowed me to catch up on my gardening." She sighed and gazed around the room. "I'm considering selling, though. Perhaps moving closer to my brother in Gloucester. Just a room is all I need, really."

"Best not to make any decisions too hastily," Phoebe cautioned, and the woman nodded. "And if you need any assistance . . ."

"Now there's the surprising thing." Mrs. Mathison sat on a small chair near the hearth. "It seems Mr. Perkins laid a bit by for me in his will. And to think, I never much liked him." She gasped and pressed her fingertips to her lips. "Forgive me, I shouldn't have said that. It's not that I didn't have a certain regard for him. He was a good employer, rarely complained of my work, but he *was* rather curmudgeonly, in a general sort of way."

"We understand," Eva assured her.

"Yes, perfectly." Phoebe sounded so eager in her agreement that Eva was tempted to tap her foot in a gentle admonishment. "But the reason we're here," she went on, "is to ask you a question about the morning the chief inspector died."

"Was *murdered*," the woman corrected her. "We mustn't understate it. Curmudgeon or not, he didn't deserve such an end."

"No." Phoebe crossed one ankle over the other and sat forward a little. "The chief inspector appears to have eaten a Cornish pasty for breakfast that morning. Did you prepare it for him?"

"Why, no. I never made the chief inspector's breakfast. I always came later, after he went to work. Now, lunch and supper, yes, but not his breakfast."

"And you didn't make a pasty for him, say, the night before?" Eva asked.

"No. I'm quite sure I'd remember if I had. But he wasn't a man for much in the way of breaking his fast. Made do with a piece of toast and jam, which he was perfectly capable of managing, mind you, and his coffee, which he also brewed himself."

Eva and Phoebe came to their feet. Phoebe said, "Thank you, Mrs. Mathison. If there is ever anything you need . . ."

"Is that all?" The woman looked bemused as she rose from her chair.

"One other thing, actually." It suddenly occurred to Eva the woman might yet be able to offer useful information. "Did the chief inspector sometimes purchase a meal for himself in the village, and if so, where?"

"Only very occasionally. He came home most days for lunch, you see. But if I were unable to work on a particular day, I believe he took his meals at the Houndstooth." She frowned slightly. "But I don't think he ever brought the food home with him."

After leaving the cottage, they walked down the High Street to the Houndstooth Inn and Tavern. "I didn't think I'd be back here so soon," Eva said as they went through the door. The interior was cool and dim, with the curtains half drawn against the afternoon sun and the gaslights burning low. Much of Little Barlow still depended on gas rather than electricity, although Eva suspected the proprietor, Joe Murdoch, preferred the murkiness of the old-fashioned lighting. The better to hide the night's sins.

This being late afternoon, however, there wasn't much sinning going on. Only a few were in at this hour, mostly workmen enjoying a plowman's lunch, shepherd's pie, or a bowl of the Scotch broth Eva and Miles had shared earlier. Joe Murdoch stood behind the bar, setting out pint mugs in preparation for his after-work regulars.

Ordinarily, they wouldn't have approached the bar. Women were expected to be seated and wait to be served, reserving the bar area for male patrons only. But at this time of day, they wouldn't be offending anyone with their presence.

"Mr. Murdoch," Eva greeted the man when they reached the bar.

"Miss Huntford, back so soon? More Scotch broth? How did the constable like it?"

"He liked it just fine, Mr. Murdoch. More than fine. But that's not why we're here."

As Mrs. Mathison had, he did a double take upon noticing Lady Phoebe. He sputtered a bit and hurried out from behind the bar. "Such an honor, Lady Phoebe. Let me escort you to a table."

He led them across the room, to a table a good distance from those that were occupied. Eva and Phoebe let him, and then surprised him when they asked him to join them for a few moments.

"We have a question to ask you," Phoebe explained, before launching into the same line of inquiry as with Mrs. Mathison.

Joe Murdoch sat back in his chair and mulled the question

over. "That's going back more than a few days, now . . ." He scratched the side of his head, then ran the same hand over his beard. "But no, I don't remember anyone coming in that morning or the night before, asking to take food away with them." He gave a chuckle. "When you think about it, why would anyone order a meal, and then not sit down and eat it here? Except in cases like yours, Miss Huntford, where the constable isn't supposed to leave his flat. And a travesty it is, too, when a good man like Brannock is accused of such ill doings. We all know he's innocent."

"Thank you," Eva put in quickly, before the innkeeper could continue running on. "It means a lot to us both to know the villagers are behind him."

Mr. Murdoch rose from his chair. "Now, what can I bring you ladies?"

After the repast she had shared with Miles, Eva wasn't the least bit hungry, and she guessed Phoebe wasn't either. But to leave without ordering anything seemed rude. She and Phoebe exchanged a glance.

Before either could say a word, Mr. Murdoch said, "I see. You've already eaten. But we've an Eve's pudding that'll make you think you've died and gone to heaven. I'll be right back with it." He ran off, returning with two plates of steaming baked apples with custard and crumbly cake topping. Curls of steam rose from each plate and sent tantalizing aromas to tease their senses. "Here you are. Warmed it for you." He sauntered off and returned once again, this time with two mugs and a pot of tea. "Nothing fancy, but it'll go with the apples."

Eva smelled cinnamon emanating from the spout of the teapot. "You know, Phoebe, I'm beginning to think Pippa Young has serious competition in Joe Murdoch."

"Agreed. But speaking of which, let's finish this lovely repast and make our way over to the tearoom."

About fifteen minutes later, they were outside and on

their way to Pippa's Delights. "This time," Eva said as they trekked along the pavement, "let's not let Miss Young show us to a table. I couldn't eat another bite!"

"Nor me." Phoebe placed a hand on her stomach and made a face.

"I'm sure she'll be surprised to see you again, twice in one day. You haven't told me what you learned when you visited there earlier."

They looked both ways and, after waiting for a horse and carriage, a donkey cart, and a motorcar to pass, they stepped down from the pavement and crossed the street. "Let's slow down a bit so I have time to tell you. We can pretend to be looking in the window at the milliner's shop."

Once they'd waited for several pedestrians to pass by, exchanging greetings with each, Phoebe said, "Miss Young confirmed much of what Giovanna told me, including that Giovanna has been a frequent visitor to the tearoom. She added that she believes Giovanna is disappointed in the marriage. Apparently, she believed my uncle had more money than he does."

Eva pulled her gaze away from a darling felt hat sporting a cluster of roses fashioned from ribbon on its band. "He must have led her on."

"Which doesn't surprise me. Miss Young also said they're deep in debt and scrounging for funds."

"Debt can drive people to desperate acts."

"It can. But when I asked Miss Young just how desperate they had become, she became defensive and refused to answer." Phoebe shrugged. "It appears I crossed a line."

"Perhaps your uncle's wife has crossed a line as well," Eva said. "Her jaunts to the tearoom would have taken her past the chief inspector's cottage. Is there any way to know if she left the house the morning of your wedding?"

"Short of asking her or my uncle, perhaps not. The house was in quite an uproar that morning, as you'll remember. We were all busy, and the only people I can vouch for is you, Grams, and my sisters."

"The same for me, adding in Hetta and most of the servants belowstairs. I truly don't believe it was one of them. However, once again, rather than ruling out suspects, we are adding them. Or in this case, one. Giovanna Renshaw."

Phoebe placed a hand on Eva's forearm. "At least this proves that suspicion doesn't fall solely on the constable."

"Indeed not."

They began walking again and soon reached the tearoom. Unlike earlier, the tables swelled with patrons, their voices a dull roar marked by bursts of laughter. To Eva's ears, it didn't sound much different than the pub during its busiest hours, except an octave or two higher.

They stood by the door until they spotted Miss Young taking an order at a table in the far corner. A waitress, a village girl who came in during the busy hours, was serving a table of six. Eva and Lady Phoebe waited until Miss Young noticed them and hurried over.

"Goodness, Lady Phoebe, I didn't expect you back so soon," she said breathlessly. "We're having our afternoon rush, but if you can wait a quarter hour or so I'm sure I can fit you in . . ."

"No, Miss Young," Lady Phoebe said, raising her voice slightly to be heard, "we're not here for tea this time, but to ask you a quick question or two."

"Oh." Miss Young regarded them with obvious surprise. Blinking, she gazed over her shoulder at the crowded room, and then toward the street door. "Perhaps we should step outside."

Eva opened the door and let the other two precede her

out onto the pavement. They all blinked as their eyes adjusted to the sunlight. Miss Young, hatless, shielded her eyes with the flat of her hand. "Now then . . ."

Lady Phoebe looked right and left, and obviously satisfied there was no one close enough to overhear their conversation, she said, "Thinking back to the morning the chief inspector was murdered, do you remember anyone coming in for a Cornish pasty, one to be wrapped up and taken away?"

"What time in the morning? I don't open the shop until ten. Until then, I'm here preparing and taking deliveries."

"I see." Lady Phoebe considered this.

"What about the evening before?" Eva asked.

"I close at six and sometimes a customer will take something home with them. Usually scones or a tart or other pastry . . . something they'll eat in the morning." She thought a moment, then shook her head. "I don't remember anyone having me wrap up a Cornish pasty, although I do occasionally serve them. Sorry. I wish I could be more help." She leaned in closer and lowered her voice. "Has this to do with the murder?"

Lady Phoebe hesitated and flicked a glance at Eva. Opting not to answer the question, she said, "My aunt Giovanna never came in for a Cornish pasty?"

"Giovanna . . ." Miss Young's eyebrows rose in surprise, then gathered tightly. "No, never. I'm quite certain of it. Now, if you'll both please excuse me, I—"

She left off suddenly, her posture stiffening, her expression frozen in perplexity as she stared across the road.

"Miss Young, is something wrong?" As Eva asked, she followed the other woman's gaze to find Peregrin Blackwell standing on the pavement outside the post office. He was staring directly back at them. No, not staring, scowling. Foreboding uncurled in the pit of Eva's stomach.

"What can he want?" Phoebe repositioned herself with her back to Peregrin Blackwell, partly blocking Eva and Miss Young from his view.

"He's angry, my lady." Eva craned her neck to peek at him over Phoebe's shoulder. He was still there, still scowling. "With me, mostly, although he can't be too happy with you either, I'm afraid, since his wife is sheltering at your family's house."

"Insolent baggage," Miss Young declared without another glance in his direction. "There's your murderer, if you ask me."

"What makes you say that?" Eva asked.

Miss Young pursed her lips, then said, "Look at him. Well, I'm not about to let him unsettle me, although I make sure my doors are locked at night. I really must get back now, if you ladies will excuse me."

"Of course," Phoebe said. "Thank you, Miss Young."

"Do come for tea again soon," the woman said as she shouldered her way back inside.

Once they were alone, Eva glanced back across the street. The spot where Peregrin Blackwell had stood was now empty. Farther down the way, she saw the back of him disappear around a corner onto a side lane. She let go a breath of relief. She had feared he might make a scene.

Phoebe also sighed, but her thoughts had already moved on, as her next words proved. "Someone *had* to have ordered a Cornish pasty that morning, or the evening before. I knew mentioning Giovanna's name was a long shot, but I watched Miss Young closely for her reaction. What did you think?"

"I think it genuinely took her by surprise that you'd ask so bluntly."

"And what did you think of her accusation about Mr. Blackwell?"

"Equally blunt," Eva said, and tsked. "If she had any evidence, I'd take the accusation seriously. But she makes no secret of disliking him and his people simply because they're gypsies."

"Very true. We're no better off than we were before we went asking questions today, are we?" Phoebe began leading the way back to the Vauxhall.

"Aren't we? I feel this may rule out your uncle's wife as well as your uncle himself, provided the person who murdered Mr. Perkins also brought him the pasty that morning. And your aunt Cecily as well. If no one purchased a Cornish pasty from the pub or from the tearoom, we once again have to consider Mrs. McGowan, who not only makes pasties and supplies them to various establishments, but also has access to motor transportation. She easily could have made her way to Little Barlow that morning. And Miss Young's accusation aside, there are still the Blackwells, or anyone from the gypsy encampment, for that matter. Remember, they were selling pasties at the fete."

"Small ones, ones they were able to bake in makeshift ovens over their cookfires," Phoebe reminded her.

"But do we know how large Mr. Perkins's pasty was? There were only bits of it left on the plate that morning."

"Good point. Then it may well have been a small one." They reached the motorcar and climbed in. Phoebe patted the flats of her hands against the steering wheel. "I need to think about this. All of it."

"Perhaps sleep on it," Eva suggested. "Answers sometimes come when we're not trying too hard to find them."

Phoebe sat up in bed that night, her mind racing over the most miniscule details of the case. Suspects—she counted them off on her fingers: Peregrin Blackwell; Serena Blackwell; Uncle Greville; Giovanna; Mr. and Mrs. McGowan, and though she didn't wish to think it, she included Aunt Cecily on the list.

Each suspect but Aunt Cecily had a motive: money, revenge, or fear of incarceration. Each suspect, including Aunt Cecily, had opportunity. None of them could prove they weren't at the chief inspector's house that morning.

She hadn't realized she had been murmuring out loud until Owen rolled over, sat up, and peered at her in the darkness. "What?"

"You know what," she replied in a subdued tone, as if she didn't wish to alert any of those suspects as to what she was thinking. "How can you sleep so soundly when an innocent man's life is at stake?"

He chuckled softly and reached an arm around her. "Not so soundly that you didn't wake me with your muttering and your *aha*s."

"I never said *aha*. I'm not acting in a Sherlock Holmes play."

He pulled her against him. "Tell me everything you're thinking."

She did. The alibis or lack of them, the motives, the opportunities. "A lot may depend on who brought him his breakfast that morning. Any of them could have. Except perhaps Aunt Cecily."

"Earlier you said it was unlikely Greville or Giovanna could have done so."

"Well . . . they'd have to have gotten to the village first thing. But both Joe Murdoch and Miss Young deny anyone buying a Cornish pasty that morning."

"Could either be lying?"

The notion sent Phoebe more upright. "Honestly, I hadn't considered that one might be lying. Joe Murdoch I believe without reservation, but now that you mention it, Miss Young and Giovanna *have* become friends, and she *did* become defensive when I mentioned Giovanna's name. Perhaps she's trying to protect Giovanna. No one likes to believe their friend is capable of murder."

"No, no one does." He mulled that over while she waited in silence. "The pillow that silenced the gunshot was found near the gypsy camp."

"Yes. And we know they're capable of baking pasties at their camp."

"So they can't be ruled out."

"Blast it!" She grabbed the pillow from behind her, slammed it down, and thrust her fist into it. "This is impossible. If only there had been a witness, or some more significant clue."

Owen stroked her cheek with the backs of his fingers. "What about the child who saw Peregrin Blackwell walking down the village road?"

Phoebe shrugged in her frustration. "She didn't see him approach Mr. Perkins's house. And you checked with the farmer, who said Peregrin did report for work that morning."

"Yes, he did . . ." He trailed off, shaking his head. "We do appear to be at an impasse—"

"Which is unacceptable!" Phoebe punched the pillow again. Owen reached over to wrap his hand around her wrist. Gently he brought her still-fisted hand to his lips and kissed each knuckle. She felt her resolve melting and fought against it, keeping her fingers curled. "I owe it to Eva to solve this. Miles Brannock is *not* guilty."

"I know." Rather than being patronizing, he sounded thoroughly confident in his agreement. That helped. She blew out a breath. "I need a plan to bring this all to a head."

"Then make a plan. What first?"

Phoebe thought it over. "Something to bring everyone together, and to goad one of them into . . ."

"Confessing?"

"Don't be glib." She poked him in the ribs. "But if not actually confessing, giving something away. Something that will finally connect one of our suspects to the chief inspector's house that morning."

He nodded. "Let's sleep on it."

"That's what Eva said."

"So far you haven't taken her advice. You haven't slept a wink yet, have you?"

"I've had important things on my mind."

"Well, then." He took her pillow and set it behind her against the headboard. Then he pressed her down onto it, looming over her with a devilish expression. "Perhaps I can find a way to take your mind off such matters, for a while at least."

CHAPTER 17

Dawn was but a feeble suggestion on the other side of the curtains when Phoebe next sprang upright in bed, jolting Owen and prompting him to do the same.

"W-what? What is it?" he stammered, still half asleep. He rubbed his eyes.

"Aunt Cecily," she said, and compressed her lips as she once again reviewed the events of the past several days.

He shoved a shank of hair off his brow. "You think Aunt Cecily murdered the chief inspector?"

"No, silly. But she's the key to all of this. She always has been."

He shook his head, looking utterly bewildered. "I don't see how."

She grabbed his shoulders and kissed him, then swung her legs over the side of the bed. "You don't have to. I could be wrong. But I don't think so."

"Where are you going?"

"I have lots to do today. I need to get started." Despite his entreaties, Phoebe didn't wish to explain her theory. It seemed ludicrous, even to her, formulated on flimsy happenstance, and yet . . . "I have to get over to the house and wake Eva. I'll need her to do a couple of things for me today."

Owen was already out of bed and searching through his wardrobe closet. "I wish you'd share whatever brainstorm you've had."

"I will, as soon as I get back."

"I'll have breakfast ready."

"Good."

Eva was up and in the servants' hall when Phoebe arrived at the house. However unexpected her appearance might have been at that hour, Eva took it in stride. She merely drained the last of her tea and waited for Phoebe to explain her errand.

"I'm going up to the Rosalind sitting room," Phoebe said once she had finished telling Eva the basics of her plan and the reasons for it. She explained her theory about Aunt Cecily. But she left some of the details vague. "I'll find stationery and envelopes with the Wroxly crest in Grams's escritoire."

"And when you're done, I'll see that your missives are delivered." To her credit, Eva didn't ask questions or demand further details.

Would Phoebe's efforts today bring the desired results? She could end up blundering spectacularly and making things worse. Could be putting herself and others in danger. But clearing Constable Brannock's name, for Eva's sake—Eva, who had been a mother, sister, and friend to Phoebe these many years—seemed worth the risk.

A shade of doubt overcame the buoyancy that had brought her to Foxwood Hall. "Eva, do you think I'm right about this? Am I making a terrible mistake?"

"Your instincts don't usually play you false."

"Yes, but . . ." She couldn't finish the sentence, for to do so would be to admit she was grasping at straws and perhaps rushing into an error of judgment because of how badly she wanted to see Constable Brannock absolved. But to say that to Eva would be to dash her lady's maid's hopes, and Phoebe couldn't bear to do that. Perhaps she shouldn't have confided in Eva just yet. Perhaps she should have arranged everything first.

Too late now. Instead, she changed the subject. "How is Mrs. Blackwell?"

"Sad," Eva replied. "She keeps busy. So much so I believe Mrs. Sanders would hire her if she thought Serena would take the position. She would not, though. That much is clear. But when she thinks no one is looking, a deep veil of sorrow seems to come over her."

"She still feels trapped here, then."

Eva shook her head. "In all honesty, I believe she misses her husband."

"He didn't treat her very well, though, did he?"

"No, but . . ." Sadness seemed to come over Eva, as well. "I think there are things about the man she values. If only she could have the good without the bad."

"If only," Phoebe agreed. "But no one can change a man if he doesn't wish to be changed."

She stood up from the table and ascended the two flights of stairs to the Rosalind sitting room. No one else appeared to be up yet. Leastwise, no sounds emanated from the family's bedrooms. As for the guests in the wing on the other side of the gallery, Phoebe didn't know, but she doubted anyone would disturb her before she completed her task.

She wrote out six invitations to an affair that would take place the following day—short notice, she knew— and addressed each envelope. Three of them hadn't far to go to be delivered, as the recipients currently resided at Foxwood Hall: Greville and Giovanna Renshaw; Serena Blackwell; Lucille and Aunt Cecily. When she was finished, she handed all six missives to Eva, along with a seventh that wasn't quite an invitation. Then she returned to the hunting lodge.

Eva managed to deliver Phoebe's invitations to Greville and Giovanna Renshaw and Serena Blackwell without anyone else taking notice. It was part of the plan that only those individuals who had been invited would arrive at the hunting lodge tomorrow afternoon, and no one else. Phoebe had even staggered the arrival times. Eva was not to share the names of the other invitees. For all each knew, they, or they and their spouse or, in the case of Lady Cecily, she and the dowager Marchioness of Allerton, were the only people joining Lady Phoebe and her husband for tea tomorrow afternoon.

However, if one of Phoebe's siblings caught wind of an affair they were not invited to, their noses would undoubtedly be put out of joint and they might decide to show up unannounced. Phoebe said she wished to avoid that at all costs.

Eva wished she knew the rest of this plan, but Phoebe had chosen to keep her in the dark. She might have pressed, but something in the set of her lady's features had spoken of a single-minded determination, and that, coupled with the doubts Phoebe had expressed, had stilled Eva's tongue. And Eva had spoken true when she'd said Phoebe's instincts had rarely played her false. For now, she would trust that all would soon become clear.

Eva had enlisted Douglas to deliver three of the invitations. He would drive to the McGowans' farm to deliver theirs, and then stop by the gypsy encampment to deliver one more, to Peregrin Blackwell. First, though, he would drop off Eva in the village. She could only imagine the McGowans' reaction when the motorcar pulled up to the house and a footman in livery climbed out to hand them an envelope embossed with the gilded Wroxly crest. She almost wished she could go with him to see their eyes pop out of their heads, but she had a matter to attend to in Little Barlow. As for Peregrin Blackwell, she guessed he would merely scowl.

After waving Douglas on, she made her way to Pippa's Delights. The tearoom wasn't yet open, but through the window she spied Miss Young and her assistant bustling about the room, readying tables for brunch. Eva tapped on the glass. Miss Young saw her, smiled and waved, and crossed the room to unlock the door.

"Why, Miss Huntford, such a pleasure. We're not open yet, but—"

Eva held up a hand. "I realize that and I don't mean to take up your time. I only wish to give you this from Lady Phoebe." She handed her yet another of the sealed envelopes.

"I see. Is it anything urgent, do you know?" Miss Young pressed the missive to her breast.

"Not at all. It's a request for your services. You see, Lady Phoebe wishes to entertain tomorrow and doesn't have her own staff yet. She hopes this isn't too short notice. Everything is explained inside, and as you'll see, her soiree is scheduled during your afternoon lull here." Eva pointed at the envelope. "You can look it over at your leisure. I've some errands in the village, so I'll come back later and you can give me your reply to Lady Phoebe then."

"I'm honored. Thank you, Miss Huntford. I'll see what your mistress wishes and do my best to accommodate her."

That done, Eva hurried down the side lane to Miles's flat. She had no fear of awakening him at this early hour; she knew he'd be up. Poor man, having to spend long days cooped up, for the most part alone, except when she had time to visit.

"Something is happening," she said as soon as he'd opened the door. She strolled in past him, then turned and stepped into his open arms.

"Good morning to you, too. What are you on about?"

"Lady Phoebe has a plan. I don't know all the details, but I gather it has to do with an afternoon tea she's planning to hold tomorrow."

"Tea?"

"Yes, please."

He laughed. "I wasn't offering. I was questioning how Lady Phoebe hopes to resolve matters tomorrow *at* her tea."

"Oh. That's what I don't know yet. For some reason she has chosen not to inform me of all the details. I've no idea why not."

"That *is* odd. She trusts you with everything else."

"I don't think it's a matter of trust. Perhaps she doesn't want to raise my hopes too high, or yours. Or perhaps there's some amount of risk she doesn't wish me to share. I don't know. Now, about that tea."

Miles laughed again and led the way to the kitchen area. He took down the tin of tea while Eva filled the kettle and set it on the hob. They made toast in the oven and spread it with blackberry preserves. For a short while, Eva pretended nothing was wrong. It felt wonderful.

That feeling persisted the next day when she walked over to the hunting lodge to help Phoebe prepare. Together they brought out the brand-new, never-before-used Crown Lily china that had been a wedding gift from her grandmother, each gold-rimmed, monogrammed plate, bowl, cup, and saucer unmarred as yet by the ravages of forks and knives. The pure ivory porcelain glowed beneath the gentle caress of the dining-room chandelier. Next came the Baccarat crystal water goblets. Then the sterling silver flatware.

"You're not pulling any punches today, are you?" Eva remarked.

Phoebe surveyed the table, straightening a fork here, moving a teacup there. "Everything must be perfect."

"Why won't you tell me what's up your sleeve?"

"What I'm doing today, Eva, *is* like a slight of hand. I want everyone to be taken wholly by surprise."

"So you can gauge their honest reactions to whatever you've got planned."

"That's right."

"Why keep me in the dark?"

"Because I could end up being wretchedly wrong. There's been a precious lack of evidence in this case, so I've taken to considering that lack of evidence very carefully."

"Considering the lack of evidence," Eva repeated slowly. "Considering what, then? Nothing? Empty air?"

"Believe me, Eva, there is a world of detail floating in that empty air."

"My lady, you speak in riddles." Eva leaned over the table and fussed with the flower arrangement. "What if they don't all come?"

"They'll come."

Eva straightened to regard her. "You sound awfully confident."

"I am." Phoebe smiled. "In the invitations, I told each of them that I was prepared to reveal the identity of Mr. Perkins's killer, as well as apologize for having ever implied that they were guilty. So yes, they'll come. All of them."

"Indeed." Eva shook her head and gave a laugh. "Who could possibly resist that?"

Pippa Young arrived at the hunting lodge at three o'clock sharp the next afternoon. "Our rush is over and I've left my assistant to handle the stragglers," she assured Phoebe as she carried the last of the carboard boxes of savory and sweet treats into the kitchen. "And I'll be back there in plenty of time to prepare for high tea this evening."

"Very good," Phoebe said, "because I surely didn't want to cause you any hardship with your regular customers."

"Not at all. I was up before the roosters this morning getting everything prepared, but I'm happy to do it."

"I'm so glad to hear that, and I hope this is the first of many such occasions. Now then, the oven is already pre-heated for anything you need to warm up. The larder is through there"—she pointed—"and the icebox, as you can see, is in the corner. Please acquaint yourself with the kitchen and make use of anything you need."

"The guests should be arriving within the hour, I be-lieve?"

"That's right. But we don't stand on ceremony here. Un-like my grandparents," she said with a laugh, "we have no strict schedules or rules. I want today to be enjoyable and relaxing for everyone. Even you, Miss Young."

"A modern hostess," Miss Young commented heartily.

Lady Cecily and Lucille were the first guests to arrive some twenty minutes later. Though they had been driven over by motorcar, Lady Cecily showed signs of fatigue the moment she stepped into the foyer.

"She tires so easily these days," Lucille said with an air of both apology and regret. "Might we go somewhere for a lie-down before tea? I'll of course stay with her."

"Assuredly. Aunt Cecily, would you like that? A brief rest before we enjoy ourselves?"

"You are a dear, yes," the elderly lady replied with a look of relief. "It was quite a journey to get here, as I'm sure you realize."

It was barely more than a mile, but Phoebe said, "Yes, Aunt Cecily. Quite."

"Oh, but first a kiss from this handsome husband of yours."

"Did you think I'd let you get away without one?" Owen, who had been standing by, eagerly but carefully caught Aunt Cecily up in an embrace and kissed her cheek. She blushed and tittered, pressing her palm to the spot as if to preserve something precious.

While Phoebe didn't wish ill health on poor Aunt Cecily, she had already planned for this possibility, and in fact, much of her plan depended upon it. "Eva?" She glanced over her shoulder to find her lady's maid waiting to escort their guests upstairs to a guestroom. They traded significant looks. "We'll let you know when tea is ready," she said in parting as the women ascended the stairs.

About a quarter hour later, Uncle Greville and Giovanna came bustling in with shouted greetings, laughter, and an armful of hothouse flowers. Phoebe and Owen accepted the flowers, joined in the laughter, and led their guests into the salon.

Uncle Greville wasted no time in niceties. "What have you got to wet my whistle?"

"Champagne," Owen said, eliciting a sideways glance from the other man, along with a *tsk*.

"I'm afraid you'll have to do better than that, old man."

Owen relented with a grin. "How about a whiskey?"

"Now you're talking sense."

"I'll have champagne," Giovanna said to Phoebe. An ice bucket sat on the sofa table, along with two flutes. Phoebe poured and handed one to Giovanna. The woman sipped, scrunching her nose as the bubbles tickled it. "I must say, we were surprised to be invited today, considering no one else in the house was, or even knows about this."

"Yes, well . . ." Phoebe took a sip of champagne. "Owen and I were hoping to have a more intimate occasion with you. We'll have everyone here another time soon."

"Now see here, my girl." Uncle Greville held his whiskey tumbler on his knee as he leaned forward. "When you say, 'intimate occasion,' what exactly does that mean? In your invitation you said you were going to tell us who murdered the chief inspector. You're not going to accuse one of us, are you?"

"Relax, Grev." Owen poured another finger of whiskey into Uncle Greville's glass. "This is more of a social occasion."

After a few minutes, Phoebe discreetly consulted her wristwatch. "If you'll excuse me, I need to check on things in the kitchen."

"Do you need help?" Giovanna began to stand, but Phoebe waved her back down.

"Not at all. I'm just going to see that the caterer is coming along all right."

Giovanna seemed only too happy to remain where she was. Thank heavens, Phoebe thought. By the time she reached the kitchen, another guest had arrived. The invitation to Serena Blackwell hadn't been completely honest, however. Instead of an invitation to tea, Serena had been invited to earn some extra money by helping out. Now Phoebe had to smooth things over with Pippa Young before the tearoom owner tossed the Romany woman out on her ear.

Which was in the process of happening. "You're not needed here," Phoebe heard Pippa Young state in a curt tone. "I've got everything under control. I can't imagine why Lady Phoebe asked you to help."

"She did, and I won't be leaving unless she tells me to."

"Please do stay, Mrs. Blackwell," Phoebe said as she rounded the corner from the short hallway leading into the kitchen. "Miss Young, I asked Mrs. Blackwell here today. She's to help serve. She's been working at Foxwood Hall and has shown herself to be exemplary in serving at table."

That was mostly a lie. While Serena Blackwell had been working diligently at whatever task Mrs. Sanders set her, she had not been required to serve in either the family dining room or the servants' hall. True, she had helped clear the table in the servants' hall after meals and had put away the clean tableware—and she had done so without a mishap. That qualified her, didn't it?

Phoebe had needed some excuse to lure Mrs. Blackwell here today—a believable excuse, and inviting her to tea would have been met with suspicion, not to mention most likely reducing the woman to a bundle of nerves.

"I thought Miss Huntford would be helping me serve," Miss Young said.

"Yes, but it seemed such a task for only the two of you."

After a hesitation, Pippa Young said, "Lady Phoebe, might we have a word?" She gestured to the hallway, and, with a nod, Phoebe followed her out. Miss Young sighed before getting to the point. "Are you quite certain you want this creature in your house? She's already been arrested for theft. And you know how these people are. I'm only thinking of your well-being."

"Miss Young, I appreciate your concern and it's well noted. But I am satisfied that Mrs. Blackwell did not steal the items found in her bag that day, that someone who wishes her and her people gone slipped those things in to make trouble. Furthermore, Miss Huntford and the housekeeper at Foxwood Hall both vouch for Mrs. Blackwell's trustworthiness. She could use the employment for reasons I shall not go into, but trust me when I say that she is eager to make her own way in the world."

This speech seemed to take Miss Young aback, for as Phoebe finished the other woman blinked and remained silent for several seconds. Then she merely said, "Yes, Lady Phoebe. I . . . er . . . shall make an effort to get on with her."

"I'd appreciate it if you would. Thank you." Phoebe retraced her steps to the salon, but a knock sent her detour-

ing to the front door instead. She opened the door upon
Ian and Brenda McGowan. They appeared to be wearing
their best, probably the clothes they wore to church each
week, and Mrs. McGowan sported a darling hat of glossy
pale blue straw with a rolled brim and a spray of fabric
flowers on one side. "Thank you for coming. Please do
come in." Phoebe stepped aside to allow them to enter.

The pair hesitated, trading glances, before stepping over
the threshold. Mrs. McGowan said, "This seems terribly
irregular, Lady Phoebe. My husband and I didn't know if
we perhaps should go around back."

"Good heavens, no." Phoebe closed the door behind
them and turned to them with a smile. "I asked you here
as my guests."

"As I said, it seems terribly irregular," Mrs. McGowan
persisted. "After all, you're a . . . well, you know, and
we're merely farmers, and our sort and yours . . ."

"As I often tell people, my husband and I don't stand on
the same ceremony as the rest of our family. Please, make
yourselves at home. Shall we go into the salon?"

She held out an arm to point the way, but when neither
of the McGowans made a move, she went first and hoped
they would follow. Uncle Greville was in the middle of re-
lating a story when he glanced over, spotted the newly arrived couple, and fell silent. His forehead became a mass
of ridges, and Phoebe cringed inwardly as she followed the
path of his gaze up and down both Mr. and Mrs. McGowan.
Giovanna did the same, although with a puzzled half smile
on her lips.

"Uncle Greville, Giovanna, this is Ian and Brenda
McGowan. They'll be joining us for tea. Mr. and Mrs.
McGowan, my uncle, Greville Renshaw, and his wife, Giovanna Renshaw." Phoebe added nothing more by way of
explanation. The silence became deafening. Then Owen
came to his feet.

"Good to see you both again," he said. "What may I get you? We have champagne, but if you'd like something with a bit more bite . . ."

"We were told we'd been invited to tea." Mr. McGowan's hands rose to his hips in a challenging stance, but he just as quickly dropped them to his sides.

"And so you have been," Owen assured them. "But there's nothing wrong with a small nip, is there?"

"My husband and I never imbibe, sir." Mrs. McGowan pinched her lips together.

"Please, have a seat," Phoebe hastened to say. "Tea will be served shortly."

All but one of the invited guests had arrived. Phoebe suspected Eva was already upstairs helping Lucille rouse Aunt Cecily and prepare her to come downstairs. Then she would head into the kitchen and signal Miss Young to begin serving.

Uncle Greville, apparently over his initial shock at the McGowans' appearance, leaned comfortably back in his chair and swirled the contents of his glass. "So much for an intimate occasion," he murmured, but loud enough for all to hear.

His wife shot him a glare before turning to Brenda McGowan. "You and your husband farm? What do you grow, or do you raise sheep?"

Phoebe raised her eyebrows in pleasant surprise. Perhaps her uncle's wife wasn't as self-absorbed as Phoebe had come to believe.

"Wheat and rapeseed," Mrs. McGowan replied. Beside her, her husband sat nervously, his hat dangling from between his hands.

"In Italy, my family grew olives. But between war and politics, we no longer own the land."

"I'm terribly sorry to hear that, ma'am." Mrs. McGowan looked sincere, if puzzled. Phoebe had no idea exactly what Giovanna meant by her cryptic statement and suspected there was no easy explanation for the loss of her family's olive groves.

Before anyone could prompt Giovanna to elaborate, Eva appeared in the doorway. "Tea is ready to be served, my lady."

"Ah, very good. Everyone, shall we adjourn to the dining room?" Phoebe stood, prompting the others to do the same.

As they began filing into the other room, Giovanna held back until she walked beside Phoebe. "Just what are you playing at, my dear?"

Phoebe tilted her chin. "I don't know what you mean."

"Yes, you do." Giovanna smiled shrewdly. "There is nothing ordinary about this little tea you planned or about the company you invited."

She didn't wait for a reply, for she sped her steps to catch up with her husband. Phoebe checked her watch again. A knot of tension grew in her stomach. She wanted this group seated before the last guest arrived, which should be any moment, along with someone else she and Owen had conferred with the day before. This latter person, however, would not be shown to the table. In the next half hour or so, the truth of who murdered Chief Inspector Perkins would be revealed.

Or so Phoebe hoped.

CHAPTER 18

Eva tapped on the door of the guestroom and went inside. She was relieved to see the dowager marchioness and Lady Cecily standing before the dressing table mirror, preparing to join the other guests downstairs.

"Miss Huntford, I believe I heard voices from below," Lady Lucille said as she straightened the silk jacket over her aunt's frock. She patted Lady Cecily's coif and declared her as pretty as a picture, which made the older woman grin and blush. "Are there other guests?"

"There are, my lady."

Lady Lucille sucked in her cheeks. "But we thought it was to be only the two of us."

"The . . . er . . . plans changed, my lady. I hope it's not any reason for concern."

"Only that my aunt tires easily, and a house full of people is sure to be taxing for her."

Eva didn't point out that Foxwood Hall presently contained a house full of people. Then again, perhaps being around all those people had taken its toll on the elderly woman, which might explain such reckless acts as taking pistols outside and shooting them into the air. "Would you like me to ask Lady Phoebe to come up, ma'am?"

"No, that won't be necessary. I suppose it will be all right."

"What are you going on about, Lucy?" Lady Cecily continued primping and posing in front of the mirror. "Isn't the party starting yet? How lovely of dear Phoebe to invite us to tea. Now, there's a young lady with manners."

Eva forewent rolling her eyes at yet another of Lady Cecily's implied admonishments about people not inviting her to tea. About to suggest they make their way downstairs, Eva went utterly still. Her pulse raced along with the sudden turn her thoughts had taken. A vein in her temple thrashed with anticipation. She realized she was holding her breath . . .

"Miss Huntford, are you quite all right?"

Eva blinked, snapping out of the trance that had taken abrupt hold of her. "Quite, my lady. Shall I escort you down now?"

"No need. I'm sure you're wanted below to help serve. Aunt Cecily and I can make our own way down."

"Very good, ma'am." Eva left them to finish their preparations.

Taking the back stairs, she reached the kitchen in time to hear Miss Young scolding Serena Blackwell about how she had mixed up the varieties of finger sandwiches, rather than separating them according to their ingredients.

"Deviled ham, all on one platter. Salmon and caper, on another. It's not that difficult, Mrs. Blackwell. They must be redone. Oh, here, I'll do it. If you want something done right . . ." Miss Young left off, muttering. Then she shot Serena a look and pointed to the two steaming teakettles on the stove. "You can fill the teapots and brew the Darjeeling. And be quick about it. They'll be in the dining room at any moment."

"They're already there," Eva informed them as she came into the room. She had been pressed against the stairwell wall, eavesdropping. Now she took the bowls of candied fruit out of the icebox, along with the clotted cream and lemon curd Miss Young had brought with her from the village. "These look divine," she said, genuinely admiring the swirls in the curd and the peaks in the cream.

"Quickly, bring them to the dining room!" Miss Young made shooing motions at Eva with both hands. "And you too, Mrs. Blackwell. Bring in those teapots and start pouring. Goodness, why wasn't I warned sooner?"

Because Lady Phoebe wants everyone off-balance. Outwardly Eva only shrugged, placed the curd, cream, and fruit on a tray, and carried them through the pantry and into the dining room. The McGowans, the Renshaws, and Phoebe and Lord Owen were already seated. Greville and Giovanna Renshaw each held an alcoholic beverage and appeared relaxed, if slightly bemused. The McGowans, on the other hand, sat stiffly in their chairs as if ready to spring up and bolt. Eva couldn't help feeling sorry for them. Even she had to acknowledge that aspects of Lady Phoebe's plan seemed downright devious. Then again, if either or both were responsible for the chief inspector's death . . .

She went back into the kitchen to help carry in the now corrected platters of finger sandwiches, each tray accompanied by a pair of serving tongs. Miss Young led the way. She paused and questioned Lady Phoebe with a glance as to whether she would be serving the sandwiches or merely leaving each platter on the table.

"We'll help ourselves, thank you, Miss Young."

Eva noticed the quick look that passed between Giovanna Renshaw and Miss Young. Pippa's Delights had become a haven for the former woman, and the two were friendly. But here, among the others, neither openly acknowledged the other.

Serena brought in the teapots and set one at either end of the table. The deep aroma of Darjeeling filled the room. When she and Miss Young returned to the kitchen, Eva followed, but only as far as the pantry. There she remained, watching the goings-on in the dining room while remaining out of sight. From the front hall came Lady Lucille's and Lady Cecily's voices. Greville Renshaw turned to his niece with an accusing look.

"*More* guests?"

When the two ladies came through the doorway, the men around the table came to their feet. Ian McGowan was the last to stand, and he and his wife appeared as though panic had begun to set in. Phoebe gestured the latest arrivals to the two empty places on one side of the table, and Lord Owen came around and held their chairs for them.

"Everyone, please, help yourselves," Lady Phoebe said gleefully. "We're going to be very casual here today. Don't be shy."

Giovanna Renshaw reached for the tongs on the platter nearest her. "No one has ever accused me of being shy."

Her husband, however, merely drained the contents of his glass and stared pointedly at Lord Owen, who in turn ignored him. Then Uncle Greville apparently noticed something. "Why is there still an empty place at the table?"

"My goodness, I almost forgot." Lady Phoebe glanced around at her guests with the expression of a solicitous hostess. "Would anyone like champagne? Mr. and Mrs. McGowan, you've already said you don't indulge in spirits, but perhaps some lemonade?" She pointed to a pitcher near the center of the table. "Lucille, Cecily, would you like some champagne? Giovanna, more?"

Without waiting to be asked, Lord Owen filled the flutes at each place setting, except for the McGowans'.

"Bubbly!" Aunt Cecily raised her glass and took a dainty sip. "How lovely. I haven't had any in ever so long."

"You drank champagne at Phoebe and Owen's wedding, Aunt," her niece reminded her, and then cautioned, "Only a little, now."

A knock at the front door sounded, and Eva walked back into the dining room. "I'll get that," she said, and kept going.

"What the devil is going on here?" she heard Greville Renshaw murmur behind her.

"Ian," Mrs. McGowan murmured as well, "we don't belong here."

"No, and I think it's time we were going." As Eva reentered the dining room, Ian McGowan stood and offered his hand to his wife to help her up. "We thank you for the invitation, but—" His brow furrowed tightly, and his wife stared at Eva. Or, rather, the individual behind her.

At the same time, Serena Blackwell stepped out from the pantry carrying a covered platter of scones, taken fresh from the oven. When she saw who followed Eva, the platter nearly fell from her hands. As it was, it tipped to one side and the cover slid partway off, releasing curls of savory steam.

"Perry, what do you think you're doing here?" Mrs. Blackwell set the scones down on the corner of the table with a bang that dislodged the cover the rest of the way. It fell to the rug with a dull clunk. She ignored it. "Lady Phoebe, I'm sorry about this. He has no right showing up here like this. Perry, you mustn't be here."

"But . . ." Peregrin Blackwell's nervous gaze darted from his wife to Lady Phoebe to Eva and back. "I was invited. I'm a guest."

*   *   *

"The day you'd ever be a guest of these people is the day I'm invited to dine with the king and queen." His wife snapped her hands to her hips, her lips compressing to a thin, angry slash.

"I'm telling you I was." He reached into his trouser pocket and pulled out a creased, half-crumpled rectangle of thick paper bearing the Wroxly crest. He waved it back and forth. "I'm no liar."

"I invited Mr. Blackwell." Phoebe came to her feet. She smiled encouragingly, taking in Peregrin Blackwell's attempt to dress for a house party in an ill-fitting cutaway coat and pinstriped trousers that needed hemming. At least he had tried, and Phoebe knew very well why he had.

Serena Blackwell rounded on Phoebe. "Have you lost your wits?"

"Don't you dare speak to my niece that way," Uncle Greville admonished in a half-slurring voice. Mrs. Blackwell didn't spare him a glance. She'd gone back to staring her husband down.

Meanwhile the McGowans had sunk back onto their chairs, while Giovanna looked downright gleeful. Aunt Cecily began muttering something under her breath. Phoebe tried to make out the words, but the woman spoke too softly. Much to Phoebe's chagrin, Lucille stared daggers at her for putting the elderly woman in a potentially confusing and taxing situation.

"Please, Mr. Blackwell, sit." She gestured toward the one unclaimed chair at the table. He hesitated a long moment, as if deciding whether to comply or cut his losses and run. Phoebe held her breath until the former won out and he sidled to the indicated place at the table. She took her seat as well. "Now then, everyone, let's continue. Mr. Blackwell, we're helping ourselves. Mrs. McGowan, would you please pass that platter of tea sandwiches to our newly arrived guest?"

The woman did so with a look of bafflement.

"Now then, I realize you're all wondering why I've invited you here."

"That's an understatement," Uncle Greville griped.

Phoebe stole a glance at Owen. He nodded his encouragement.

"You did mention something about an apology in your invitation," Brenda McGowan said with a self-righteous look that told Phoebe she was still interested in hearing that apology.

"You're quite right," she admitted, "I did. The apology is for suspecting each and every one of you, at one time or another, of having murdered Chief Inspector Perkins."

If she had expected gasps or cries of surprise, she would have been mistaken. They merely sat stoically, waiting. She cleared her throat, but before she could speak, Aunt Cecily caught her eye.

"Even me, my dear?"

Phoebe hadn't expected Aunt Cecily to follow or understand what she had just said. That the woman had took her aback for several seconds. Then, reluctantly, she confessed, "Yes, Aunt Cecily, I'm sorry to say, even you."

"Of all the nonsense." Her niece tossed her napkin to the table. Phoebe expected her to leap to her feet, urge Aunt Cecily to hers, and stomp off. But she remained seated.

"Well, how exciting!" Aunt Cecily exclaimed in a bubbling voice. She pressed her hands to her bosom and simpered with delight. "To be a murder suspect. Who'd ever have thought?"

Lucille reached over and grasped her shoulder. "That's enough now, Aunt. Say no more."

"What, are you afraid the old . . . er . . ." Uncle Greville appeared to struggle to find the right word. Phoebe could only imagine what he had intended to call her. He finally said, "Afraid the old soul will incriminate herself?"

"You hush your mouth, Greville Renshaw," Lucille shot back.

"The point is," Phoebe said loudly to recapture their attention, "each of you has fallen suspect, except you, Lucille. You're merely here to be with Aunt Cecily. But I do sincerely apologize to most of the rest of you."

"What do you mean, most?" Mr. McGowan grabbed his wife's hand, once again making Phoebe think he was preparing to flee. "Are you saying the killer is among us?"

"I'm saying potentially, yes, there is one person in this house today who had motive, opportunity, and means. And that last, you see, is key. The way I see it, most of you had a motive for wishing ill on Isaac Perkins. And many of you cannot account for your whereabouts at the time of the murder. There are no witnesses to corroborate your claims. But not all of you had the means to carry out the crime."

"But aren't opportunity and means the same thing?" Giovanna asked in an almost academic way, as if they were colleagues discussing a hypothetical scenario.

"No, not in this case." Phoebe stood and began slowly walking around the table. "Mr. McGowan, you certainly had a motive for wanting revenge against the chief inspector. No, please don't interrupt. Because of him, you spent eight years of your life in prison. For that matter, your wife could be said to have had the same motive. Isaac Perkins destroyed some of the best years of your life, and . . ." She swallowed and spoke her next words in a gentle voice. "Had it not been for Mr. Perkins intercepting Mr. McGowan that night, your son might be alive today."

Tears trickled down Mrs. McGowan's cheeks and she raised her hands to her face to hide them. Angrily, her husband demanded, "Must you twist the knife?"

"I'm sorry, truly I am, but I am getting to an important point." Phoebe waited while Brenda McGowan wiped her tears away. "While you had motive and perhaps opportunity, neither of you had means. The chief inspector was found shot in his favorite chair in his parlor, his breakfast beside him. There were no signs of a struggle. Had either of you gone to his home that morning, I sincerely doubt he would have let you in voluntarily. You certainly wouldn't have made it as far as his parlor. At least not without a struggle."

She walked the length of the table and stopped beside Uncle Greville's chair. "Uncle, the chief inspector had been blackmailing you—surely a motive to commit murder."

"Now see here, Phoebe." He came to his feet. "The old blighter may have deserved it, but I did no such thing."

"I don't believe you did, either." Phoebe patted his shoulder until he lowered himself to his seat. "Because, you see, I believe whoever murdered Mr. Perkins brought him that breakfast, and that's something I cannot see you doing. Why would you even think of it? No, had you wished to murder the man, you'd have been much more straightforward about it."

"Well . . . yes, that's quite true." He stroked the side of his face, nodding. "Why bring breakfast to a man one intended to kill?"

"Exactly," Phoebe said.

Giovanna frowned and fingered the pearls hanging around her neck. "If it wasn't the McGowans and it wasn't Greville, then it must be that man." Her finger shot out, aimed at Peregrin Blackwell.

The McGowans turned their heads to gawk at the man. Mr. McGowan held up a fist. "If he makes one move, I'll pummel him."

"There'll be no pummeling at this table," Owen warned.

"Phoebe, *is* it this man here?" Lucille, too, pointed at

Peregrin Blackwell, who only stared back at her with his black eyes and his dark scowl. "Or . . . wait a moment . . . what about her? Giovanna? You just said the chief inspector was blackmailing Greville. Maybe his *wife* murdered him." Lucille narrowed her eyes at the Italian woman. "You're a greedy thing, aren't you? You don't even bother to hide it."

"Me? We all know your aunt likes to play with guns, Lady Lucille." Giovanna scoffed. "It was probably she who murdered the man."

"Don't try to distract us by talking nonsense," Lucille countered. "Phoebe, what about Giovanna?"

"Yes, Giovanna, too, had a motive, assuming she knew about Mr. Perkins's latest attempt to blackmail her husband." Phoebe watched for a reaction and was rewarded by a rare darkening of the woman's complexion. With a nod, she went on, directly addressing her uncle's wife, "You probably would have gained entry to the chief inspector's cottage and might even have made it as far as his parlor. However, I very much doubt you would have brought him a Cornish pasty. You'd have left too obvious a trail if you had, having to either ask Mrs. Ellison to bake one or buy one in the village. I think you're too clever to have made such a mistake."

"*Grazie.*" Giovanna frowned. "I think."

"I believe we need more tea. Excuse me." Phoebe went into the pantry toward the kitchen.

Uncle Greville called out, "Where the devil are you going?"

"Phoebe, come back here," Lucille joined in. "Finish what you started."

Phoebe ignored them and poked her head into the kitchen. "Miss Young, we could use more tea, if you would."

"Where is that Mrs. Blackwell?" Miss Young was obviously fuming. "I sent her out there ages ago with orders to come right back. Lazy girl, she's probably disappeared, no doubt."

"No, she's in the dining room. There was a spill and she's cleaning it up. I'd appreciate it if you'd bring out the tea."

"Oh, I see. Yes, right away. I've kept plenty of water hot."

Phoebe returned to the dining room. Within minutes Miss Young entered with two fresh pots of tea. She set them on the table, then pulled back with a start.

Peregrin Blackwell surged to his feet, his finger pointing. "You!"

At the same time, Aunt Cecily spotted Miss Young and huffed, loud enough for all to hear.

CHAPTER 19

Even Lady Phoebe hadn't anticipated this development. Eva was certain of that simply by the look of utter surprise on her face.

Not to mention the satisfaction.

But Eva herself still didn't understand what had just happened, or why. She longed to demand what link existed between Peregrin Blackwell and Pippa Young. Surely, his outburst could not have been the result of his wife's arrest or Miss Young's contempt for his people.

Could it?

Miss Young inched backward the way she had come, but without looking behind her she missed the pantry doorway and hit the wall beside it. Eva didn't think the woman noticed Lord Owen suddenly rising and going to stand in that very same doorway, blocking any escape she might wish to make. Serena, too, had backed away from the table, but not nearly as far as the wall. She hovered with a shocked look in her eyes, her mouth agape.

Phoebe's gaze lingered for a moment on Lady Cecily before angling back toward Peregrin Blackwell. "Why did you just say that?" she asked the man.

He came around the table to stand some ten feet away from Pippa Young, facing her as if they were about to fight a duel. "She tried to have me arrested when I was a boy."

"For what?" Phoebe gripped the back of the chair closest to her, occupied by her uncle.

"Accessory to murder," the young man snapped. "As if I had anything to do with her sister's death."

"What?" This utterance came from everyone in the room. Serena's knees suddenly appeared in danger of buckling. Eva went to her and wrapped a supporting arm around her.

Peregrin took a menacing step toward Miss Young, prompting her to press herself tighter against the wall. "I was *fourteen*. My family and I were camping in the area, and I got some work on her sister's farm in Pennington on the outskirts of Gloucester. The husband was a brute of a man. Kicked me a time or two and slapped me around, once hard, on the face. All because I hadn't mucked out his stable to his liking, or splashed a bit of water on the horses' hay, or simply looked at him the wrong way." He slapped a fist into his open palm.

"What's that got to do with Miss Young?" Lord Owen asked the question calmly enough, but Eva heard the undertone of tension in his voice. The readiness to spring to action.

"It's got *nothing* to do with me," Miss Young cried out, then pressed a hand to her mouth.

Mr. Blackwell ignored her. "I wasn't the only one the swine liked to slap around. Thank God they hadn't had children yet."

An uneasy silence gripped the room. Eva whispered, "You mean he beat his wife, don't you? Miss Young's sister."

"Regularly." Mr. Blackwell turned his head as if to spit, but apparently thought better of it. "I'd hear his shouts, her cries. Once I went running to the house thinking there'd been an accident, and he turned on me. Grabbed me by the shoulders and hurled me out the kitchen door so hard I landed in a heap on the ground, like a ragdoll."

"Why did you stay working there?" Giovanna procured a cigarette case from somewhere—a pocket in her dress, perhaps. As if sitting at an outdoor café, she snapped it open and plucked one out. "Why did you not go elsewhere?"

"Work wasn't easy to find and we needed the money. Anyway, do you think that was the first time I'd been backhanded by an employer? It was par for the course. What *wasn't* usual was seeing the . . . the . . ." He obviously groped for a word suitable for mixed company, glanced at the women at the table, and settled on, "Seeing a man treat his wife the same way he treated me."

"Where does Miss Young fit into this story?" Phoebe turned to that very woman, still cowering against the wall like a felon before a firing squad. "Or would you care to enlighten us?"

Pippa Young shook her head vigorously. "He's lying. He's a baldfaced liar."

"Is he lying about your sister's treatment at her husband's hands?" Feeling Serena tremble as she asked the question, Eva tightened her arm around her waist.

"No . . . n-not about that. Fran was always bruised. He was a beast—he should have been the one to die. I'd tried telling the constable . . ." With a gasp, Miss Young whisked both hands to her mouth to stop her words.

She had said too much. More than she had intended, certainly. A realization crept over Eva. She glanced over at Phoebe through the cloud of smoke from Giovanna's cigarette. That initial look of satisfaction had become so much more, signaling that this was all going according to plan. Eva held her breath, waiting for the rest to unfold.

"Your sister died," Phoebe said. "No, was murdered. How?"

"He pushed her down the stairs," Miss Young said flatly. "She broke her neck."

Phoebe's expression lost its satisfied look. "And then what happened?"

"He tried to hide the body." Her chin jerked in Peregrin Blackwell's direction. "With *his* help."

"Never," he shot back. "I wasn't even there when it happened. But that didn't stop you from insisting I was part of it. Tried to have me charged with murder."

"You were just as responsible," Miss Young cried. "You should have helped her."

"I was just a lad, and I wasn't there when she died."

"Excuses."

Peregrin took a step forward and stopped. "The constable didn't agree with you, or I might not be here right now."

"You *shouldn't* be here," Miss Young charged in a hissing voice. "You or that wife of yours. Beggars, both of you. You and all your people."

Peregrin started forward again, but Serena pulled away from Eva and caught her husband by the arm. "No, Perry. Leave it. It doesn't matter what she says."

"Will someone kindly explain what this has got to do with today?" Greville Renshaw reached with two fingers for the cigarette in his wife's hand. He took a long drag and handed it back. Accompanied by a long trail of smoke, he said, "Seems to me this is all neither here nor there and has nothing to do with the rest of us."

"Yes, it does," Eva said so quietly no one seemed to hear her. The pieces were falling into place. Then, as a sudden realization came over her, she added, louder, "When Lady Phoebe and I stood outside the tearoom with Miss Young, I thought you were glaring at me, Mr. Blackwell. Because I'd encouraged and then helped your wife to leave you. All that anger—I believed I was its target. But I wasn't, was I?"

Their arms around each other now, he and Serena turned to face her. "No, not you. Serena's leaving me is my own fault." He broke off, his face filled with remorse. Serena whispered her encouragement, and he continued. "Seeing *her* brought it all back, Serena, and I realize what an arse I've been, hardly better than that scoundrel years ago." He slipped his arm free of his wife and turned back to Miss Young. "It's been about a decade since I laid eyes on your face. When I saw you there, across the street . . . it took me a minute to place you, but that first sight of you made me feel like I was stepping into a nightmare. Then I remembered. You've aged, but I can still see the woman you were. The bitter shrew. Your sister wasn't like you. She was kind. When her husband wasn't nearby, she'd bring me things to eat. She didn't hate me because of who my people were."

"That's all well and good," Ian McGowan said. "But we've yet to learn what this has to do with why we're here today."

"One of the reasons we suspected you and your wife," Eva explained, "besides your possible motive, is that she bakes savory pies for some of the tearooms and inns hereabout. The inspector had a Cornish pasty for his breakfast that morning, and his housekeeper hadn't baked it for him."

Mrs. McGowan sat up straighter. "But how would the chief inspector have gotten ahold of one of *my* pasties? I surely didn't bring it to him." A little gasp escaped her. "He could have gotten it from *you*."

Brenda McGowan's attention homed in on Pippa Young. The woman shrank further against the wall. "So what if he bought a pasty from me and had it for his breakfast?"

"You told us no one had bought a Cornish pasty from the tearoom to take home with them," Eva reminded her.

"I simply forgot. Yes, the chief inspector did come in. It was the evening before he died. What are you saying, then, that I poisoned him?"

"No." Phoebe went to stand in front of the woman. "We are saying you visited him that morning. Perhaps you'd done so before, gaining his trust over time. That morning, an opportunity arose. His gun must have lain on the table beside him, waiting to be brought to work. While he ate the delectable breakfast you brought him, you saw the gun, snatched it up, and shot him at point-blank range. You even had the presence of mind to muffle the report with a pillow. Which means this was surely no crime of passion, but rather one planned and awaiting an opportune moment."

"Lady Phoebe, your imagination has run away with you." Pippa Young released a brittle laugh. "Why on earth would I do something so beastly?"

Eva went to stand beside Phoebe. "My guess is that Isaac Perkins was the very same constable who refused to listen to you when you tried to get help for your sister. It'll be easy to verify, but you can save us the time, Pippa. Is this the truth? Did Mr. Perkins meet your entreaties with a deaf ear? A refusal to interfere between a husband and wife?"

"That's absurd." The woman had gone pale, the only color in her face the icy blue of her eyes. "You've all come unhinged. You can't prove a word of this."

"Then you admit there *is* something to prove here?" Lord Owen, unseen by Miss Young, moved out of the doorway and stood close enough to take hold of her arm.

She lashed out, slapping at his hand and lurching away, then charged forward and shoved both Eva and Phoebe out of her path. They both went down. With nary a hesitation, Pippa Young sprinted the length of the room. Ian

McGowan jumped to his feet. He and Peregrin Blackwell moved to follow in pursuit.

"Don't bother," Phoebe called to them. "Let her go. She won't get far."

By then, Lord Owen was helping his wife and Eva to their feet. Eva felt a slight ache in her wrist where she had broken her fall, but otherwise felt sound enough.

From the table, they heard a *harrumph*, and Eva turned to see Lady Cecily shrug. "That's what the insolent baggage gets for being too rude to invite me in for tea."

Pippa Young made it out of the house, but only just. Within moments, she came trudging back in, chin down, her upper arm in Detective Burridge's grip. He sat her down in Phoebe's vacant chair at the end of the table.

Phoebe approached her, and Eva felt the urge to step between them. But there were enough people in the room to restrain Miss Young should she get any further ideas. "How long have you been planning this?" Phoebe demanded. "Since you moved to Little Barlow? Is that why you came here? Because you'd learned Isaac Perkins had been assigned to the village?"

The woman narrowed her eyes and seethed. For Eva and, she suspected, Phoebe too, that seemed admission enough.

Peregrin Blackwell also went to stand before Miss Young. "You hoped we'd be blamed. One of us at the encampment. I'd wager you counted on it."

Miss Young met the accusation with a look of defiance. "I surely didn't want Constable Brannock blamed."

A burst of fury sent Eva to that end of the table as well. She stood over Miss Young, hoping the woman felt every spark of her ire. "But you'd have allowed him to hang nonetheless." Without waiting for an answer, she turned to Detective Burridge. "What changed your mind about Miles?"

He shrugged, his lips skewing to one side. "Your mistress and her husband can be quite persuasive. The only way I could dislodge them from the police station yesterday was to agree to this little farce." He issued a hearty sigh. "Which turned out not to be a farce at all. Now, if you three will excuse me, it's my turn." He gestured for Eva, Peregrin, and Phoebe to step away. He took up position in front of Miss Young. "Pippa Young—"

"Philippa," she said with a sneer. "If we're going to be official about this."

"Oh, we're going to be official, all right." The detective cleared his throat. "Philippa Young, I am arresting you for the murder of Chief Inspector Isaac Perkins. You are not obliged to say anything unless you wish to do so, but what you say may be put into writing and given in evidence."

"I have nothing to say."

"Perhaps not now, but eventually you will. I find that, in the end, most murderers are eager to bare their souls. I wonder . . . How *did* you manage to take that gun from wherever it lay and use it against its very owner? Was Perkins so besotted with you he never saw it coming? The autopsy didn't show laudanum, but the coroner might have missed it."

Her nostrils flared; her jaws ground together.

"Well, as I said, you'll spill it eventually. Miss Young, please come to your feet." He pulled free the pair of handcuffs hanging from his belt beneath his coat. "Hold out your hands."

The metallic scrape of the handcuffs ratcheting into place sent a chill through Eva. Such a forlorn sound, and she could imagine the cold, unforgiving touch of the steel encircling each wrist. Miles had suffered the restraint of such cuffs—perhaps the very same ones—unfairly, unjustly.

Suddenly the how and why Pippa Young had committed murder no longer mattered to Eva. All that mattered was getting to Miles and telling him it was over, he was free— *they* were free. No plan formed in her mind as she made her way to the door, other than getting to Miles's flat, even if she walked all the way to the village. She'd done it before . . .

Another hand reached around her to grip the latch and open the front door. Eva stepped out, with Phoebe right behind her. "I'll drive you," she said, and they climbed into the Vauxhall.

In the village, Phoebe left her on the lane outside the flat, blew her a kiss, and drove off. Eva went through the street door and ran up the stairs. When his door appeared before her, she pounded on it.

"Miles! It's me. Let me in."

His pale face greeted her, his eyes filled with dread. "What's happened?"

In reply, Eva threw herself into his arms, her own tight around his neck.

"What's this? What's happened, my love?" His voice was taut, his breathing strained, and Eva realized she held him too tightly. She loosened her arms, but only slightly, enough to tilt back her head and whisper into his ear.

"It's over. You're free. It was Pippa Young. Lady Phoebe solved it. Miles, do you understand? This nightmare is finally over."

It puzzled her then, that he pressed her face to his shirtfront, stroked her hair, and whispered soothing words. Why on earth would he be comforting *her*? He'd been through hell, his life very nearly forfeit—she should be comforting *him*.

"It's all right, my darling. It's all right now . . ."

Only then did she feel the tears leaking from her eyes to soak his shirt, and how she clutched feverishly at his muscled arms, and how she could hardly draw breath without it dissolving into a sob that was at once sorrowful and joyous.

She made a fist and pressed it against her open mouth, struggling to gain control over the emotions pouring from her as if from an unstopped bottle turned on end. "Miles . . . what a blubbering ninny I am. I'm sorry."

He cupped her face in his hands. "You say I'm free? That I'm no longer under arrest for murder?"

She nodded vigorously while wiping at her eyes.

He still looked disbelieving, but he tossed back his head and let out a groan of relief. "Then I might not show it, but believe me, inside I'm as much a blubbering ninny as anyone. Can this be happening? Dare I trust I won't wake up to find your being here was just a hopeful dream?"

"It's no dream, Miles, but you have woken from the nightmare."

He took her hand and practically pulled her to the sofa. "Tell me again. *Who* did this? Surely you didn't say it was Pippa Young from the tearoom?"

"I did. The pasty—she brought it to him that morning. And Detective Burridge suspects she had either seduced him or laced the pasty with something to make him groggy. Or perhaps both," she added, "but it was Lady Phoebe who figured it out. Or, mostly. I believe a thing or two happened today that surprised even her."

He leaned back against the sofa, resting his head on its back. "Tell me everything that happened. Leave nothing out."

The front-door knocker sent an echo through the house. Phoebe rose from the breakfast table, leaned over Owen's shoulder to press a kiss to his cheek, and went to let her visitors in. She opened the door upon Julia, Amelia, Grams, and, smiling at her over the shoulders of the rest, Eva. "Good morning, everyone," she said as she stepped aside and bade them enter.

Once inside, Grams paused and perused the hall with a puzzled gaze. "Why on earth are you answering your own front door?"

"Because it *is* my front door, Grams." Phoebe embraced her grandmother, then reached for Julia and then Amelia.

Grams sniffed. "I understand you haven't had time to hire staff, my dear, but I told you you could borrow someone from up at the house."

"Owen and I have decided we don't want a house full of servants," she explained. "A cook, yes, since neither of us has much skill in that area, I'm afraid. All we'll need beyond that is someone to clean a few times a week and a man to keep the garden tidy, and they can come on the days they're needed."

"Good heavens, Phoebe." Grams sounded scandalized. "How very modern of you. How do you suppose you'll get yourself dressed in the mornings? Who'll do your hair? Oh, yes, you'll have Eva while you're here, but when you're not . . ." Grams left off and turned to Eva. "You did say you'll remain here and tend to Amelia? Or has that changed? Need I hire a new lady's maid for my youngest granddaughter?"

"Grams." Phoebe lightly grasped her grandmother's hands. "First of all, I'm perfectly capable of readying myself in the morning. Look." She twirled, showing off the simple, scallop-hemmed frock she wore. Draping her figure in taupe silk with a smattering of embroidered red poppies and delicate white daisies, it had only needed to be slipped over her head and buttoned down the back. Owen had been only too happy to perform that task. She nearly blushed as she remembered that for each button, there had been a gentle kiss along each ridge of her spine.

She shook the memory away, or, rather, saved it for later. Now she touched her hair, which had required little

effort to put up. Just a twist, two hair combs, some pins—
she thought it had come out rather fetching.

Grams pursed her lips. "Yes, you look well enough today. Quite stylish, if one must admit to it, but what will
you do for your next formal evening?"

"We'll cross that bridge when we come to it." Phoebe
caught Amelia's eye. Her sister was doing her best to hide
a grin; she herself had been the object of Grams's scrutiny
nearly as often as Phoebe. Owen's footsteps saved Phoebe
from further interrogation, as in the next instant he wished
them all good morning and deposited kisses on their cheeks.
Once that had been accomplished, Phoebe clapped her
hands. "Shall we?"

"Yes, let's!" Amelia led the way, running up the stairs
and to Phoebe and Owen's bedroom. Here was one aspect
of Phoebe's married life Grams would not object to, that
of her and Owen sharing a bedroom. Unlike so many of
their peers, Grams and Grampapa had rejected the tradition of separate bedrooms, a fact Phoebe knew many of
their acquaintances would have eyed askance had they
known.

By the time Phoebe and the others entered the room,
Amelia had the armoires open and had disappeared into
the dressing room. Three brass-studded, brown leather
Louis Vuitton trunks sat on the floor at the foot of the
bed. Two were Phoebe's, one Owen's. Amelia had opened
all three, displaying the as-yet empty interiors, lined in
monogrammed canvas.

Grams made a show of peeking inside each one, *tsking*
all the while. "I see we are very much needed, if the two of
you are ever to set off on your honeymoon."

Julia went to the largest of the two armoires and began
thumbing through frocks and suits. "Let's see . . . No. No.
No . . . *hm* . . . Oh, *this* is nice." She took a frock of pale
yellow silk with a matching jacket off the rack, went to the

tall mirror, and held it up in front of herself. "Yes, very nice. Phoebe, why don't you have more like this?"

Phoebe sighed.

Amelia bustled back in from the dressing room with an armful of lacy silk underthings and nightclothes. She placed them on the bed, then joined Julia at the armoire. "I like this very much," she declared, and reached in.

"Heavens, you're not serious?" Julia snatched the peasant-like blouson top that was worn belted over a matching pleated skirt from Amelia's hands and hooked the hanger back on the rack. "No."

"Oh, Julia, you're too picky." Amelia clucked her tongue. "If you have your way, Phoebe will go naked on her honeymoon."

"Amelia, really!" Grams shook her head. "Personally, I happen to like that one. Take it out and let's start a pile on the bed for Eva."

While the others continued debating the merits of this or that outfit, Eva unwrapped the bundle of tissue paper she had brought with her. As she had always done whenever they traveled together, she would fold each piece of Phoebe's wardrobe between layers of tissue paper, ensuring they came out of the trunk wrinkle-free and ready to be worn.

As the pile on the bed grew, and Eva carefully and lovingly prepared each piece for its journey inside the trunk, Grams called Phoebe over to the window. "I have something for you. It was my mother's and her mother's before that, and so on. It's been passed down from second daughters to second daughters, with each of us receiving it upon our honeymoon, and now it will be yours."

Grams held her handbag. Now she opened it, reached inside, and drew out a velvet-covered box. She opened the lid and Phoebe gasped. Against the black satin lining lay a gold necklace set with three emeralds about two inches apart, with a large teardrop pearl hanging from each stone. Phoebe's eyes misted. "Oh, Grams . . ."

"Now, I realize it might not quite suit the taste of a modern woman—"

"It does, Grams. Of course it does."

Grams waved away Phoebe's assurances. "Perhaps, perhaps not, but I want you to have it, and to wear it whenever you need to remember where you came from. Where we all came from. The world is changing, and yes, I realize we must all change with it, but Phoebe, we must also remember the women who came before us, those who quietly helped mold this world we now inhabit. We've got much to be proud of, you and I and your sisters, and I want you to always remember that, even if some of our old traditions no longer seem pertinent."

Phoebe opened her arms and wrapped them around the formidable woman who had raised her from an early age, who had praised, encouraged, and sometimes scolded, who had quietly and sometimes not so quietly shaped the woman Phoebe had become. She turned around. "Put it on me? Just for now. But I promise I'll wear it for Owen's and my every formal occasion."

Phoebe was admiring the sheen and sparkle of the necklace before her dressing-table mirror when Owen knocked on the open door. "Someone's here to see Eva."

Eva, bent over a trunk, straightened with a hand at the small of her back. "Whoever could it be?"

Owen affected an innocent expression. "The constable."

"Oh! Nothing the matter, I hope?" A bit of the color drained from Eva's cheeks. Phoebe understood. With the challenges of the past couple of weeks finally behind them, and Constable Brannock at liberty to leave his flat and return to work, all any of them wanted was a nice, long stretch of time where life remained uneventful.

"No, I shouldn't think so." Owen glanced at his fingernails in an offhand manner. "Although, now you mention it, he did seem rather agitated."

"Agitated?" Eva's eyes filled with worry.

"Go," Phoebe told her. "This can wait."

Owen moved out of Eva's way as she set off at nearly a run. When she reached the corridor, she stopped abruptly. "Where is he?"

"In the garden."

With a nod, she set off again. Phoebe beckoned Owen over. "What is this all about? And you needn't play innocent with me, I can see you know something." He reached out a finger and touched the center emerald of her necklace, puzzlement putting a faint crease in his brow. "A gift from Grams," she succinctly explained. "Don't change the subject."

"Well . . ." His grin was infectious, even if she didn't yet know the cause. "As it happens, the constable's errand also has to do with jewelry."

"What on earth are you on about . . . ? Oh." As she realized what he meant, her pulse leaped with excitement. He had said Miles waited for Eva in the garden. That lay on the other side of the house. Without a thought as to right or wrong, Phoebe set off nearly as quickly as Eva had, her destination being a guest bedroom overlooking the garden.

Amelia's voice followed her. "Phoebe, where are you going in such a hurry?"

Phoebe crossed the bedroom and took up position at one side of the window. She herself had slid it open that morning to let in the temperate June breezes. It also let in the sound of Eva's and the constable's voices, though she couldn't make out most of the words. Shame on her perhaps, for eavesdropping, although in actuality she wasn't, not from this high up with their words being so indistinct.

They were just below, standing between the chestnut

tree and a wispy border of bluebells. Suddenly the constable was on his knee. Phoebe gasped, her heart brimming with excitement for her friend.

"Phoebe, whatever are you doing?" Amelia came up beside her. Glancing out, she gasped, then gave a laugh, then turned around and ran out. From the corridor, Phoebe heard her voice. "Julia, Grams, come quick! Eva's life is about to change."

CHAPTER 20

Eva was breathless from her race down the stairs and through the house when she came upon Miles. He was pacing back and forth just beyond the terrace, kicking at stones and whatever other detritus lay in his path.

Yes, he certainly appeared agitated, and she braced herself for more bad news. At the same time, she wondered how much more they could take, how many more storms before forces beyond their control tore them apart.

Could that happen? Miles had spoken of marriage... hadn't he? In her heart, she believed he had, or had she only heard what she had wished to hear? His intentions had seemed to be implied, but now... Each step she took as she crossed the terrace seemed to take an eternity.

"Eva." He saw her and strode to her, taking her hands in his. How large they were, how strong. Had she ever noticed before? Funny, she didn't think she had ever quite appreciated his hands, but now as they wrapped around hers, she thought she would never find a man with hands as fine as his.

"Lord Owen said you wished to see me. Here I am," she blathered rather stupidly. Of course he had come here to see her. What else? "I hope there's nothing wrong." Then, before he could gather breath to reply, she said, "Is there any news about Pippa Young? Has she confessed?"

"I . . . er . . ." His brow creased with perplexity. For a moment he seemed uncertain how to go on. But then he said, "Yes, she has, actually. Last night. She simply broke down and poured it all out to Detective Burridge and me. She basically confirmed everything either said or implied here that day. The sister at the hands of her brute of a husband, how Miss Young had tried to get help for her. How Isaac Perkins said it wasn't his place to interfere."

"Did she explain how she gained Isaac Perkins's trust? Didn't he recognize her from all those years ago? Peregrin Blackwell had."

"Apparently he didn't." Miles shrugged. "It doesn't surprise me much. At the time, she was barely out of her teens, a girl who he perceived as making a nuisance of herself, butting into matters that didn't concern her. Now, she's an attractive, grown woman who showed him kindness, every so often making little gifts of food from her tearoom."

"Not a romance, then?"

He shook his head. "I don't think so. Simply a village business owner showing her gratitude for his services. She was subtle, and her actions were measured while she awaited just the right moment."

"The arrival of the caravan."

"Yes, but things didn't go as she had planned. She believed one of them would be blamed and arrested, and the case would be closed. She hadn't wagered on me being accused, or on the determination of you and Lady Phoebe." His gaze traveled over her features. "But this isn't why I came."

He looked so serious again, so ill at ease, that the worry

returned to clutch at her insides. "Then something else is wrong?"

"No, Eva, nothing is wrong. Quite the opposite."

Relief poured through her in buckets, so much so her knees went a little weak. "I'm so glad. When I think of the last time you were on the estate—"

"It was to tell you Isaac Perkins had been murdered."

"Yes." A billowy breath escaped her.

"Nothing like that has happened this time." He took her hands in his. "Actually, I have wonderful news. I'm to be promoted to inspector."

"Inspector? Oh, Miles! That *is* wonderful." She surveyed him with pride. "And so deserved. It's long overdue."

"Eva, it's more than that. Don't you see?" He beamed at her, yet a ghost of apprehension flitted across his features. "Now that I'll be making a decent salary, why . . . we can marry."

"Miles . . ." Her heart paused a beat, then reached up into her throat as he sank before her and reached into his pocket. "Miles . . ." She'd gone all but speechless; every word she had ever known had flown quite out of her head. All but one. *Miles.*

He reached into his trouser pocket. "Eva Mary Hunt-ford, will you do me the great honor of becoming my wife?" He held up a gold ring into which was set a small opal. In the sunlight, the stone flashed milky tones of pink and yellow against subtle shadows of blue. Then it blurred before her eyes. He came to his feet, reached out, but let his hand linger in the air, as if afraid to touch her. "Eva? Will you?"

"Yes," she whispered, as faint and shaky as a moth's wings. She gathered her breath, her longings, her joy, and louder, said, "Of course I'll marry you. Miles Brannock, I cannot wait to marry you."

"Eva!" Shakily, clumsily, he slid the ring onto her finger. His arms went around her and he held her tight—so very tight. For a precious few moments there was nothing else, no one else, only the two of them and this boundless happiness. But as with all intense emotions, this could not be sustained indefinitely. His embrace loosened, his face came away from hers, and he showed her a rueful smile that immediately raised a wariness inside her. "There is one small catch, a compromise we'll have to make."

Compromise? She gave a laugh. Her entire life, it seemed, had been one long compromise, and she had weathered each one. "Whatever it is, we'll manage."

"I'm so glad to hear you say that." He took her hand, his thumb caressing her knuckle above the ring as he spoke. "Because the position is in Gloucester. We'll have to relocate."

"Gloucester?" She took a step back, her hand nearly sliding from his. "Miles, that's so far away. Couldn't they let you take over the Little Barlow station, or somewhere hereabout? There are so many villages in the area . . ."

"They want me in Gloucester. It can't be helped. But Gloucester's not so very far. We'll come back to visit your parents, I promise."

"Goodness, yes, my parents. They're getting older, how will they get by with both Alice and me so far away? And my ladies. Yes, Phoebe is married and determined to make a go of it without servants, or without many, but Amelia still needs me. She's only now coming into her womanhood. I've always promised I'd be here for them . . ."

"Eva, you've given them so many years of your life. It's time you lived for yourself, don't you think? I believe they'd agree—"

"They'd say they agreed, Miles, but would they really?"

"Yes, I believe they would. Eva, please."

She shook her head. "I need time to think."

"To think about whether you wish to marry me?" He looked so crestfallen, so puzzled and hurt, that her heartstrings pulled to breaking. But she had made promises. She had a duty to the Renshaw family.

"No. Yes. I don't know, I need some time." Blindly she turned and retraced her steps into the house, leaving Miles standing all alone, undoubtedly watching her go and wondering what the blazes had just happened. She barely knew herself. She knew only that she owed so much to the Renshaws, that she loved her ladies beyond compare, and the thought of leaving them so entirely left her feeling empty, bereft. Guilty.

"Eva, stop right there."

She was halfway across the parlor when she found her path suddenly barred. Phoebe stood in front of her, hands on hips, with a stern-looking sister flanking her on either side. "My ladies. What do you need?"

"We'll have no more of that," Phoebe said. She sounded angry. All three of them looked angry. No, perhaps not quite anything as severe as anger, but they certainly weren't happy.

"No more of what?" Eva blinked, which made her aware that there were tears in her eyes. That blink sent them spilling over, down her cheeks, and dripping onto her shirtwaist. "Forgive me, I don't know what's wrong with me. What do you need, my lady?"

"Nothing." Amelia spoke sharply. "We are not in need of anything but your friendship and, at this precise moment, we are in need of your happiness, Eva."

"Yes." Lady Julia's lovely features took on a defiance that baffled Eva until she spoke her next words. "You see, we were all upstairs spying on you. We heard and saw everything—or almost. How could you, Eva? How could you deny yourself and that honorable man waiting for you outside the happiness you both deserve?"

"And use *us* as an excuse?" Phoebe demanded. "We won't have it, Eva. Change can be frightening. Believe me, I understand that. But if your life is to be a happy one, you must be willing to have faith and take a risk."

"She speaks the truth." Eva hadn't noticed Lady Wroxly standing across the room. She came forward now, a woman as tall as most men, moving with dignity and pride, and not to be argued with. "I doubt there's ever been a woman born who didn't hesitate at least a moment or two when it came to marriage, nor a man, for that matter. I'm sure your constable was a bundle of nerves on his way here, but he put it aside, stiffened his upper lip, and did what he came here to do. If you're smart, you'll do the same."

Yes, Miles had been nervous, she had perceived that much. But he had plowed through rather than allow his fears to rule him, because . . . because he loved her and wanted to spend his life with her. Didn't she want the same? Was she using her ladies as an excuse? For what? She searched their adamant faces, yet the duty she had lived by, sworn by, continued to tug. "But . . . Amelia . . ."

"Will be fine, I assure you," Lady Wroxly said firmly.

"More than fine, Eva. Look at me." Amelia held out her arms. "As you can see, I'm no longer a child. I've had you and Grams and my sisters as my good examples, and I will continue to have them and even you. As the constable said, Gloucester isn't so very far, and Phoebe has promised to teach me how to drive."

"Heaven help us," Ladies Wroxly and Julia murmured simultaneously.

Amelia ignored them. "So, if you're hesitating because of me, you can stop it right now. As Phoebe told you, we'll have none of it."

Phoebe came forward and took Eva's hands. "We've been through so much together, all of us. You were there when we received the news about Papa, and you helped each of us through that terrible time. You worked side by side with us collecting and packaging supplies during the war. You have listened to our troubles, soothed our hurts, encouraged us, and advised us, not to mention laundering and ironing our clothes to perfection." That got a laugh from all of them, even Eva. "You've gone far and above anything we could have asked of you."

"I've loved every minute," Eva whispered through her tears.

"So have we." Phoebe gave her hands a squeeze before releasing them. "But now it's time to love every minute of the life you build with Constable Brannock."

Lady Wroxly moved to Eva's side and placed a hand on her shoulder. "Assuming the good constable hasn't left already . . ."

Eva gasped, her heart thumping wildly in her chest. How could she have turned away from him and run off? How could she have been so callous, so dismissive? So stupid?

She once again found herself running, and as she ran, she called out his name. Was he gone? *Please, don't let him be gone . . .*

She found him standing where she had left him, still staring after her, still waiting. She wasted not a moment in rushing to him and throwing her arms around him.

"Miles, yes."

"Yes? Eva, are you certain?"

"Oh, yes."

Six Months Later

Phoebe and Owen sat side by side in the family pew, their hands joined beneath the muff she had carried into church. Around them were Grams and Grampapa, Julia and Theo, Fox and Amelia. And snuggled warm and safe inside her, the newest family member who would grace their lives come May.

The organ music began and the congregation came to their feet. Directly across the aisle were Betty Huntford and other members of the family: aunts, uncles, cousins. Clasped in Betty Huntford's hands and pressed face outward against her bosom was a framed photograph of Eva's brother Danny, whom they had lost in the war.

A side door opened and Miles Brannock strode out to stand in front of the altar, accompanied by his cousin Seamus from Ireland. Miles's widowed mother and other family members who had been able to make the trip from Ireland sat behind the Renshaws. The organ music, quiet up until now, gathered volume and the doors into the sanctuary were opened. Beneath an arch festooned with ribbons, a slightly older, plumper version of Eva stepped through. Her sister, Alice, matron of honor, smiled with such happiness it might have been her own wedding.

Eva followed on the arm of her father, Vincent, a bearded, burly farmer whom she adored. Eva looked lovely in white satin—the fabric a gift from Grams—cut to the latest style at calf length, with a simple veil and headpiece that had been her mother's. Over ladies' hats and men's bared heads, their gazes briefly met, but in that scant moment Phoebe saw that Eva had indeed found the faith to take a risk—faith that Phoebe and her sisters no longer needed her in the way they once had, and that she, Eva, felt nothing but certainty about the life she was about to embark upon.

They had all of them—Renshaws, Huntfords, Brannocks, and everyone filling the church—found a new kind of faith since the war ended, one that allowed them to trust in themselves, in each other, and in the forces of change that set them on new, once unimaginable, paths. Phoebe squeezed Owen's hand and smiled, excited to see what life would bring them next.